Blood Double

Also by Neil McMahon

Twice Dying

Blood
Double

Neil McMahon

■ HarperCollins*Publishers*

BLOOD DOUBLE. Copyright © 2002 by Neil McMahon. All rights reserved. Printed in the United States of America. No part of this book may be used or reproduced in any manner whatsoever without written permission except in the case of brief quotations embodied in critical articles and reviews. For information, address HarperCollins Publishers Inc., 10 East 53rd Street, New York, NY 10022.

HarperCollins books may be purchased for educational, business, or sales promotional use. For information, please write: Special Markets Department, HarperCollins Publishers Inc., 10 East 53rd Street, New York, NY 10022.

FIRST EDITION

Designed by Nancy B. Field

Library of Congress Cataloging-in-Publication Data

McMahon, Neil.
    Blood double : a novel / Neil McMahon.
      p. cm.
    ISBN 0-06-019766-8
    1. Medical examiners (Law)—Fiction. 2. Human experimentation in medicine—Fiction. 3. San Francisco (Calif.)—Fiction. I. Title.

    PS3568.H545 B56 2002   2001039961
    813'.54—dc21

02 03 04 05 06 WBC/RRD 10 9 8 7 6 5 4 3 2 1

For Dan Conaway,
whose guidance, patience, and trust made this happen

If God afflicts somebody,
we ought all to profit from it.

—*John Calvin*

Carroll Monks was standing on the spot he thought of as the bridge of Mercy Hospital's emergency room. It was like the command deck of a ship, the point from which he could monitor most of what was going on at any given time: the eight private cubicles, six of which were occupied; the trauma room, which was not; the activities of his resident, nurses, and other staff; the softly bleeping monitors and blinking lights of the complex instruments; and the main desk, where the charge nurse worked at a computer. Monks could glimpse through the glass doors into the waiting room, which held a further group of postulants, most of them in discomfort, none in severe distress. He could hear the ongoing radio report of a team of paramedics in the field, attending to a mild heart attack that did not require his intervention.

This was the way the ER was most of the time, busy but stable—and tensed for whatever might burst through the doors that would throw it into organized frenzy.

It was a damp Tuesday evening in March, 7:07 P.M.

Monks sensed a stir in the waiting room, a tiny ripple of movement that caught his gaze. A woman was coming in. He got an instant impression as she yanked open the door, framed in its light. She was about twenty, pretty, sturdily built, with black hair and golden skin:

Asian. Heavily made up, wearing a short black dress. On her own feet, with no obvious injury.

But moving fast. Half-running, on spike heels, to the desk. Speaking urgently to the receptionist, pointing back outside.

The receptionist leaned forward, puzzled.

The Asian woman closed her eyes and quickly placed her palms together beside her tilted face, a child's gesture of sleep. Then she jabbed her finger toward the outside again.

Monks said, *"Nurse!"* and moved for the door.

The cool wet air of the San Francisco night blurred his eyes, and he squinted to focus in the orange-yellow glow of the parking lot's lights. Twenty yards ahead, a figure lay sprawled on the sidewalk, with another crouched over it. Their faces were touching. Monks felt an instant of eerie terror, the shocking sense that he had stumbled onto an act of desperate passion gone wrong, or even a vampire ripping into its victim's throat.

But then the crouching man's face lifted, and Monks saw one hand pinching the downed man's nostrils, the other positioned behind the neck. This was not violence, it was mouth-to-mouth resuscitation.

Monks turned to yell behind, "I've got an unconscious man, he's not breathing, let's *go*," and dropped to his knees beside the sprawled figure. His fingers touched the neck to find the carotid artery's pulse. It was barely detectable. He thumbed an eyelid open and could just make out the blank round iris, the pupil shrunk to a pinpoint. The body was shutting down.

The crouched man, like the woman, was Asian: small, wiry, gaunt-faced. His eyes watched Monks.

"Ovahdose," he said. His hands moved to make a quick gesture of jabbing a needle into his arm.

The other man was Caucasian, in his late thirties. His face was dirty and abraded, as if from falling. But his shirt was hand-woven, tailored cotton, and his shoes leather loafers that also looked handmade. His teeth were beautifully cared for. This was not the sort of junkie Monks was used to, and his first guess would have been respiratory failure from another cause—except for what the Asian man seemed to be telling him.

Monks said, "Are you sure?"

The Asian shook his head in incomprehension. "Ovahdose," he said again, and bent back to the mouth-to-mouth. He was quick and efficient, obviously trained; had sustained the fragile hold on life for critical minutes.

Monks decided to believe him.

Monks craned around. Two nurses were coming fast with a gurney, kneeling with the Ambu bag to take over breathing. The Asian man exhaled one last breath into the receiving lungs, then moved out of the way in a crouching roll that made Monks think of a paratrooper's landing fall.

He strode ahead into the ER, calling orders, stepping into gloves and barrier gown. The nurses prepped the patient, putting a rolled towel behind his neck, hooking him to a cardiac monitor, preparing an IV. A respiratory therapist took over the Ambu bag, now hooked to an oxygen source. A third nurse arrived with a clipboard to note procedures and times.

His gaze swept the room. His daughter Stephanie, in her first year of medical school, was working part-time as a hospital attendant. When Monks was on duty, she liked to visit the ER, getting a feel for it. She was standing against a wall, hands clasped like a shy girl waiting to be asked to dance: eager to help, afraid to interfere.

He called to her, "Take over recording." It would free up the nurse, and give Stephanie a look at why she might want to choose another specialty.

"I'm having trouble breathing for him, Doctor." The therapist was holding the mask against the patient's face with one hand and squeezing the plastic sack hard with the other, but the lungs were not inflating well. Monks stepped in, pulled the jaw forward, and leaned close to listen. Over the weak breaths came the harsh sound of stridor: vocal cords or tongue had swollen, obstructing the passage.

He said, "Let's get an oral airway in." He held the mouth open while she inserted the device, a flanged four-inch tube, to allow air past the tongue. He realized he was taking deep breaths himself, that he was unconsciously resisting what was happening, reassuring himself that it was not happening to him. He braced himself for the next step, the insertion of an endotracheal tube. It was a risky procedure under any circumstances, and if the constriction was severe, the ET tube would not work; it would require a cricothyrotomy, cutting a hole through the throat into the trachea.

He scanned the vital signs: blood pressure at 90/60, heart rate showing on the monitor at 45, oxygen saturation meter, clipped to a finger, at 80 percent.

Not good.

"Give me an intubation tray." He started to add, *Let's make this fast*: the Ambu bag could remain off the face for perhaps fifteen seconds. But everybody knew.

He prepared the laryngoscope and tube and positioned himself over the patient's head. He nodded to the therapist. She gave the Ambu bag a couple of rapid squeezes, then lifted it. Monks pulled up on the tongue with the lighted scope and tried to ease the tube between the vocal cords. They were tight, resisting. He tried again. They still would not yield.

"Get a scalpel ready," he said.

One nurse held out the gleaming knife in her fingers for him to grip. The other leaned in to towel sweat off his forehead. The fifteen seconds were up.

He probed the tube between the vocal cords once more and said, "Give me a Selleck's." The therapist pushed down on the larynx. Monks felt the cords part slightly. He pressed harder, and closed his eyes in relief as the tube slid home.

"I'm in," he said.

He spent a minute catching up on his own breathing while the apparatus was secured, a balloon inflated to seal air in and vomit out, the tube taped into place. Now the chest rose and fell easily.

"Breath sounds symmetrical, good on both sides," Monks said, listening with his stethoscope, speaking to Stephanie. She looked a little shell-shocked. The whole thing had taken less than two minutes. "Oxygen saturation and blood pressure are starting to rise. He should be okay now." He added kindly, "You're supposed to be writing that down, hon."

"Sorry." Flustered, head lowered, she started scribbling.

To the others, he said, "Get a chest X-ray to make sure of that tube position." It could still slip: into the right-stem main bronchus, inflating only the right lung, or back above the vocal cords, doing no good at all. "Start lab and an IV. Give one milligram Narcan, IV." He caught surprised looks from the nurses; this was not the sort of junkie they were used to either.

"I have a reason," he said. "Let's try it."

While they set up the IV and drew blood samples to take to lab, Monks gave the patient a once-over, looking, touching, listening. There were no apparent injuries besides the facial lacerations. Monks unbuttoned the left sleeve and pulled it up, noting, besides the expensive clothes, a heavy silver and turquoise bracelet and a similar ring, both of fine workmanship. The inside of the forearm was bruised and pocked, with several needle marks. But it was not the flesh of a serious user, and offered a possible explanation for the overdose: a well-to-do thrill seeker getting more than he could handle.

"IV started, Narcan in," Monks told Stephanie, and added, "Let's get restraints on those wrists." Narcan worked fast, often within a couple of minutes or even less. Once, early in his career, he had seen a patient sit bolt upright some thirty seconds after the Narcan went in, grab the endotracheal tube in her throat, and yank it out, inflated balloon and all.

With the patient stable, there was time to think about other things, such as who he was. Monks patted the front pants pockets, then slipped his hand beneath each buttock, but could not feel a wallet. The obvious explanation was that he had been rolled, but it was hard to understand how a thief would have missed the bracelet and ring. Monks stepped to the cubicle's door to see if he could find out anything from the people who had brought him in.

The young Asian woman was standing at the main exit, gripping her purse, in intense conversation with Mrs. Hak, a receptionist whom Monks knew to be a native South Korean. He turned to tell the nurses that he was going to talk to them. But at that moment, the patient wheezed and tried to sit up, yanking at the restraints, hacking and gagging around the tube.

Monks let the nurses handle it, laying soothing hands on the struggling man, pressing him gently back down, talking: "You're in the emergency room, you're going to be okay."

When the man was settled, Monks stepped into his line of sight. "You overdosed," Monks said. "You stopped breathing."

The eyes widened. It gave him a fishlike look that quickly went from incomprehension to dismay. Narcan brought lucidity almost immediately.

That sweet narcotic high was gone, and trouble was here.

Monks said, "Relax. You're fine. Just stay still a few seconds and we'll get that tube out. Okay?"

He stared at Monks, eyes bulging, then nodded.

Monks made sure the suction apparatus was ready in case of vomiting, then reversed the procedure, deflating the balloon, withdrawing the tube. It went smoothly this time. The patient coughed and gagged, but recovered. Monks released the restraints, and the man sat up, sagging forward with his face in his hands.

The respiratory therapist left, her work done. Monks motioned the nurses to the door and said quietly, "Give me a minute alone with him, huh? You can call off X-ray."

"Do you still need me?" Stephanie said. Monks could not quite tell whether she hoped the answer would be yes or no. He considered. This had happened so fast that the phlebotomist, who usually drew and handled blood samples, had not yet appeared.

"Why don't you go ahead and take those samples down to lab," he said.

She glanced around nervously. The tubes of blood were usually transported by cart, but there was no cart to be had. "You mean, like, just carry them?"

Monks nodded. "Try not to drop them," he advised. "They make a hell of a mess."

She moved away practically on tiptoe, the tray with its half dozen tubes encircled in her arms and cradled to her bosom, as if it were a relic being borne to worship.

Monks walked back into the cubicle, went to the sink, and wet a hand towel with warm water, then pulled a stool to the bedside and sat.

"I'll clean up those cuts," Monks said.

"I'm all right," the patient said. "I've got to get out of here." He shifted his weight, preparing to stand.

Monks put a hand on his shoulder. "Not just yet."

The return stare was stubborn. This was a man not accustomed to being crossed.

"Is this about money?" he demanded.

"This is about the fact that you came into my emergency room nearly dead, call it five minutes ago," Monks said. "Not breathing. Heart almost stopped. Another minute or two, and we wouldn't be having this conversation, that's how close it was.

"And it's not over. You might still have enough dope in your system to kill you. It will last longer than the reversal drug I gave you. Meaning you could walk out of here and two hours from now drop dead of another OD. For real this time." Monks watched the words register. "Is that what you wanted? Was this a suicide attempt?"

The patient looked away and shook his head.

"I'm Dr. Monks. This will be easier if I know your name."

"Smith. John."

Right.

"Okay, John Smith. I'll release you as soon as I'm satisfied you're out of trouble. Is there someone you'd like us to call, to come get you? Family, friend?"

"You haven't called the police?" The question was quick and wary.

"I have no reason to. The legal aspects of this are somebody else's job."

John Smith's relief was evident. "How long are we talking?"

"If everything looks okay on your lab tests, and you stay awake?" Monks said. "Maybe four hours."

John stiffened in outrage. "That's impossible. You have no right to keep me here." He moved again to swing his feet to the floor. Monks placed a palm in the center of his chest, less gently this time.

"I know you're trying to cover your ass, John, with the phony name and all," Monks said. "You don't want this made public, and I don't blame you. Let's face it, you'd look like a dork."

John's face tightened. A dork was not something he wanted to look like.

"But I've got to cover my ass too," Monks said. "If I let you out of here and you go down again, I might as well put a gun to my head. There'd be lawyers all over me and this hospital like coyotes on a bunny. So you're going to stay where I can see you, and if you give me a hard time, I *will* call the cops. Now settle back, this is going to sting."

"Why don't you give me a shot?" John Smith mumbled. "For the pain."

"For Christ's sake," Monks said. "The whole reason you're *in* here is because you took a shot that just about killed your pain for good. Grit your teeth, it won't take long."

Monks carefully cleaned around the facial lacerations, with John wincing as the crusted blood and bits of grit came free. The impression was that he had been raked with a concrete cheese grater, leaving a patchwork of bloody furrows.

"You took a pretty good header," Monks said. "What happened?"

"I don't remember," John said sullenly.

None of the wounds was severe enough to require stitches. Monks applied Bactroban and taped on a bandage.

"You don't look like an addict," Monks said. "How does a guy like you start shooting up?"

"I don't want to go into it."

"Did you do your usual dose?"

"Yeah. Are you finished?"

Monks went to the sink to wash his hands. "For now."

"Then how about giving me a phone. And some privacy."

Monks had been working on his temper for the last forty years or so. It was getting better.

He said, "If you're going to go out and blast yourself again, do me a favor: Get far enough away so you won't end up back in my ER."

Monks got a cordless phone and took it to John Smith, who accepted it without thanks. When Monks left the cubicle this time, he found Stephanie waiting, peering in. She beckoned him a few steps away. Her whisper was urgent, her eyes wide.

"Daddy, I mean, Doctor, I didn't mean to spy, but I saw him when you were taping him up. You know who he looks like?" Her voice was brimming with excitement. "*Lex Rittenour.*"

Monks blinked in surprise. "That guy in there? With the vomit stains on his shirt?"

"Just because he's brilliant doesn't mean he's a Boy Scout. He did a lot of wild stuff. There's been at least one paternity suit."

Dinosaur that Monks was, even he knew the name. Lex Rittenour was a legend of the computer world, a wunderkind who had started designing revolutionary software while still in his teens. But he had raised eyebrows—and hackles—by a glaring disregard for the corporate world, often appearing at important functions barefoot, wearing ragged jeans and beads. Monks seemed to recall that there was a publicized association with eastern religions too. But then, for the past several years, Rittenour had dropped out of sight.

Monks took an unobtrusively closer look at John's face, trying to resurrect the glimpse he had gotten between the crusted blood and Ambu bag and the bandage that now covered most of one cheek from temple to jaw. It was clean-shaven, with a somewhat beaky nose and a thick brown shock of hair that was long but obviously carefully cut. The overall impression was of a rich forty-year-old hippie. Monks recalled photos of Rittenour and admitted the resemblance.

But it was a look that was in vogue; there were plenty of men around who had it. As far as the ER was concerned, John Smith was a John Doe junkie who had caused them some moments of serious tension, and in spite of his assurances, was likely to cost them a fair chunk of money.

"What if he *is* Lex Rittenour?" Stephanie said. "With that IPO about to happen? There's a huge story here."

"That's not our concern."

"It's everybody's concern," she said heatedly. "It's a scam. They're going to screw people big-time and make a fortune doing it."

More severely, Monks said, "Whether or not that's true, Stephanie, that's not the issue here. The issue here is a patient's confidentiality being foremost. I'd advise you to keep your speculation to yourself."

She let out a sound of exasperation, a sort of *uh*, and spun away, a gesture so reminiscent of her mother that it startled him. She looked like Gail at that age too—athletic, taffy hair cut short for swimming, not so much pretty as brightly energetic. He had not spent much time with her over the past years, and there came the bittersweet sense that she was grown, becoming lost to him.

"I'd also advise you to sign your chart," he called, and stepped away with mock alacrity from her withering gaze.

Monks was somewhat familiar, from news accounts, with the issue Stephanie was talking about. At its center was a software program that worked off the recently mapped human genome, offering a sweeping diagnostic test for potential diseases and birth defects.

The genius behind this was none other than Lex Rittenour, stepping again into the news. Within the next few days, an initial public stock-offering was scheduled to open, estimated at upward of a billion dollars.

But criticism was furious and bitter. At the controversy's center was a fear that tore deep into the human heart—that this was an attempt to identify and even engineer a genetically superior race, which would have privileged status and dominate its inferiors.

Monks walked to the nurses' station, where Leah Horvitz, the charge nurse, was working at her computer.

"Are those Asian folks still around?" Monks asked. "The ones who brought the guy in Cubicle Seven?"

"They disappeared."

Monks was not surprised. "Let's go ahead and enter him."

Leah typed something with machine-gun speed. "Name?"

"He gave it as John Smith."

There was an infinitesimal pause, while Leah registered what that probably meant: several hundred dollars minimum for the hospital, plus at least one unpaid physician, namely, Monks.

"Middle initial *Q* by any chance?" she asked acerbically.

"Probably."

She typed in the name, adding it to the other thousands of John and Jane Does in the accounts receivable files.

"Any other information?"

"Not yet," Monks said. "I'll let you know."

Whoever John Smith was, there remained the question of what had happened to him. A suicide attempt was possible, with him lying to cover it—but injected narcotics were not usually suicide drugs of choice. It seemed more likely that he had been trying a new kick and miscalculated his dose. Had fallen, causing the lacerations to his face. He would have stopped breathing within a minute or two—but the Asians had had the skill to keep him alive, the presence of mind to bring him here.

However it had gone, John Smith was a lucky man.

Monks walked back into Cubicle Seven. "Breathing okay?" he said.

"I've got someone coming to get me," John said, sounding a little smug.

Monks gripped John's wrist, feeling the pulse through his fingertips. It was much better, firm and steady. He released it and stepped back, folding his arms.

"Physically, you're coming along fine," Monks said. "It's my professional advice that you get a psychiatric evaluation. I can arrange one if you'll agree."

"I like my head the size it is." John's tone was sharp.

"It seems plenty big enough," Monks agreed.

John stared combatively. But then he deflated, rolling wearily to the side, knees rising into a fetal position. One hand rose to touch his own skull.

"You see this brain? This brain founded an empire."

"Very impressive. Maybe it'll break a record when the pathologist weighs it."

"I feel like shit." This time the words came out in a dead, miserable tone. Monks found himself liking John a little better. "This wouldn't have happened, except I was trying to do the right thing," John said. "You probably don't believe me."

"I don't get how 'doing the right thing' involves shooting narcotics," Monks said, but felt a touch of shame for being judgmental. He had spent more than his own share of time wrapped in the inflamed insulation of alcohol, shielding himself against his failings and rage.

"I'm Frankenstein, man," said John Smith. "I created a monster."

"Monster?"

"A *perfect* monster." John made a cackling sound, which Monks interpreted as the bleak amusement that stemmed from despair. "Worst kind. Now I want to lock it up, but—" His hands turned palm up in a gesture of futility. "It's gotten huge."

"Try to get comfortable," Monks said. "We'll leave the IV in, in case you need more of the reversal medicine. There's a buzzer if you have trouble."

"Doctor?"

Monks paused on his way out. John had not moved, his gaze still on the wall.

"Yes?"

"What did you say your name was?"

"Monks."

"Is that German?"

"Irish. From gaelic *manachan*, a monk."

"What, they shortened it when they got to this country?"

"Yeah," Monks said. "They tried 'Smith' first, but nobody bought it."

Monks saw John's lips curve in a smile before his eyes closed again.

Less than fifteen minutes later, Monks was in another cubicle, examining an elderly woman who complained of intestinal discomfort, when a tap came at the door. It was a nurse, looking nervous.

"You'd better come out here, Doctor."

Monks could hear a voice now, across the room. It was not loud, but had an intense abrasive tone that overrode the ER's other sounds. Its owner was a man leaning over the main desk, gripping the counter as if he were about to vault it, talking to—or more accurately at—Leah Horvitz. He was in his mid thirties, trim, wearing the young executive look: dark moussed hair, expensive suit with tie loose at the collar, tasseled shoes, Burberry overcoat. Two other men, similarly dressed, stood in the waiting room with the air of guards: one just inside the door to the ER, the other at the main entrance, talking on a cell phone. Both had the broad-shouldered look of ex-football players.

Monks gave the worried old lady in the cubicle's bed his best reassuring smile, which he secretly feared made him look crocodilian.

"You're going to be fine," he said, patting her hand. "I'll be right back."

"I'm not sure I'm getting through to you, miss," the man at the desk was saying as Monks approached. His voice was edged with contained

menace. "Your lack of cooperation could have very serious consequences for this hospital."

Leah, true professional that she was, ignored him with icy calm, her
gaze on her work. "Why don't you try getting through to Dr. Monks?"
she said, without looking up.

"Where do I find this Dr. Monks?"

"Right behind you."

The man swung around to face Monks, thrusting his jaw forward
like a boxer rising to the bell. "Are you in charge here?" he demanded.

"I'm the senior physician on duty."

"You have a patient named John Smith? Where is he?"

"He's being cared for."

"He told me you're refusing to release him. I strongly advise you to
do so, *now*."

"Mind if I ask, by what authority?" Monks said.

Impatiently, the man pulled an embossed business card from his
wallet and held it up for Monks's inspection. It identified him as
Ronald Tygard, attorney, with an office in the Bank of America Building. It was a prestigious address, and Tygard obviously knew it.

"I'll take care of the bill right now," Tygard said.

Monks said, "That would be nice. But I'm afraid you can't have
John Smith just yet. There's a question of competence."

"Are you suggesting I'm not competent?" Tygard said, bristling.

"I'm telling you *he's* not, in the medical and legal sense. Not in full
control of himself. He could still go down again."

"We won't let him out of our sight."

"The keyword is *medical*, friend," Monks said again. "He needs full-
time medical attention, until he's out of danger."

"You have no idea of the league you're dealing with." Tygard spoke
quietly, with narrowed eyes.

"This is not my personal preference, Mr. Tygard. I'm talking about
liability exposure." Monks could not resist adding, "Surely, you understand. As an attorney."

"This is bullshit," Tygard said disgustedly, and signaled to his crony standing guard inside the ER door. "Andrew, go find him." Andrew took a striding step into the room, as if to start yanking open cubicle doors.

Monks threw the rope around his temper again, but not by much. "Mr. Tygard, if your man's not here because he needs emergency medical attention, he's interfering with people who do. So are you. Kindly leave, both of you."

Tygard ignored him.

Monks was abruptly aware that the ER seemed still, hushed. Personnel were paused in their movements as in a tableau, none watching openly but everyone tuned in to see how this was going to work out.

He said to Leah, "Call Security. Let's get the SFPD here too."

"Hold on, now." Tygard spun toward Leah with palm outstretched. She watched Monks, phone receiver in one hand, finger poised over the button.

Tygard bowed his head—a somewhat theatrical gesture of being overwrought by circumstances, struggling manfully for control. Then he inhaled deeply and extended his hand to Monks.

"I'm sorry, I'm under a lot of pressure," he said. "Let's start over."

"I'm likely to have touched something contagious," Monks said. "Nothing personal."

Tygard's hand dropped, rubbing unobtrusively against his slacks. "It doesn't have to be *your* medical attention," he said.

"That's true," Monks conceded. "We could have an ambulance take him to another hospital. Of course, there'd be several more people involved, another check-in procedure, all that." He waited, letting the point sink in; it would not help the cause of John Smith's anonymity.

"His own doctor, then," Tygard said.

Monks considered. To be safe, in terms of covering his and the hospital's ass, he knew he should insist on keeping John Smith the full four hours. But John was stable, and by the time a physician could arrive and sign him out, the acute danger period would have passed.

Most important, Monks's sum total of training, experience, intuition—*feel*—satisfied him.

"If that doctor's willing to come here, I'll release John into his care, AMA," Monks said.

"What's AMA?"

"Against medical advice."

Tygard smiled thinly. "We can handle that." He snapped his fingers at Andrew, who was hovering nearby, a powerful physical force waiting to be directed. "Call Dr. Rostanov," Tygard said. "Get her here, now, I don't care what she's doing." Andrew produced a cell phone and cupped it to his ear.

Monks said, "If you'd ask your friends to move outside."

"It will only be for a short time, Doctor," Tygard said. "We just want to make sure nobody comes in who doesn't belong."

"Mr. Tygard, this is a hospital emergency room, not an executive suite. *I* decide who belongs. This has already taken up a lot of time, and my patience is wearing thin."

Tygard gave him another cold, measuring look, then issued the order. Andrew threw Monks a similar look, making it clear that he was tolerating this only because he had to, then walked stiffly out. He and his partner took up positions flanking the main door.

Eyes widened mockingly, Tygard said, "Satisfied?"

Monks would have let it go except for what he saw in Tygard's face. It was young, unstamped by hardship or real adversity, living smugly on the surface of a glossy world and untroubled by concern for the great weight of those who struggled below. Monks did not like bullies under any circumstances, but especially bullies who had not paid dues.

"When I run into people like you, Ron," Monks said wearily, "I always want to tell them, 'You don't have to flaunt your inner child so much. It's real obvious.' "

Tygard's gaze narrowed. "What the hell's that supposed to mean?"

"You could save yourself a lot of work."

There was a longish moment of eye contact. Monks got the unsettling sense that it was not about menace or even dislike, but about two different species that did not comprehend each other. And neither wanted to share the planet.

"I'd like to see John now," Tygard said.

Monks pointed toward Cubicle Seven. "It's my opinion he should have a psychiatric evaluation. I offered to give him one here, but he refused. I'd urge you to make him reconsider. If not here, then Dr. Rostanov should arrange one."

Tygard walked to the cubicle, shutting the door hard behind him.

Monks stood where he was for a minute, aware that he was breathing deeply, his body catching up; that he was shaking a little. He was angrier than he had thought. Taking care of the ER was trouble enough, without having to put up with this. At least it looked like the hospital stood to get paid after all.

Best of all, this goddamned mess was soon to be somebody else's problem.

He made a visual inspection of the ER, an automatic move before returning to the elderly lady with the bowel trouble. Stephanie, helping one of the nurses, caught his gaze and mimed an exaggerated I-told-you-so look.

Whether John Smith was, in fact, Lex Rittenour, Monks did not much care; but he admitted that, judging from the drama, John was indeed a man of some consequence.

Found dying on a San Francisco sidewalk, with a needle barely out of his arm.

When Tygard had referred to John Smith's personal physician as "she," and added the name Rostanov, Monks had formed an unconscious image of a tall, imperious Valkyrie type of hardy northern stock, sweeping in from the steppes wearing furs and boots.

He did not realize this until he was called to the desk to meet her, and his mental picture shifted abruptly. Martine Rostanov was a small, waifish woman of about forty, with a short thick mop of dark hair, slender, veined hands—and a stirrup brace, just visible on her left foot beneath the cuff of her slacks. She swung the leg a little from the hip as she walked. She was dressed casually—heavy Shetland wool cardigan over a soft white turtleneck, with a simple gold bracelet that seemed to flow like mercury with its own fire. Monks was no judge of women's clothing, but the ensemble was tasteful and, he was sure, expensive.

The introductions this time were civil. Her eyes were dark and anxious, but Monks imagined something else in the way she watched him: as if they had met in the past, and she was waiting to see if he would remember. He did not, and he was pretty sure he would have.

He stepped into the hall with her and gave her a quick rundown of the situation.

"This is horrible," she said. "It never should have happened."

It was not clear whether she meant the overdose, the emergency room treatment, or something else entirely.

"Are you sure you want him?" Monks said.

"Is he going to go down again?"

"Realistically, it's not likely."

"Then, yes. I have Narcan with me. I'll get him into treatment immediately."

The door from the ER opened into the hallway. It was Stephanie. Monks waited for her to pass by on whatever errand. But she lingered, with a tentative smile. Monks was surprised. It was not like Stef to be forward with strangers.

"Dr. Rostanov, my daughter Stephanie," he said. "First year med at UCSF."

Martine Rostanov's eyebrows arched: appraising, sensuous, even suggesting a potential for cruelty. Monks feared that she would say something cutting, impatient with the introduction in what was hardly a social situation.

But she said, "You must be very proud."

Stephanie stammered thanks. "Any advice?" Monks's surprise deepened: His daughter was blushing.

"You have to be better than the men," Dr. Rostanov said. "*Keep being better.*"

Then, in a gesture that was odd but just right, she touched Stef's cheek lightly with her fingers: a gracious dismissal. Stephanie hurried away, leaving him bemused at his daughter's boldness, and at the powerful presence he had glimpsed beneath Martine Rostanov's slight exterior.

"That was kind of you," he said.

"I know who you are." She spoke the words quietly, even timidly. Her eyes seemed to suggest sympathy.

Monks was puzzled. "I'm sorry. Have we—"

"No. From the newspapers, a couple of years ago."

Comprehension hit him with an abrupt tingle of adrenaline, a stark instantaneous flashback to a moment when he lay bleeding from knife slashes on the stone floor of a wine cave, while a psychopath's psychopath knelt on his back, about to hamstring him. With a clarity laced with nausea, he felt the shock of his cheek hitting the cold stone, the knife's sharp point piercing the flesh of his leg with practiced confidence, and he tasted the metallic but strangely sweet flavor of his own blood in his mouth. The events of that same night had spilled over into Mercy Hospital, most notably when another physician had had his heart removed on an autopsy table—while still alive at the time.

The hospital had done its best to downplay publicity, and like most news, it had blown quickly through the public's memory. Monks was left with a certain notoriety among coworkers, a sort of two-edged awe; in the eyes of some he was heroic, while others feared that he was like a man prone to being struck by lightning—bad luck and a danger to be near.

"A past life," Monks said. It was almost literally true.

She lowered her gaze. "I guess I should see—the patient—now."

Monks led her to the cubicle where John Smith waited. When she stepped inside, John's face turned sheepish, the expression of a boy who had been caught doing mischief. She shook her head in dismay, then sat beside him on the bed and smoothed his hair back, a maternal movement that suggested long-standing intimacy. Monks left.

A few minutes later, Ronald Tygard came out of the cubicle and walked to the main desk. Monks was already there, busily writing.

Tygard said to Leah Horvitz, "What do we owe you?"

Monks's hand paused and Leah looked up in surprise. This did not happen often.

"The bill won't be ready for a couple of days," she said.

"You must have a ballpark," Tygard said impatiently. He pulled a wallet from his inside coat pocket. "Five thousand? Ten?"

"Oh, I don't think nearly that." She looked to Monks for confirmation.

"Maybe two," Monks said. "Maybe less."

Tygard stripped three bills off a sheaf, as if he were dealing cards, and dropped them on the counter. They were thousands.

"We can't accept this," Leah said, flustered.

"It's legal tender, miss." Tygard was on top again, the high roller, obviously enjoying it.

"We'll put it in the safe," Monks said. "When you get the bill, send someone around to pick up the change."

"You can keep it."

This time, Monks let it pass. "I need to talk to you and your associates for a minute," he said. "You'd probably prefer it in private."

John Smith was sitting on the edge of the bed when Monks reentered the cubicle. He looked inquiringly at Martine Rostanov.

"Breathing and pulse are good," she said. "He says he feels all right."

"Go ahead and stand up," Monks said.

John rose to his feet, with her steadying him. He lowered his head briefly, dizzy, but then recovered.

"You going to be able to walk, or you want a wheelchair?" Monks said.

"I can walk."

"Okay," Monks said. "Listen up, please. I need to make it very clear that you're leaving this hospital against my medical advice. I'm only allowing it because I'm releasing you into the care of your personal physician. You still have narcotics in your system. There's the possibility of another overdose and even death for the next hours. Do you understand that?"

John nodded perfunctorily. He seemed to be regaining his haughtiness again, perhaps absorbing it from Tygard.

"Then, if you'll sign this, it's all written out here," Monks said. He handed John a release form with his admonitions scribbled on. "Mr. Tygard, since John doesn't have any identification and you're representing him legally, I'd like you to cosign."

"The bill is paid," Tygard said. "There's no need for any of this."

"Liability, Mr. Tygard, liability. I'll get another witness if you object."

Tygard took the clipboard and scrawled contemptuously across it.

"You too, Dr. Rostanov," Monks said. "And I'll need to make copies of your driver's license and California medical license."

Her eyes cooled. Monks had expected it, but it still hurt.

"I'm sorry," he said, "but you would too."

Silently, she handed him the licenses.

Monks said, "Good luck, John. I've given you my professional advice. Now I'll add some that's unprofessional. Be more careful about what you put in your arm. You probably got hold of something purer than what you're used to. That's how an overdose like this usually happens."

John's face took on an odd look, quizzical, uncertain. Monks got a little grim satisfaction from the thought that his words had registered.

The group left quickly, with Tygard and Martine Rostanov close beside John Smith, holding his arms to support him—or to shield him from other eyes. No one else seemed to be paying attention. It occurred to Monks that most of the ER staff had been aware of a wealthy thrill seeker and his arrogant lawyer, but only he and Stephanie had gotten good looks at John Smith's face.

Monks stepped to a window that looked into the parking lot. The two bodyguards met the group at the outer door and flanked them to a waiting vehicle, a black 600-series Mercedes with smoked windows. Tygard opened a rear door for John Smith to get in. Monks caught a glimpse of another man waiting in the backseat. He was perhaps fifty, handsome, hair just graying at the tips. Dr. Rostanov leaned in to talk with him. The exchange lasted perhaps a minute.

Then the graying man's hand came to rest on her wrist. It was a gesture that could have been consoling or grateful. But something about it—an excessive firmness, the sense that it pinned her to the car—suggested ownership.

The graying man released her. She moved back, and the Mercedes drove off.

Another car pulled up immediately, a silvery, new-model Volvo. Andrew, the bodyguard, jumped out and held the door open like a valet. She got in, alone, helping her left leg with her hand.

"She's beautiful, isn't she. Dr. Rostanov, I mean."

Monks turned quickly to find Stephanie beside him, watching the Volvo drive away. She wore an expression he had never quite seen before: admiration, tinged with longing.

"I don't mean pretty," Stef said. "*Strong*. Smart. It really hit me. Think of what it must be like for her, being in with those people."

"I'm sure it has its pros and cons," Monks said.

"What cons?"

He looked at her again, realizing how little he knew about the adult that his bright, idealistic child—straight-A and straight-arrow student— was becoming. He realized too that this experience was arguably the most exciting thing that had ever happened to her—even if only in her imagination.

"Suppose that was Lex Rittenour," Monks said. "And you were Dr. Rostanov. Think you'd be criticizing his billion-dollar brainchild?"

"I'd have told him what I thought, yes."

"In that case," Monks said, "I seriously doubt you'd still be with him."

Her mouth moved in a quick little pout, an expression he was much more familiar with. It meant that she knew he was right, but was damned if she was going to admit it.

He put his arm around her and squeezed her shoulders. "I'll be packing up pretty quick. You should too."

"To what, an empty bed and a hot water bottle?"

She stalked away, leaving him taken aback. The night was deepening the lesson that his daughter was a human being, with her own life, perhaps even desires.

Monks walked back into the ER and took up his position on the bridge. His watch read 8:38 P.M. He would be done at ten, the last leg of a three-shift stint, with the payoff of six days of freedom. He tried to refocus on a briefing for his relief. It was harder than usual.

He recalled the brief vignette he had glimpsed earlier, of the Asian woman who had arrived with John Smith, talking heatedly with Mrs. Hak. Monks walked to the admissions desk where Mrs. Hak was working. She was small-boned, attractive, and looked forty. But Monks had heard that in fact, she had been a child during the Korean War. She certainly remembered the hellish winter of 1950–1951, when most Koreans starved and many froze, with U.S. troops faring not much better, in the fighting that savaged them everywhere. He had never seen her look surprised.

He said, "I saw you talking to the lady who brought that patient in. I wondered if she left a name. In case something comes up."

Mrs. Hak shook her head. She spoke clear if choppy English that sometimes took a little deciphering, but she understood everything that was said to her.

"From Korea," she said. "Scared of trouble. No names."

"Did she say what happened?"

"Find him on sidewalk."

"They were just passing by?"

"Taxi driver."

A taxi driver who had obviously had some degree of emergency medical training. "He knew CPR," Monks said.

"Maybe solja first."

Monks remembered the man's parachute-type roll. Monks had not had personal contact with troops of the Republic of Korea in Vietnam, but they had been legendary. To the enemy—anyone or anything labeled Communist—they were a nightmare. In the early 1970s, while serving in the navy, he had passed through Seoul, where the downtown streets were strung with banners warning against spies from the north. Martial law and 10:00 P.M. curfew prevailed, with uniformed soldiers patrolling the streets, eager for the sport of beating or even shooting student offenders. Caution was an essential survival skill in Korea, and it was entirely possible that this pair were illegal immigrants, to boot.

"Okay. Thanks, Mrs. Hak." Monks turned to go.

"Docta? What you think might come up?" She watched him with her neutral gaze.

"Nothing, really," Monks admitted.

There was no reason anything should.

THREE

Monks had hardly started reviewing his next chart when lights began flashing on the ER's walls. He knew it was only a fire alarm, but for the first instant, the bright strobelike bursts brought a memory of the far-off trails of tracers. Immediately, a muffled bell started sounding in a 2–3–2 pattern.

Leah Horvitz stood, supervising while the other nurses hurried around closing doors. Monks listened for the PA message that would announce the fire's location. These alarms were almost always drills; even if it was real, it would not affect the ER unless it was very close.

"Dr. Red is on One-North," the PA said, the message, like the alarm, coded to prevent patient panic. Monks stopped paying attention. One-North was at the other end of the building, near medical records and the pathology lab.

But then he heard another sound, faint and faraway, one he probably would not have picked up, except that he had spent a lifetime listening for it:

Sirens.

City fire inspectors sometimes supervised the drills, but emergency vehicles would not come out for one.

Monks walked into the waiting room. The fifteen or so people there watched him anxiously; they could hear the sirens too, and see the flashing lights coming fast.

"Don't be scared," Monks said loudly. "There's a minor incident at the other end of the hospital." A few people moved closer to the door anyway, obviously unimpressed by his reassurances. Down by One-North, two trucks pulled up, with city firemen unloading equipment on the run. Monks went back into the ER, moving faster.

"This might be for real," he told Leah. "Cover the room a minute, I'll go take a look." If patient evacuation did become necessary, it would be a good thing to have a jump on it.

Monks turned a corner and met Stephanie, hurrying toward the ER, looking breathless.

"You were supposed to go home," he said.

"I went to see what was happening," she panted, grabbing his lapel and turning back. "Come on, there's something weird."

Monks trotted alongside her. Strobe lights were flashing all down the hall, and he began to smell the acrid reek of smoke.

"Weird?" he said.

"I saw two firemen go into the lab," she said. "They were apart from the others."

"What's weird about that?"

"It's not where the fire is."

"Are you sure?"

"It's in a conference room, down by Records," she said impatiently. "I saw them spraying it."

The hallway outside the lab was empty. Farther along, around another corner, Monks could hear a sizable commotion, raised voices, and the sounds of heavy-booted feet.

"In there," Stephanie said, needlessly whispering, pointing at the lab's closed doors. "I heard one of them say, 'This is it.' They, like, trotted in and closed the doors behind them."

Monks went to the double metal doors and felt them with his palms. They were cool. He knocked, then tried the handles. The doors were locked. It was not something that happened automatically. There was another exit from the lab, but it struck him as very odd that firemen would seal off any potential escape route.

He knocked again, louder, pounding. "Are you all right in there?" he called. "What's going on?"

After half a minute, there was no response. He walked down the hall and turned the corner toward Records, Stephanie hurrying along with him.

Several firemen in full gear were standing watchfully outside the door of a conference room, holding extinguishers, with a heavy hose snaked across the floor. Smoke hung in the doorway. What he could see inside the room was wet from sprinklers, and globs of extinguisher foam clung to surfaces.

"Two of your men went into a laboratory," Monks said to the group. "The door's locked. I think you'd better check it out."

One of them stepped forward and raised his mask, revealing an earnest face with a walrus mustache. It looked puzzled.

"My men are all here, sir," he said. He turned to his crew and demanded, "Any of you go into a lab?" There was a general shaking of heads.

"Can you describe them?" Monks asked Stephanie.

"They looked the same as these guys," she said defensively: covered from head to foot in helmets, heavy rubberized slickers, gloves, and boots.

"Let's go take a look," their chief said. "Anybody got a key?"

Other hospital personnel were gathered at a distance, evacuated or drawn there to see what was going on. A couple of the hospital's security personnel were there too, including the night chief, Joaquin Gutierrez. Monks had gotten to know him fairly well over the years; the ER did a lot of business with Security, especially after dark.

Monks beckoned to him. Joaquin approached with a sort of waddle; he was not a fat man, but had a barrel-like torso that bottomed into stubby legs and almost no hips. He wore a perpetually woeful expression.

"We need to open up the lab," Monks said.

Joaquin searched the ring of a couple dozen keys that hung from his belt. "Looks like a coffeemaker," he told Monks quietly as they walked. "The plastic housing melted, like it shorted. Caught some paper napkins on fire, they caught the drapes." Joaquin shook his head. "I don't know. Lot of coincidence."

The implication touched Monks with queasiness—there might be an arsonist in the hospital.

Joaquin singled out a key, unlocked the lab doors, and pulled them open.

Monks stared in disbelief. The room's far end looked like it had exploded. The stainless-steel storage refrigerator doors were gaping open; racks of blood were strewn across the floor, many smashed, pooling into a gory swamp glittering with broken glass. The whole mess was covered with extinguisher foam.

"Jesus," the fire chief said. He wheeled to the men who had come with him. "Whoever did this better have a damn good explanation."

But nobody did. There was another round of head-shaking, and steadfast denials from the firefighters that any of them had even entered the lab.

Within a couple of minutes, janitors wearing barrier gear against possible contagions arrived to clean up the blood. The fire chief was talking to lab personnel, assuring them the city would cooperate if they wanted an investigation.

"There's nothing we can do here," Monks said to Stephanie. "Let's get back."

"You think it was an accident?" she said.

"What else?" The obvious scenario was that two of firefighters— overzealous, pumped up on adrenaline—had attacked the wrong area, and were understandably trying to cover for it.

She shrugged. "It's still weird."

"You watch too much TV," Monks said.

It got weirder a few minutes later. Joaquin Gutierrez reappeared, coming to the ER doorway and motioning Monks into the hall. He looked even more unhappy than before.

"You mind coming back down, Doc? Seems like most of what they smashed was from the ER. Like it was deliberate."

Monks was startled. "Really."

"Yeah. They stole some stuff too."

"What kind of stuff?"

"Blood."

Monks was more startled. He walked with Joaquin to the lab.

The senior lab tech on duty—a spectacled, owlish man named Ollie Burstall—had started taking inventory.

"As if this wasn't bad enough," Ollie fumed, flailing his hand toward the violated storage refrigerators. "They took blood samples off our *desks*. *Oafs* are one thing. *Ghouls* are another. What are we going to find in the broom closets, cattle mutilations?"

"You're sure that most of what's missing is from the ER?" Monks said.

"That's what tipped me off," Ollie said emphatically. "I was about to recheck one with a high differential count when the fire started. When I came back, it was gone. I started looking at the rest, and that's the common denominator." His finger tapped Monks's chest. "*You* people."

This implied a number of things. That whoever had done it was familiar enough with hospital procedure to know the various places where the samples were likely to have been stored. That it was, in fact, intentional. And that the intent was something specific, although Monks had not a clue what. It occurred to him that the two firemen Stephanie had seen might have been phonies; might even have set the fire in the conference room as cover.

But that was a hell of a lot of trouble to go to, to destroy some blood samples. If the object was theft, what could be done with several test-tubes? The blood was useless for a transfusion or anything of that sort: all of different types, and it could easily have contained a spectrum of diseases, possibly including HIV, hepatitis B and C, or other virulent agents. Monks had known of all kinds of items stolen from hospitals—money, equipment, supplies, and, of course, drugs—but this was nonsensical.

Still, Joaquin's words reverberated: *Lot of coincidence*.

"I'll have replacements sent down for any patients still here, Ollie," Monks said. "If there's anything else, let me know."

Outside in the hall, Joaquin said dolefully, "This isn't gonna make me look good. What do we do, sue the fire department?"

It was not going to make the hospital look good either. But the damage was not as bad as it had first appeared. With the ER's fast turnover, most of its patients had already checked out. Any samples that remained necessary, along with the main hospital's samples that had been dragged off the racks too, could be redrawn without causing much flap.

"Take it easy, Joaquin," Monks said. "Nobody could have seen this coming. Chances are it will just go away."

Monks trudged back upstairs, grateful that his shift was almost over. He went to the main desk and explained the situation to Leah Horvitz. The ER's admission list for the past hours would have to be compared with the lab's inventory and necessary samples retaken. He was not surprised to notice that Stephanie was hovering nearby, listening.

She cornered him immediately afterward, her eyes afire.

"That's *it*," she said.

"What's it?"

"They can't afford to have it known that Lex Rittenour's an addict, especially with that big IPO coming up. So they trashed all the blood samples from the ER. It wasn't any accident, they knew what they were looking for."

"Whoa, whoa," Monks said. "Who's 'they?' "

"Aesir Corporation. His company."

"I'm still not following you, honey."

"The paternity suit," she said, with the patience of speaking to someone very slow. "His DNA signature's a matter of record."

Monks finally got it. Establishing that John Smith was really Lex Rittenour would be very difficult. But if a sample of John Smith's blood from tonight had been subjected to DNA analysis and matched the known signature from Lex Rittenour's paternity suit—that would constitute positive identification.

"You're suggesting the company staged a raid?" Monks said incredulously. "In that short a time? They'd have to operate like the CIA."

"Are you kidding? They're huge, worldwide. They have floors of offices in the Bank of America Building. Dad, where've you been?"

Monks tried to dismiss the idea: It was an absurd amount of trouble, not to mention highly illegal, for insurance against something that was unlikely anyway.

On the other hand, having a megacorporation's presiding genius identified as an addict would be infinitely bigger trouble—especially with a billion-plus dollars at stake within the next days. Money was no object to a company like Aesir. Certainly, they had their own highly trained security, and it was not too much of a stretch to assume they were capable of commando-type activities.

Offices in the Bank of America building, where Ronald Tygard also happened to be based. The BOA was a big building, but it was still another notable coincidence.

"You *have* to call them on it," Stephanie declared.

"Why?"

"They set fire to the hospital. You can't just let it go."

"On the contrary, Stephanie, that's an excellent reason to let it go. Christ knows what else they'd be willing to do." He was only half-joking.

"Come *on*. This is fascinating. Aren't you curious?"

Curiosity did not play a large part in Monks's life when he was trying to stay on top of an ER with several patients inside, a bunch more waiting, paramedics in the field, and the chance of a serious crisis at any moment.

Although it was true that that was over for the next few days.

"Okay," Stephanie said, with the air of releasing a pent-up confession. "*She's* fascinating. Dr. Rostanov. I wish I could get to know her."

Monks's perplexity deepened, but he grasped dimly that this went along with losing the child she had been. She was turning into the adult she was going to be, but was not yet sure who that was; casting about, eager and a little scared, looking for people who would define her.

"You think so too," she said. "Admit it."

"Stephanie, I can't imagine that Dr. Rostanov was involved in the fire or the theft. And if I went walking in to see her, waving a couple of felonies, it wouldn't exactly warm the air."

"What have you got to lose?"

Monks drew himself upright. "I'm glad I stand so high in your estimation."

"I'm sorry, Dad, I didn't mean it like that. You could just go talk to her." She raised her palms in exasperation and left again, this time for good.

Monks was left standing alone, feeling a little sorry for himself: unjustly condemned. He had not seen fit to point out that Martine Rostanov, with the high-powered company she kept, was not likely to be very interested in a curmudgeonly fiftyish ER doc, or his no-matter-how-bright-and-charming student daughter, in return. Not to mention the fact that he had annoyed her by demanding her licenses.

But there had been that moment of near-intimacy. *I know who you are.*

It was also true that the hospital would investigate the matter, internally and maybe officially as well. For Monks to bring these suspicions to light could have huge consequences. The more information, the better.

Then there was the point that Stephanie had made: He had nothing to lose.

Monks went on into the ER to close out his shift.

FOUR

Martine Rostanov's licenses identified her as an internist with an address in Burlingame, an affluent area south of San Francisco. They gave no phone number, and there was none listed for her. Monks walked out into the hospital's parking lot and got into his '74 Ford Bronco. He located her street, Mirada Avenue, on a city map. It was toward the west end of Burlingame—just about dead on top of the San Andreas Fault—and this time of night, taking Nineteenth Avenue and Interstate 280, it should be an easy twenty-minute drive.

He sat for a moment longer, feeling like a high-school boy, then started driving south.

Nothing to lose.

Traffic was light. Monks settled into the warm comfort of the old truck, feeling the city around him in a way that was usually lost in tension and haste. San Francisco was one of the world's most beautiful places, its Mediterranean profile, in clear weather, breathtakingly sharp against the blue Pacific sky. But Monks loved it like it was tonight, softened by the mist, lights blurred, outlines indistinct. The sense was something like a striptease: intimate, mysterious, exciting, not because of what it showed, but what it promised.

He passed the San Francisco State campus, then the last of the stop-lights, and accelerated into the concrete-banked valley onto 280. His mind turned to what Stephanie had been talking about: a genetics breakthrough which not only involved huge sums of money, but which epitomized the influence on human life that this new science was certain to have.

When Monks had been in school, the science of modern genetics was just beginning its explosion. The discovery it rested on—the double helix structure of the DNA molecule—had taken place only in 1953. Since then, knowledge had been amassed with bewildering speed; it was impossible for him to keep up with it in any kind of detail. But the scheme that had taken shape in his mind—very rough, vastly oversimplified, and with many exceptions—went like this:

Every cell in the human body (about one hundred trillion) contained a genetic component that was something like a city, tiny but very densely populated. All of these cities were almost identical. All had the same number of streets (chromosomes), twenty-three pairs, with one member of each pair coming from the mother and one from the father. If the last street at the outskirts of town dead-ended part way (the Y chromosome), you were male instead of female.

The streets were divided into blocks (genes); there were somewhere upward of 25,000 of these. Each block had thousands of houses. As in some 1950s-style subdivisions, the houses were available in only four models, A,C,G, and T (for adenine, cytosine, guanine, and thymine). They were arranged in three-unit complexes—about a billion of these per city. Together, they created the building blocks (proteins) which made for the actual construction of flesh and bone.

All humans were 99.9 percent alike genetically (bad news for racial supremacists). The layout, size, and shape of the streets, blocks, and even the arrangement of houses, were just about the same. Moreover, there was not any extra or fundamentally different genetic material that caused humanity's huge variety of characteristics. This came from the statistically slight, but still almost infinite, variations in order.

For years, scientists steadily had been filling in the city map, locating the blocks and even specific houses. Very recently, in what some considered the greatest scientific breakthrough in history, the map had been essentially drawn. The next step was staggering in its complexity: figuring out what the individual houses did. Each gene might have many functions; it often seemed to work in conjunction with other genes; to be active at different levels in different circumstances; and to be influenced by a host of other factors, many yet unknown.

But there was no doubt that gene decoding was the key to the future health of the human race. Some genes that caused malfunctions—disease and birth defects—had already been identified; finding more, and learning how to control them, was being worked on feverishly. Entire new fields of medicine were burgeoning, and every part of the puzzle that was filled in might yield concrete results, tangible help for the suffering of real human beings. That was the dream.

It was also the dream of big business around the world. The potential for profit was almost unimaginable

And now a new player had appeared on the scene, promising a quantum leap in making it come true: a hero, arisen to battle the raider cells that sailed through the bloodstream, ravaging peaceful organ communities.

This was Lex Rittenour's brainchild: REGIS, the Rittenour Gene Identification System.

Tests to identify some genes which caused defects or disease already existed. But this technology was limited, there were comparatively few such tests, and they were like arrows that had to be shot at specific targets.

REGIS was a software program developed by combining biochip technology, laser scanning, and computer analysis to yield a sweeping genetic test, shooting a barrage of arrows at numerous targets. In theory, this would allow quick identification of many troublesome genes all at once. Eventually, a single blood scan would lay out an individual's potential to develop disease or pass on damaging genes. Those conditions could then be treated or avoided.

But the downside of the dream was the fear that REGIS would be used to label and even create genetic superiority—and its opposite. It was further inflamed by the fact that the name REGIS suggested a Latin cognate for royalty.

And it had not gone unnoticed that the computer giant corporation backing REGIS was called Aesir: the name for the pantheon of Norse gods, with its mighty figures like the warriors Odin and Thor, who guided the Vikings on their raids, and Freya, the goddess of love, who rode with the armorclad Valkyries to carry dying heroes to Valhalla, there to brawl and carouse until the day of doom.

Aesir, the gods, creating REGIS, the king. All taken together, Monks thought, it did suggest that ordinary human beings did not loom very large on that particular map.

He drove on, with John Smith's words resonating in his head: *I'm Frankenstein, man. I created a monster. A perfect monster. Worst kind. Now I want to lock it up, but it's gotten huge.*

Monks was starting to wonder if that monster's name was REGIS.

Monks took the Trousdale exit off the freeway and found his way to an older section of Burlingame, a sheltered enclave of grandiose mansions with extensive grounds, hidden behind high hedges. He turned in at 2735 Mirada. The house was stone, with tiled roof and ivied walls, definitely in the seven-figure range.

Not bad for an internist.

There were lights on downstairs. The single car in the drive was the silver Volvo he had seen her leave the hospital in, two hours earlier. He climbed the steps to the porch. The old beveled-glass panes in the door gave him a glimpse into an entry hall that opened into a spacious, high-ceilinged living room.

Monks rang the bell, not sure what to expect. He had noticed that she had not worn a wedding ring. But he remembered the gray-haired man in the limousine, the casual ownership that had seemed implicit in his touch on her wrist.

Martine Rostanov came into sight a moment later, walking cautiously with her slight limp, and switched on the porch light. Monks thought he saw a small shiver when she recognized him, like shock at an abrupt and intrusive reality.

But she opened the door quickly and said, "Well, hello," in a way that seemed shyly welcoming.

"I'm sorry to disturb you," he said. "I would have called, but I don't have the number."

"It's been a disturbing night. You're the first one to apologize." She stepped back, holding the door open, a gesture inviting him in.

"I should probably tell you why I'm here," he said, not yet moving. "There was an incident at the hospital after you left. Another incident, I should say. A fire, then the lab was sacked, by firemen who seem to be phonies. They destroyed or stole dozens of blood samples."

Her face became troubled. It deepened the darkness under her eyes that makeup did not quite conceal.

"That's terrible," she said. "Why in the world would someone do it?"

"The samples included all of John Smith's. With your people so bent on protecting his identity, we suspect those were the target. To prevent possible DNA identification of John."

She said, "Oh," a quiet exhalation that combined shock, disappointment, and weariness. She turned back inside, leaving the door open. Monks followed her, feeling a little guilty for not pointing out that "we" consisted of Stephanie and himself.

The living room was old plaster, painted a color between brindle and peach. The woodwork was Victorian-style, clear fir stained a deep mahogany. The result was a subdued glow. The furniture matched: early American chairs and pine sideboard, oak coffee table, an old couch of deep burgundy pile, all unobtrusively elegant.

Martine moved to a window, rubbing her bare upper arms as if she were cold. "So? What can I do for you?"

"I'm not sure what's going to happen with this," Monks said. "The hospital administration may or may not want to press an investigation. I have to decide whether to tell them what I think, or withhold it. I thought talking to you might help me make that decision."

"Ah, yes. You're an investigator, aren't you?" she said, perhaps with a trace of sarcasm.

"In a minor league. If this does turn official, you're going to be dealing with people a lot tougher than me."

"Well, what does the hospital have to press?"

"I don't know yet," Monks said. The fireman's words that Stephanie had heard—*This is it*—did not amount to much, and he did not want to bring his daughter into it. "Some kind of physical evidence may turn up, or an eyewitness. But—with John Smith's resemblance to Lex Rittenour, I'm sure all this would be interesting to the media."

Her hands stopped moving on her arms. "That resemblance is nothing but your guess," she said coolly. "And making it public in a damaging way would be libelous."

"It might not gain the hospital anything tangible. But our chief administrator's an ex-marine who likes to even scores."

"Why come to me? Why didn't you call Ron Tygard? He's the lawyer."

"Mr. Tygard and I didn't get along," Monks said. "Quite frankly, I had my fill of him in a real short time."

"You think you and I can do any better?"

Monks hesitated, then said, "My daughter admired you."

Her face flashed surprise, then amusement—but it was not displeased. "Really."

"I think she's at an age where she's looking for who she wants to be."

"I'm afraid I'm not much of a role model."

"Me either," Monks said. "But she doesn't seem to see it that way."

Martine turned away, gazing out the window. Her reflection in the glass was like a pale shadow.

"You don't know anything about me," she said.

"True," he admitted.

"You must have a lot of faith in your daughter's judgment."

"It's not just hers," Monks said.

He thought he saw Martine's eyebrows rise, the same appraising look as when Stephanie had first approached her. For another half minute, neither of them spoke.

Then she turned back, folding her arms, businesslike now.

"All right, Dr. Monks. First off, I don't know anything about the fire or the rest of it. I don't have any reason to think anyone at Aesir was involved. But strictly between you and me—" She moved a little closer, with a confiding air. "There are people who think they're above the law."

Monks was impressed by the admission. Martine Rostanov seemed to have no hesitations once she made up her mind. "Meaning?"

"Meaning the company would like to head off trouble," she said. "There are other people there who'd do anything to make it right."

"You're in position to speak for them like that?" he said.

"Not officially. But I'm well connected there."

"What *are* you, officially?"

"I'm the company's on-call physician," she said. "And I take care of occasional delicate problems. Like tonight."

"Do you know Lex Rittenour?"

"I've met him. He doesn't come down into the trenches much."

"Was that him tonight?" Monks said. "Aka John Smith?"

She tilted her head, eyes narrowing.

"Lex Rittenour doesn't have anything to do with this. John Smith is another Aesir executive who happens to look like him."

"Okay," Monks said, spreading his hands. "I don't have any stake in proving it one way or the other. I'll just remind you that something might turn up to contradict your statement."

"You're right, the confusion could be very damaging," she said quickly. "Especially just now. So why don't we get back to the people who'd be glad to take care of it?"

Monks weighed the situation. Without proof, the hospital had nothing. Even if substantive evidence did turn up, bringing it to bear would involve a David-and-Goliath fight with Aesir Corporation: a court battle that was likely to drag on for years, cost a lot of trouble and money, and end up a pyrrhic victory at best.

On the other hand, there was the principle of the thing. An assault on a place of healing, felony theft and destruction, outrage and insult to the institution itself, to what it stood for, to the people who worked there. Monks had become less hard-edged about principles over the years, but there were still lines drawn deep within his consciousness. Often, even he did not know where they were until something got close to crossing one.

This was close.

"What would 'taking care of it' involve?" he said.

"Let me make a phone call."

She left the room. Monks looked over the paintings on the walls. Like everything else, they were tasteful, a mix of modern and more classical styles. But he was drawn to the smallest, a rough-textured Impressionist landscape of muted blues, greens, and browns, about sixteen inches wide by twelve inches high. The scene was a somber afternoon in a late autumn countryside with a single small figure bowed in a weary walk, a tableau that evoked with almost painful intensity the lonely distances between human beings, before those could be filled by televisions and phones. Monks was pretty sure he recognized the small signature at bottom right, but he stepped close to be positive. It was Renoir.

Martine came back into the room and said, "I can't reach the person I need. How about tomorrow morning?"

Monks nodded. "Give me a number. I'll talk to administration and call you."

She went to an antique secretary desk and leaned over to write. There was something about her profile, face intent, her braced leg a little bent at the knee, that touched him with a quick, fierce emotion he could not quite identify. Then he had it: an urge to protect.

She handed him the paper, then walked with him to the entryway and stepped into shadow.

"About that admiration," she said. "When I told you that you don't know anything about me—let's say there was a girl who let her head be turned, a long time ago."

"Turned how?"

"Into a world where right and wrong get blurred."

"I think that happens to most people, in some way," Monks said.

"Maybe. But she moved further in. Now she can't even look back and see her footprints, they're covered in sand."

It sounded like the flip side of his own dilemma. But representing your own or your employer's best interests was one thing. Covering a crime was another.

"So what's that girl telling me?" he said.

"She's not sure there's really much you'd admire."

"She doesn't look like the devious type."

"That's part of what made it fun, at first. Nobody would have dreamed it. She was a cripple, overachieving to make up for it. Then one day somebody important noticed her. Cinderella."

Monks glanced around the elegant room. "Doesn't look like she regrets it too much either."

Anger came into her eyes. "It's not about money, it's about comfort. She found out she couldn't trust people. Especially men. So she bought nice things instead. Those, she can count on."

Monks said, "Comfort, or armor?"

The anger in her eyes deepened and her mouth set in a thin line.

"What happened to that woman who killed Robby Vandenard?" she said. "Alison, wasn't that her name?"

Monks blinked, taken off balance. For the second time tonight, he recalled the man who had almost killed him with a grape-picker's knife. Earlier, when Martine Rostanov had put her finger on that raw wound of terror in his memory, it might have been only naive. But this time it was a counterpunch. He supposed he had asked for it.

"Alison left the area," he said. "I haven't heard from her in a while."

"Did it change her?"

"I think it's safe to say that."

"How about you?"

"I still wake up sometimes trying to scream," he said. "If that's what you mean."

She deflated a little, the anger seeming to leave her, as if she realized that the punch was a low one.

"I'm sorry," she said. "I can't help wondering what it would be like to experience something—that powerful."

"I'd say it's best left to the imagination."

Abruptly, Monks was aware of a figure at the edge of his vision. He turned swiftly. It was a man, standing in the living room toward the back of the house, watching them. There was no telling how long he had been there.

The lawyer, Ronald Tygard.

Tygard walked toward them, right hand in his coat pocket, as if he was holding a pistol.

Martine stared at him. "What are you doing in my house? How'd you get in?"

"Something's come up," Tygard said.

"What kind of 'something?' "

Tygard ignored her question and jerked his head at Monks. "What's *he* doing here?"

Monks said, "Fire and blood."

When the implication hit, Tygard's mask of cold control slipped, just for an instant. He caught himself quickly. "What the hell does that mean?"

But it had been enough, and both men knew it.

"Dr. Monks and I are working things out," Martine said to Tygard. "I called Ken Bouldin but he wasn't in."

Then she inhaled sharply and reached out to touch Tygard—an instinctive gesture that she stopped partway. "What happened to your head?"

Now Monks saw it: a swelling on the right rear of Tygard's skull above his ear, with the hair slightly matted with blood.

Tygard shrugged impatiently. "Banged it." It looked more as if someone had banged it for him. "You'd better talk to Bouldin right now," he said to Martine. "He's in his office." Tygard moved back toward the room's far end, punching numbers on a cell phone, gesturing her to follow. "You stay here," he told Monks.

Monks bristled, starting to declare that he would do whatever he damned well wanted to. But he was not about to leave just to prove he could. He stepped to the front door and looked out. He saw Tygard's car now, a deep green Jaguar XK convertible that must have driven in without lights. It was parked behind Monks's Bronco, blocking it in. Andrew, the football player-type who had been with Tygard in the ER, was standing by. Monks's anger intensified, but so did his wariness.

There are people who think they're above the law.

It was a good bet that the bump on Tygard's head had not improved his mood.

Monks turned back just in time to see Martine hurrying from the room, looking agitated. Tygard was still talking grimly on the phone. He thrust his hand toward Monks, palm out: stand back. The hand stayed there, fidgeting, for ten seconds longer. Then it dropped, and Tygard stalked to Monks and handed him the phone.

"You're talking to the CEO of Aesir Corporation," Tygard said, with the air of warning an altar boy that he was addressing the pope.

"Dr. Monks?" the voice on the phone said. It was urbane, firm, a powerful instrument: a voice that knew its job and how to get its owner what he wanted. "Ken Bouldin here. I gather there were some problems this evening for you and your colleagues. I'd like to see if we can't smooth things over."

"I think the hospital would be interested in a meeting," Monks said.

"Any chance you could come to me, sir? I'm afraid I'm in a state of siege, here in my office."

"You mean now?" Monks said, surprised. It was 10:41 P.M.

"I'd like to resolve it immediately."

Monks realized that his usual post-ER weariness had vanished. "All right."

"My men will be glad to drive you."

Monks glanced at Tygard's sour face. "I have a vehicle," Monks said.

"Bank of America Building. They'll be expecting you at the desk."

Monks handed the phone back to Tygard. Martine had not returned to the room.

"What happened to Dr. Rostanov?" Monks said.

"She's not feeling well."

"She was fine a minute ago."

Tygard stepped close, giving Monks the hard stare. Quietly, he said, "Don't piss me off any more than you already have."

"Your car's blocking mine," Monks said. "I'll need you to move it."

On the drive back into the city, Monks could see in his rearview mirror that Tygard's Jaguar was traveling steadily along with him, a few car lengths behind. For about the first time in his life, he started to feel important.

FIVE

Monks walked through the night across the Bank of America plaza, skirting the sculpture at the corner of California and Montgomery Streets. It was a modern work, its surface hard and glittering and black as obsidian, shaped something like a large torpedo. Around San Francisco, it was known as The Banker's Heart. Fifty yards past it rose the BOA building itself, fifty-two stories of smoked-glass corporate splendor that was a dominant feature of the city's skyline.

Although it was after 11 P.M., there was plenty of activity in the lobby. Apparently an IPO like this one was big business, even here. Uniformed security guards met Monks at the doors, checked his identification, then led him to a desk where the appointment was verified by telephone. The guards rode with him up the elevator to Aesir Corporation's thirty-fourth floor offices.

Doors were open all along the wide main corridor. Personnel with the executive look—impeccable hairstyles, perfect teeth, expensive eyewear—hurried around with charged, expectant energy. The guards still stayed with him. He sensed that they were wary, confused, and even annoyed by his presence. It was not just his much-worn tweed sports coat or the Wellington-style work boots he wore for comfort through the long ER hours on his feet. He simply did not belong in this world—and yet he had been invited by the CEO. It made Monks hard to peg.

His keepers finally released him into the custody of a very attractive secretary, who told him that Mr. Bouldin would be with him in just a minute and showed him to a waiting room. Monks declined a chair but accepted coffee. It was good, a rich, strong brew that had not come from an urn. He gazed out the floor-to-ceiling windows, down on the city spreading like a glowing opulent mirage. A text from long-ago religion classes came into his mind, one of those lessons that had been imprinted so early and thoroughly, it was impossible to estimate the effect it had had on his life.

And the devil, taking him up into an high mountain, shewed unto him all the kingdoms of the world in a moment of time. And the devil said unto him, All this power will I give thee, and the glory of them.

The secretary returned. Monks followed her fillylike prance—slim taut calves and smooth hips encased in a thigh-high bandage-tight skirt—to a very large corner office.

When he stepped inside, his gaze was caught first by a banner on the far wall, shaped like a square sail and almost as big. It sported the Aesir Corporation logo: a black longboat, a replica of the Viking ship that had terrorized the civilized world for centuries, cutting across an ice-blue sea.

In front of the banner was a massive rosewood desk that must have weighed a quarter ton. A man stood behind it. He was handsome, fit, vital, with a deep, even suntan and hair just graying:

The man who had been sitting in the limousine earlier, and who had touched Martine Rostanov's wrist.

"Ken Bouldin," he said, offering Monks a handshake with just the right firmness of grip. "Thanks for coming, Doctor."

Beside Bouldin sat a woman who could have been thirty-five but was probably closer to fifty, with the kind of beauty that was gene-deep, enhanced by artifice but not depending on it. She wore a close-fitting charcoal cashmere dress that accentuated her shimmering mass of tawny hair and lithe body. She made Monks think of a not-quite-tame cat.

"Audrey Cabot, our chief of operations," Bouldin said. She inclined her head, with a look that Monks had encountered before, but never with such easy intensity. It suggested that she assigned values to everything she saw and owned what she wanted, and that Monks did not cost very much.

So: Kenneth Bouldin and Audrey Cabot were the top-ranking Aesir, the gods who controlled fabulous wealth, power—even genetic destiny.

"And Pete Hazeldon," Bouldin said.

Monks had hardly noticed the other man in the room, slumped in a chair off to the side. He was younger, even boyish looking, with long, frizzy hair, a cheap plaid shirt, and baggy pleated khaki pants—the only other person Monks had seen here who did not seem to fit. He raised his hand in an awkward wave, as if shy about being acknowledged, and went back to writing or doodling on a scratch pad.

"Pete's head of research and development," Bouldin said. "He's been Lex Rittenour's long-time partner."

There came a pause—a still, brittle couple of seconds when Monks sensed that they were waiting to see how he was going to play this, if he would suggest that what had happened at the hospital had anything to do with Rittenour.

Monks said, "I know the name. Not much else about him, I'm afraid."

The tension broke with small subliminal movements, Bouldin relaxing, Audrey brushing back her hair. Monks sensed that he had passed the test. Bouldin gestured him to a chair and took his own seat. He leaned forward, elbows on the desk.

"Martine—Dr. Rostanov—tells us you saved John Smith's life tonight."

"It was actually a taxi driver who saved his life," Monks said.

Bouldin seemed not to hear. "I can't tell you how grateful we are. It's a troubling situation: a bright man who's been acting erratic. Where the hell he got hold of narcotics, what prompted him to do it, I don't know. But his timing couldn't have been worse. Aesir can't afford even a breath of scandal now. The market can be a timid animal.

A danger signal sounds, even a completely false one, and it might panic."

"I could see where you'd want to avoid a stampede," Monks agreed.

"Exactly. We felt that we had to use discretion. As I said, we'd like to compensate the hospital for any abrasiveness."

Bouldin opened a drawer and laid a packet on the desk: sheafs of paper that looked like oversized currency.

Stock.

"The pre-IPO value is fifty thousand," Bouldin said modestly.

If the pundits were right, the sheaf on the desk was going to be worth upward of a quarter of a million dollars in less than sixty hours. There was also the fact that, on the brink of an event that had Aesir Corporation executives camped until midnight in their offices, the CEO was personally taking the trouble—

"We'd want a clear understanding of continued discretion," Bouldin said.

—to tender a bribe. Monks was starting to feel important again.

"I'll pass the offer on," he said. "But I can't speak for the hospital."

"How about for yourself?" It was Audrey Cabot, the first time she had spoken. She had a pleasingly throaty voice. The effect sounded practiced, but well practiced. "We got the impression that you were particularly offended."

"Not 'particularly,' Ms. Cabot. I get offended a lot in the ER; this was nothing special. The real issue is what happened later, the fire and tearing up the lab. There, we're talking tangible damage, in the felony range."

There was another pause. Monks understood that he had raised the stakes.

"Martine mentioned something about that," Bouldin said. "I assure you that Aesir had nothing to do with it." He spoke the last syllables with staccato emphasis and steady gaze. "Any rumors damaging to Aesir could have very serious legal consequences. For the hospital, and possibly for its personnel."

Monks ignored the obvious threat: *personnel like you.*

"There are a couple of coincidences," Monks said. "The fact that the raid occurred right after John Smith's release. That blood samples from the ER seem to have been singled out." He considered adding, *And let's face it, that John Smith is a dead ringer for Lex Rittenour*, but decided to let that rest. "That's all they are at this point, coincidences."

"What we're concerned about is those coincidences finding their way to public attention," Bouldin said.

Monks shrugged. "If an investigation comes along, I'll cooperate fully. On the other hand, attention is something I try to avoid."

He got the sense that Bouldin and Audrey Cabot exchanged nods, although he could not perceive any actual motions. It was as if they understood each other so intimately, there was no need.

Audrey stood, moving toward the door. "Nice to meet you, Dr. Monks. Oh, I understand you have a daughter entering medical school. It must be enormously expensive." She left the room, legs stretching with feline grace, steps making no sound.

Bouldin opened the desk drawer again and laid a second sheaf of stock beside the first.

"This is for you and your family," Bouldin said, and smiled. "It might perk up your interest in following the market."

A tap came at the door, and the secretary who had shepherded Monks stepped in. "Mr. Bouldin? Call for you, on line three."

Bouldin rose swiftly. When he reached her, she leaned close to his ear to whisper. Monks was pretty sure he heard the word "senator." Bouldin's lips compressed. He raised a hand toward Monks in apology or dismissal, and followed her out.

Monks was left alone with Pete Hazeldon, who had not really seemed to be a part of the interaction. But when Bouldin left, he dropped his scratch pad on the floor and leaned forward, suddenly animated.

"Nobody seems to give a damn about John Smith, you notice that?" he said.

Monks thought the trace of accent came from southern New Jersey, maybe Philadelphia. He was not as young as Monks had first thought; the boyish look was undercut by a lined face.

"He does seem to be something of an inconvenience," Monks agreed. He could not help glancing again at the sheafs of stock. Half a million bucks, half of it his—assuming nothing went wrong with the IPO.

"I think he was really feeling the pressure," Hazeldon said. "Everybody just got back from the road show. We're jet-lagged so many times over it's canceling itself out."

"Road show?"

"Hyping the IPO. Creating a global feeding frenzy. Eighteen major cities in four weeks. I mean, I could see somebody drinking too much. But *junk*." Hazeldon shook his head, as if unable to grasp the enormity of it. "Did he tell you what happened?"

"He said he didn't remember."

"Scary."

"He's a friend, I take it?"

Hazeldon flopped back in the chair, with a sort of grunt. "You don't make friends in an outfit like this."

"How about Lex Rittenour?" Monks was aware of that same sort of brittle pause that had occurred earlier. "I mean, you've worked with him a lot?"

"A lot." An expressive shrug. "Lex is so fucking smart in some ways, it's unbelievable. He's like an idiot savant. He can set up these incredibly complex software programs. But he doesn't use any logical progression, so they're full of holes. We have to go back and fill them in to make it all work."

Monks said, "Like REGIS?"

Hazeldon glanced at him swiftly. "Exactly like REGIS. He got the idea to do it. Thought about it a while, then sketched out a few pages of equations and handed it over. It took us over a year from there to get a working prototype."

Hazeldon looked at his watch. "I'd better go," he said. "Meeting down in the war room."

"War room, huh?" Monks said.

"The new corporate world's a battlefield," Hazeldon said. "A few years ago, a lot of execs were reading Musashi's *The Book of Five Rings*. Here, we're Vikings." He pointed at the logo of the dragon-prowed longboat, hanging behind the desk.

"It gets the point across."

"The company had one of those boats built in Seattle," Hazeldon said.

Monks's eyebrows rose. "That must have been pricey."

"A few million. It looks like the real thing from the outside, but it's got some improvements. Leather upholstery, gourmet bar and kitchen, and a five-hundred-horsepower Cummins diesel. They just brought it into the San Francisco Marina, a big publicity deal. You ought go to take a look."

It had occurred to Monks that Lex Rittenour's scheduled press conference tomorrow would be a litmus test for whether John Smith was, in fact, Lex. If so, he would be facing the public with facial lacerations and shaky nerves. It was possible; with good makeup, a prepared script, a few planted questions in the audience—and a judicious dose of Valium—he could probably pull off a brief appearance.

A stopover on the road to treatment.

"The boat's publicity for the press conference tomorrow?" Monks said.

"Yeah." Hazeldon stood abruptly, stooping as an afterthought to gather up his pad, and left without speaking again. He reminded Monks of engineering students he had known in school, dressed in the different uniform of those times—boot camp haircuts, narrow ties, slide rules hanging from belts, much-stained plastic packs of ballpoint pens in the shirt pockets—but with the same air of living in an invisible and much more fascinating reality, touching base with this one only when it was necessary.

So: The press conference was still on.

The secretary came back, offering Monks a smile that was noticeably less bright than the one she had given Bouldin: luminescence adjusted by an internal rheostat. It occurred to Monks that she was an Audrey Cabot wannabe. Attractive though she was, she had a long way to go.

"Mr. Bouldin sends his regrets, but he won't be able to say good night personally. He asked me to tell you that there's a time limit on the offer. Two hours, max."

She handed him a business card. It was Kenneth Bouldin's, embossed in gold on ice-blue linen, with the dragon-ship logo as background.

"I'll need to use a phone," Monks said.

Monks enjoyed a peculiar and uneasy relationship with Mercy Hospital's administration. On the one hand, he was acknowledged as competent, even exceptionally so. The performance of the ER under his direction had never been called into question.

On the other hand, the wariness his coworkers felt about him extended in spades to the reputation-conscious business staff. He was reasonably sure that most of them would fire him if they could, with sorrow in their voices and the sweat of relief on their brows.

Baird Necker, Mercy's ex-marine chief administrator, was not one of those.

"Hearing from you this late can't be good," Baird growled into the phone.

"The hospital could be looking at a tidy little piece of cash. We'd have to move immediately."

"Is it legal? Let me put that a different way. Obviously *il*legal?"

"Not obviously," Monks said.

"Keep talking."

"Can you meet me in half an hour?"

"I'll be on the roof."

On his way back out of the building, Monks was again flanked by guards, like a prisoner going through checkpoints. Ronald Tygard was standing in the lobby at the entrance to Aesir's offices. This time,

Tygard was not with the bodyguard Andrew, but was talking to a man who carried a different order of toughness: the look of the hard-drinking Irish that Monks had grown up with. He was thick-bodied, white-haired, with authority clear in his posture and the set of his jaw. His unbuttoned sports coat gave a glimpse of a shoulder holster's leather strap.

He and Tygard got quiet as Monks passed, watching him stonily.

Monks exhaled with relief when he stepped out into the night.

When Baird Necker said he would be on the hospital's roof, this was not a euphemism. He was a cigar addict who started each morning with a Tabacalero as thick as a big toe and almost a foot long, extinguishing and relighting it several times in the course of the day and finally discarded the soggy thimble-sized remnant with sighs of regret. Being called out this late would have annoyed most people, but Monks knew that Baird would welcome it. It gave him a chance to light a new one.

Monks took the elevator to the top floor and climbed the service stairs the rest of the way. The air was cool, but he could feel the building's warmth through his shoe soles, seeping up through tar, gravel, and pigeon dung. Baird was standing at the roof's edge, one foot up on the parapet, forearm leaning on his thigh, looking like Winston Churchill brooding on how to take down Hitler. Monks respected him because his main concern was to keep the hospital going. Sometimes he was not too particular about how he did it, but his reasons stemmed from a real concern for the place and the people in it.

Baird outlined, with the cigar between his fingers, a sweeping semicircle that took in the lights of the city to the north and east, the southwest quadrant stretching down to the Peninsula, the long dark stretch of ocean beyond the Great Highway, with the white lines of chilly surf endlessly crashing in.

"They're saying the Dot Commers bought up most of it," Baird said. "All done over the Net. When I was coming up, at least you had to throw some body slams to fuck people out of their money."

"You're biting the hand that feeds, Baird. That's where this is coming from. Computers."

"You're not starting some new kind of bullshit, are you? You know, there's people around here real nervous about a guy that keeps getting in trouble."

"I do know that, yes."

Scowling, Baird chewed on the cigar. "I hate to sound like the mercenary prick you think I am anyway, but how much are we talking?"

"Fifty thousand right now. A quarter of a million and still climbing, in a couple of days."

"What do we have to do for it?"

"Nothing," Monks said.

"You mind explaining that?"

Monks did.

When he finished, Baird rubbed his cheek with the heel of his cigar-holding hand, scattering ashes down the front of his shirt—taking his own look at that fine line between rulebook-legal and practical-smart. A formal investigation might find evidence of Aesir's involvement in the fire, and justice eventually would be served. But that seemed unlikely, and the cons weighed heavily. It would anger Aesir, and possibly bring litigation. It would probably strain relations with the fire department. Publicity for the hospital would be negative, and would suggest lax security.

Then there was the pro side: money which would go a long way toward any of several funds, such as the ever-deepening black hole of bills that patients could not or would not pay.

"I've been hearing about this Aesir IPO," Baird said. "It sounds shaky as hell. A lot of big people in on it. Watchdogs looking the other way."

"You don't want to be involved?"

"Hell, yes, I want to be involved. But before it crashes." Baird tapped the cigar ashes thoughtfully. "Insurance will cover the fire damage. The quarter mil would make a nice big splash in the general fund."

"That's double dipping, Baird."

"I'm supposed to worry about the insurance company, with what I pay those cocksuckers?" He bit down hard on the cigar.

"I feel compelled to say that I'm against accepting, on principle," Monks said.

"I got rid of my principles a long time ago. You ought to try it. They're like an appendix—don't do you any good and might cause you pain."

"I don't mean that kind of principle," Monks said. "I mean the kind where if this backfires, my ass is on the line."

"Anybody at the hospital know about it, besides us?"

Monks made a mental reservation about Stephanie. "I don't think so."

"Then as far as I'm concerned," Baird said, "at a quarter mil a pop, they can start a fire here any time they want."

Monks exhaled. "Okay."

Baird had a cell phone. Monks dialed the number on Kenneth Bouldin's card.

Bouldin answered with a clipped, one-word command: "Go." Monks supposed it was the modern equivalent of, *It's your dime.*

"Mercy Hospital is pleased to accept your offer, under the terms we discussed," Monks said.

"I'll have the stock sent over in the morning. How about the private sector?"

"The private sector's going to decline," Monks said. "Nothing personal."

"Meaning what? You don't agree with the hospital?"

"I'm not sure what it means," Monks said. "But like I told you, I do my best to avoid attention."

Bouldin's silence lasted for several seconds. Monks was aware of the noise of the city below him, an almost gentle sound like a river of wind flowing among the buildings.

"Good-bye, Dr. Monks," Kenneth Bouldin finally said. "I'm impressed by the way you've handled this."

Monks handed the phone back to Baird.

"What was that about the private sector?" Baird said.

"Bouldin wanted me in his pocket."

Baird grinned. "You don't figure you are anyway?"

"Yeah," Monks said. "Just not as much."

Walking back to his vehicle, he thought about the place where he had drawn his own line.

He had not even realized he was going to do it until he already had. Like most solutions to difficult problems, it did not entirely satisfy him, but it could have turned out worse.

Well, Stephanie was going to have to make it through med school without Aesir Corporation's help. But that was the other element that had weighed into his decision: The fact that they even knew about her made him nervous.

It was convenient for him, in a way. If dropping the matter was cowardice, he could blame it on his daughter.

Late at night, without much traffic, the drive from San Francisco to Monks's home near the north Marin coast took about fifty minutes. He got there just before 1:00 A.M., and walked into a house that was silent but not empty.

There were three cats hidden, waiting to get him for his lengthy absence.

Fatigue had finally descended on him. He poured a drink—Finlandia vodka over ice, touched with fresh lemon. It tasted heavenly and went down fast. He got out more ice for a second one, this time scanning the refrigerator for food possibilities. The shelves were crammed with remnants of his sporadic attempts to enliven his meat-and-carbs diet: curry and vindaloo paste, Thai chili, oyster sauce and salsa, kraut, pickled okra, a lone artichoke heart, redolent Stilton cheese, an aging pepper pâté. The sense was something like a houseful of relatives, familiar if not necessarily welcoming. But he did not have the energy to try anything fancy, and reverted to type—a sandwich made from a leftover chunk of roast beef, pasta heated up with butter and parmesan. It would do just fine.

The cats were moving in on him now, with subliminal signals calculated to destroy his nerves. A fleeting shadow barely glimpsed. A small object on a shelf in the next room knocked over by a twitching tail.

The sudden sound of claws shredding a forbidden piece of upholstered furniture. He put bits of roast beef in their bowls (they would be imperiously ignored, but it was obligatory), ate quickly, and trudged to the shower to rinse off the leavings of the day.

Afterward, he paused at the mirror for a dour self-analysis, the first time in a while—wondering, he admitted, how he would look to a woman at least ten years younger. Monks had the wiry black hair and green eyes of the black Irish, a face craggy and pitted with adolescent acne scars, a thickened nose that had once been aquiline. His fingers went to his lower back, where Robby Vandenard's grape-pruning knife had left a five-inch horizontal scar and missed, by a few millimeters, slicing into the kidney. Recovering from that, Monks had vowed never to be so physically helpless again, and had started working out. He was a long way from looking like a bodybuilder, but his wind was good now, his chest and gut tight.

With a groan of pleasure, he stretched out in bed. His hand went automatically to his nightstand, cluttered with history. Monks did a lot of reading back in time, through the vast drama that endlessly changed characters and costumes—although the basic business seemed to remain curiously the same.

Tonight he was too tired. He switched off the light and closed his eyes. An image formed in his mind: the Aesir logo, with its longboat, turned into a several-million dollar pleasure craft, for publicity or just vanity. Corporate raiders, modern Vikings, trading sword thrusts over telephone lines and controlling empires on paper.

The Vikings had called their boats *dreki*, dragons, because of their dragon-head prows, their teeth of swords and axes, their bellies that belched the fire of death in the form of fierce men. The real longboats had not even had decks for shelter; their sailors had simply endured the brutal weather of the northern seas. This gave the boats a suppleness that made them capable of enduring those storms too. Instead of breaking, they bent, slipping through the water like sea serpents, easily covering more than a hundred miles in a day.

Led by chiefs with names like Eirik Bloodaxe, Harald Wartooth,

Thorolf Lousebeard, with bearskin-clad berserkers who raged into battle gnawing chunks out of their own wooden shields, they would rove for years at a time, reaching Africa, America, deep into Asia, leisurely plundering the European coasts, the Mediterranean and Black Sea. They could attack a town within an hour of first being visible on the ocean horizon, and travel silently far up rivers and into lakes to surprise unsuspecting inlanders. Ferocious winters trapped them in frozen river mouths: groups of men on small boats, starving grimly for months, until the ice broke up enough to allow the survivors onto the sea again.

They settled in France, becoming Normans, and their raids evolved into full-scale invasions of England and Ireland. There, a Norman leader known as Strongbow left a legacy that Monks often recalled. He took his young son into battle—hundreds of howling men, hacking each other with iron into bloody hunks—and when the boy fled in terror, Strongbow had his legs amputated as punishment for cowardice.

They were a people formed by a life that was almost unimaginably brutal; it was easy to see how that savage spirit arose from it. But what fascinated Monks most was its opposite, or perhaps the converse aspect of the same thing. That had taken many forms, but it was epitomized for him by Thomas à Becket: another Norman of Viking heritage, the drinking, brawling, whoring comrade of the king of England, who had turned his back on wealth and power—and by doing so, had brought about his own murder.

Like thousands of others, Monks had stood on the spot in Canterbury Cathedral where Becket had been cut down, striving for a glimpse into that mysterious inner prompting. Monks had felt a faint echo of it in his own life, caught between the all-powerful Church in his childhood, and his intense scientific training as he grew. He lived his life by the second of the two, but the first was like a stubborn ghost that had faded through the years to a bare specter, but would never entirely leave.

He drifted toward sleep, finally allowing his thoughts to take their own direction. They turned to an adolescent fantasy of the slender limping woman he had met that night, of carefully releasing her thin leg from its brace like a wounded bird from a cage, with her arms outstretched to accept him.

SEVEN

Monks awoke groggily to the realization that he was being walked on. Specifically, his full bladder was being kneaded under the weight of determined paws. He tried to sweep them away but his fingers only brushed fur that moved agilely out of reach. He thought he could smell bacon frying and assumed he was dreaming, but a few seconds later, something sharp nipped his ear.

He opened his eyes. The wideset gray eyes of Omar, his twenty-two-pound blue Persian, were staring back a few inches from his face. When it was decided in the cat world that Monks needed disciplining, Omar acted as the heavy, both figuratively and literally.

This morning, Monks was late in serving breakfast.

The bedside clock read 6:44. Outside, the day was brightening, the silver gray of dawn turning to the thin blue of morning.

The bacon smell was real.

He got up and stepped cautiously to a window. There was another car parked in the drive, a small aquamarine Honda, pulled up next to the Bronco. Stephanie's.

He rubbed his eyes with the heels of his hands. She must have left her San Francisco apartment before 6:00 A.M. She was twenty-two, accustomed for years to dawn swimming practices, with no cell in her body ever tainted by anything unhealthier than a very occasional glass of wine.

He started remembering the events in the ER, then realized that they were confused with a dream: John Smith's face, flattened into flounderlike distortion, eyes bulging and mouth gulping to speak words that Monks had struggled to understand, but could not.

The rest of the night was coming back now too. He pulled on sweats and waded out to face the brash energy of youth.

Fur swirled around his ankles, the other two cats appearing out of nowhere to join the assault, herding him toward the savory smells from the kitchen. Stephanie was standing over the stove, spatula in hand, looking cheerful.

"Morning, Sunshine," she said. "I would have fed them, but I know they want it from you."

Monks divided up a can of Kultured Kat Salmon Feast, a choice perhaps influenced by his dream, and set the bowls down to the music of reproachful yowls. He started sleepwalking automatically into the morning's next step, making coffee, but then realized his place at the table was set, with fresh orange juice and a steaming cup of French roast. He grudgingly decided that this was not so bad and kissed her cheek.

"To what do I owe the pleasure?" he said.

She pointed to the day's *San Francisco Chronicle*, spread out on the table, open to the business section. The main headline read: WHERE'S LEX? Beneath it was a photo of a man who was a ringer for John Smith, a little younger and a lot cleaner.

Aesir Corporation announced early this morning that Lex Rittenour, principal creator of the REGIS gene-scanning program, will not appear as scheduled to tout his brainchild. Rittenour was slated to be the keynote speaker at a press conference today, topping off the fervor that has accompanied this groundbreaking technology and a massive IPO. Aesir executives declined to comment on his whereabouts.

Rittenour was catapulted to fame at the age of 20 with ViStar, a systems management programs that made others obsolete. REGIS, his latest brainchild, has aroused heavy controversy, but the market for REGIS remains strong.

The REGIS IPO will open when trading begins on the New York exchange Friday morning. The 280 million dollars in initial shares are expected to jump from twelve to upwards of fifty dollars per share.

Aesir's press conference will take place this morning at the San Francisco Marina at 9:00 A.M., Pacific time.

Monks sipped his coffee and recalled what he knew about the REGIS program. Working from a blood sample exposed to biochips, REGIS read the individual's entire active genome—then compared it to an "ideal," genetically perfect structure. Any aberration showed up, and any of these which were linked to troublesome genes were identified. As disease-linked gene sites continued to be identified, the program would be updated. Eventually, in theory, a single blood scan would map out all of a person's damaging genes. This was a hugely more thorough analysis than had been possible until now. And a computer could do it in a matter of minutes.

Proponents called this a giant step, pointing to the huge range of possibilities it opened up: for early diagnosis and treatment of disease, and for prevention of passing on hereditary diseases and birth defects.

Critics challenged the program's accuracy, charging that existing information was inadequate, with far too many complexities and unknowns, and that it had not even begun to be properly tested.

But REGIS could be used more insidiously, to discriminate in health insurance and employment, and even to stigmatize a genetically inferior caste. Genes might be identified—or claimed—as being responsible not only for disease and birth defects, but for low intelligence, violent behavior, sexual orientation. Individuals might be labeled as unfit to have children, with economic penalties imposed if they did.

The name "REGIS" itself, evoking the Latin for "king," could be seen as an allusion to a master race, with all the specters that raised.

This had gotten another twist.

The term "ideal genome" was being used to mean "free of deleterious genes." Establishing any such thing at the present was impossible: There was far too much information still unknown. The gaps in the prototype were filled in with projections and educated guesswork, to be updated as new information became available.

But a rumor had surfaced that a particular gene pool of long-lived, healthy individuals had been used in structuring the ideal model. This group happened to come from Iceland. In other words, the REGIS ideal was a tall, blue-eyed blond.

Whether there was any truth to this or it was a fabrication by opponents was not clear. Even if it were true, the point was that Icelanders were a *healthy* group, not that they were of a particular racial stereotype.

But that did add a potent spice to the brew of controversy.

Stephanie brought a plate of peppery fried spuds, thick bacon cooked to perfect crispness, and scrambled eggs with sharp cheddar cheese grated in.

"This kind of food is very unhealthy," Monks warned, salivating.

She joined him at the table with a much more modest plateful for herself. "You see?" she said triumphantly, jabbing a finger down on the newspaper photo. "John Smith *was* Lex Rittenour. They can't let him be seen in public."

Monks was slowly assembling his wits. He had to admit, this development gave her theory more whack. Apparently, last night's war-room strategy at Aesir had gone awry. He debated how much to tell her about all that had happened.

"I saw Dr. Rostanov again last night," he said.

Stef put down her fork. "Really?"

"She assured me again that the guy was really John Smith. He just looks like Lex."

Stephanie became subdued, and Monks felt bad. It was a mean trick, forcing her to abandon her theory or call her new idol a liar.

"We can prove it," she said.

Monks, crunching a mouthful of bacon, paused. "What do you mean?"

"They missed one of the blood samples."

He remained still, letting the concept settle into his brain.

"I forgot to tell you, I never made it to the lab with them," she said. "I met the phlebotomist coming up to the ER, and gave them to her. Then, after it was all over, I started thinking, maybe there were extras. So I found her cart. There was one still in the rack."

"And?"

"I took it."

"Stephanie. Are you telling me that you stole a blood sample from the hospital?"

"It's not like anybody else *wanted* it. Geez."

"It should have been dealt with officially."

"Yeah? I remember what happened to *you* with that radio tape. You and Mom might still be married otherwise."

Monks doubted that, but chose not to say so. Twelve years earlier, he had been chief of emergency services at the major trauma center of Bayview Hospital, upright husband and father, pillar of the community. Then one night a team of paramedics in the field disobeyed his orders, resulting in the death of an elderly woman. The paramedics were well connected with the sheriff's department, and within the next twenty-four hours, the tape of the conversation—the only hard evidence of the orders that Monks had given—disappeared from a police evidence room. The paramedics contradicted Monks, and memories of other staff who had been present got fuzzy. Not long after that, Monks was out of a job and a marriage, and into an alcoholic tailspin.

"Where's the blood?" he said.

Stephanie nodded toward the kitchen. "In the refrigerator."

Monks got up to look. There it was, all right, in a Ziploc bag, wedged behind the Tuong Ot sauce—a finger-sized glass tube filled with dark red liquid, sealed and tagged with Mercy Hospital's official label:

SMITH, JOHN
030601 19:16
MR # 3424659.001
ER / DR. MONKS

"You think we should freeze it?" Stephanie said.

Monks closed the refrigerator door. "I think it will be fine."

"So, who do we take it to? The FBI?"

Monks sat down again. "Honey—we cut a deal last night. Baird and I. Aesir Corporation offered a very generous donation to the hospital. In return, we agreed not to pursue the matter."

Her eyes dampened. "You're kidding."

"I've become a believer in the concept of limited good," he said. "There's nothing to be gained by tilting at windmills. But the hospital can use the money."

"Wow. You can justify anything that way."

"I don't claim that it's noble."

"Have you heard what they're saying about that REGIS program?"

"Some of it," Monks said.

"It's wildly irresponsible. Everybody at med school thinks so. There's way too many variables for predicting disease; it's just going to be used to discriminate against people."

He blinked. He had never heard her so impassioned. "I'm under the impression that there's a pro side to the argument," he said. "Especially as it gets refined over time."

"Then let them wait until it *is* refined. That Aesir outfit is a bunch of crooks. They're trying to make a quick buck, and the world's going to be stuck with all the damage."

Monks said gently, "And you think if we could humiliate Lex Rittenour, that would bring it crashing down?"

"They wouldn't have paid the hospital off if *they* didn't think so."

"It was cheap insurance for them, Stef. They've got a lot on their plate right now. This was just another fly buzzing around the room that they didn't want to deal with."

She got up and started clearing plates into the sink, avoiding his eyes. Monks's shoulders slumped. He was familiar with the saying, "No man is a hero to his valet," and he had long since stopped caring much what the world in general thought of him. But the world in general did not include his daughter.

He tried to imagine being twenty-two again. Bright, bold, outraged at injustice, ready to jump into any fray on the side of righteousness—blithely unaware of the things life had hiding up its alleys to stomp you, of the thousands upon thousands of days to be gotten through, tough enough without inviting trouble.

"I told her we'd like to see her," Monks said. "Dr. Rostanov."

She turned back to him quickly, eyes alive again. "You did? What did she say?"

"I think she was interested. Probably never been hit on by a father-daughter team before."

"That's not getting you off the hook," Stephanie said, but Monks could tell that she was pleased. He went to shave, feeling better.

So: A few milliliters of blood in his refrigerator that could conceivably shake confidence in a billion-dollar deal. Said blood having been obtained illegally, and the release of which would very certainly bring down heavy wrath on its discoverers.

In short, it carried considerable power, and Monks caught another echo of the past. There had been a lot of traffic in holy relics during the Middle Ages, many of them organic: body parts of saints, vials of Christ's blood that would liquefy on Good Friday. They were huge tourist draws. Churches and monasteries were not above manufacturing them, and even purloining them from each other. One tradition held that devotees, risking their own lives, had stolen the still-smoldering bones of Jacques de Molay, last Grand Master of the Templars, from the pyre where King Philip the Fair had had the old knight burned.

By any scientific standard, such beliefs were pure superstition. But Monks could not shake that shadowy feeling that maybe, just maybe, there was something to it.

Monks suggested to Stephanie that she needed some new clothes and prevailed upon her to accept a modest check. He sent her off—still disappointed in him but a little less so—to shop her way home through the malls and boutiques of Marin County.

He spent an hour cutting brush in what he euphemistically called his yard, in the endless defense against the fires that could rip through these dry canyons with a ferocity that was impossible to stop. Maintaining a nonburnable perimeter was about the only chance you had. His house was nothing to brag about, but it meant a lot to him.

He had bought the place twenty-odd years ago, before real estate prices had escalated, as a summer and weekend getaway. There were several acres of redwood, oak, and madrone, isolated from neighbors and far up a narrow road that most wandering traffic missed. The main house was a patchwork of additions tacked onto a cabin originally built in the thirties. Like the Bronco, it was a remnant of divorce, one of the few things he had left after a previous life.

The several outbuildings included a garage that had accumulated junk for the two decades of his ownership. But finally he had cleaned it out and hung a heavy bag. He had never trained formally in boxing. His technique came mainly from watching the Wednesday and Friday night fights in childhood, while the giants of the time—Rocky Marciano, Floyd Patterson, Gene Fullmer, Sugar Ray Robinson, Archie Moore—pounded each other with terrifying beauty around that tiny square of canvas. His father, on his knees, would sometimes mock-spar with him between rounds.

But a heavy bag was a fine workout even for an ungraceful man, and it always paid off once he got started. When he was done with chores, he wrapped his hands and put on bag gloves, and set the timer for five three-minute rounds with a minute in between. He started slow, throwing straight, hard left jabs from the shoulder, stepping in with his left foot, making the bag snap. Partway through the round, he started following each jab with a right cross, the right foot catching up to the left, pivoting on the ball to put the body's full weight behind the punch. In the next round, he worked on the third move in the classic combination, a left hook alternating to the ribs and jaw of his imaginary opponent.

At the end he let it go, hammering as hard as he could with no pretense at defense or style. When he finished he was streaming with sweat, chest aching, breath a shrill whistle.

He had kept his eye on the clock. It was just before 9:00 A.M. He went back inside the house and turned the television on to San Francisco news. He puttered in the kitchen, half-listening to the latest international troubles and warnings of more rolling blackouts, until he heard the announcer say:

"When we come back, we'll take a look at the major IPO that Lex Rittenour *won't* be there to kick off. Stay with us."

The screen changed and, for a few seconds, showed the San Francisco Marina. Among the yachts and sailboats, standing out like an eagle in a dovecote, a Viking longboat was moored. It was perhaps sixty feet long, with a hull of dark wood and a dragon-head prow painted with fierce eyes and teeth. Monks could just make out the name emblazoned on the bow, in stylized rune-like letters: *Mjollnir*.

While the TV offered yet another long series of ads for investment opportunities, geriatric medicines, and the-car-you-had-to-have-to-be-fastest-on-the-road, Monks thumbed through a volume of Viking lore and found the name *Mjollnir*. It was the thunderbolt hammer of the god Thor.

The announcer's voice came back on. This time, the TV camera swept the Marina Green, a hundred yards inland. Blue-uniformed SFPD police had cordoned off a good-sized crowd of demonstrators. Many were carrying signs. Monks glimpsed a couple.

READ OUR LIPS, NOT OUR GENES
NO REGIS

LET'S KEEP HITLER DEAD

Some of the demonstrators were shouting, pressing against the ropes that held them back.

The camera switched to a close-up of the ship's deck. A podium bristling with microphones was mounted at the bow. In the background, Monks could see Ronald Tygard talking on a cell phone. The two bodyguards who had been with him at the hospital were there too, watching the area with the air of Secret Service men. The morning was foggy but all three were wearing bug-eye sunglasses.

Kenneth Bouldin stepped up to the podium and surveyed the group of journalists gathered on the dock below.

"I know you're all disappointed that Lex Rittenour couldn't be here today," Bouldin said, his voice echoing over the microphones. "So are we. Lex is a great man, and I feel very small standing in his shoes. He's also a very private man, and he's just not interested in being in the limelight these days. He sends his best wishes to you all."

Bouldin's voice became solemn. "We're here to formally announce the greatest advance in the treatment of illness that has ever been made. I say that knowing full well what an audacious claim it is. The germ theory of medicine, the discovery of antibiotics—these were huge, but they pale in comparison to what REGIS promises.

"Think of it! A simple blood test to identify the whole spectrum of diseases that plague us. Specific treatments developed to target them. A few years from now, if you find out you have cancer, a medicine will be formulated for your individual genetic makeup. You'll take it home from the drugstore, and in a couple of months, the cancer's gone."

Bouldin paused to let it sink in. With his handsome profile, his just-graying hair, his sense of command, he was every bit the chieftain of the ship.

"REGIS embodies a great element of hope," Bouldin said. "It's not yet perfect, and I know that there are those who find fault with that. Yet, if we can help to end the suffering of millions, are we right?—do we *have* the right?—to hold back?

"*I* hope you'll join Lex Rittenour, and the rest of us at Aesir, in welcoming this great voyage we're embarking on, into a future that would have been science fiction only a few years ago. Thank you all."

Hands shot up from the crowd of journalists, like coiled springs that had been barely contained until a lid popped off. Monks caught bits of the shouted questions.

"Mr. Bouldin, where *is* Lex Rittenour?—"

"Isn't it true, sir, that REGIS is a tool to deny rights—"

"Would you address the rumor that REGIS is a racist stereotype—"

"There is no truth to any such vicious slurs," Bouldin said loudly. The clamor continued. He looked down onto the crowd with a coldness that bordered on contempt. Then, abruptly, he raised his hand in dismissal and stepped back from the podium.

The press conference was over.

The announcer cut back in. "For commentary, we have with us Dr. Joseph Krauzer, a geneticist from Stanford Medical Center." The screen switched to a bearlike, balding man of about sixty.

"Dr. Krauzer, let's start with a couple of issues that Mr. Bouldin declined to address. Proponents of the REGIS program are saying it's a huge step forward in early diagnosis of disease, and prevention of hereditary defects. But as we've heard, critics charge that REGIS will be used to discriminate against people who already *have* defective genes, to deny them health insurance, employment, and perhaps even more. What's your position?"

Krauzer's voice was authoritative, his words measured. "The moral implications are enormous. But I'd like to set them aside and concentrate on a practical issue. Quite simply, does REGIS work? In theory, it stands to be an extremely valuable tool. But it's going to take a lot of time to refine, and it may never prove out."

"So you think that marketing REGIS at this point is premature?"

"Very much so," Krauzer said. "Since it's not a drug or medical product, there's been no FDA supervision or other regulation. No actual testing has been done except rudimentary work with laboratory animals. Most of REGIS's claims are based on computerized projections, and there's simply no way to estimate how accurate those are."

"But that's not going to stop its widespread sale and use?"

"It certainly doesn't look like it from where I'm standing," Krauzer said dryly.

The television screen cut back to the anchored dragon-prowed boat. "The ship you're watching, the—" the announcer hesitated over the pronunciation "—*Mjollnir*, is an authentic replica of an actual Viking longboat. Tomorrow evening, it will sail for Belvedere, carrying Aesir executives and top stockholders to a gala celebration to launch REGIS—and a billion-dollar IPO."

It did seem like the health professionals and other critics were like a Greek chorus in the background, Monks thought: commenting, voicing protests and even outrage, but powerless to change events.

He started for the shower. The phone rang.

Monks picked it up and said, "Hello."

"I hope I'm not disturbing you," a woman said. He recognized Martine Rostanov's voice. She sounded tense and brittle.

"Not at all. I just watched the press conference."

"That's where I'm calling from," she said. "I've been trying to make up my mind whether to do this."

"Do what?"

There was a longish silence. Ten seconds. Twenty.

Then she said, "I lied to you. It *was* Lex Rittenour last night."

"I'd be lying if I said I was surprised."

"Can we get past that?"

"Get past it to where?"

"I told you to be careful about trusting me," she said. "But if I tell you this—I have to trust you."

He hesitated. Sudden trust could be a heavy weight, especially when it only worked one-way.

"Go ahead," he said.

"Lex disappeared last night. That's what Tygard came to my house to tell me."

"Disappeared how?" Monks said.

"He ran away. They'd taken him to Ken Bouldin's house. Put him to bed, trying to get him ready for the press conference. When they checked in on him later, he was gone."

Monks grappled with the concept of a junked out, billionaire computer expert "running away."

"Tygard wanted to know if I'd heard from Lex," she said. "But I'm afraid that really—he might have been killed."

Monks realized that his body had turned and he was staring at the refrigerator, and what it contained. The Precious Blood of Saint Lex, Patron of Corporate Megabucks.

"Do you have a reason for thinking that?" he said.

"He was getting in the way. There was someone else before him who got in the way. Who turned up dead."

"Why aren't you taking this to the police?"

"If I do that, it puts me there too," she said. "In the way."

Over the years, Monks had started looking back at his life as a series of choices. It was something like quantum theory in nuclear physics. Most of those choices were tiny inconsequential decisions, routine, barely conscious, that occurred during every infinitesimal subinstant of time blending into the next. And yet, they added up like a weight gain, until they tipped the scales into larger choices. These might lead in turn to a moment of life-changing significance.

Then there were the ones that were somewhere in between, where you stepped from one pathway to another.

"Take down this address," he said. "I'll meet you there in an hour."

The windows of Stover Larrabee's third-story office looked out on the east end of Howard Street. Past the Embarcadero, a collage of gray concrete piers and the derricks of tankers rose against the fog-bound sky and steely waters of the Bay. Gentrification had landed around Larrabee, but had not yet found him. The weathered warehouses with broken windows reminded Monks of his own boyhood on Chicago's south side.

The office floor was scarred old hardwood, sagging in places from the weight of bearing walls. The doors had transoms and the ceiling was ten feet high, made of pressed lead and probably backed by asbestos, an environmentalist's nightmare. Larrabee lived in adjoining rooms, which was illegal, zoning-wise, but nobody troubled him. His presence put a damper on crime, and the building's management was glad to have him.

Larrabee was leaning against a wall, arms folded, a burly man in his forties with a thick mustache and roosterlike shock of dark hair. He was a former SFPD cop, now chief investigator for a doctor-owned malpractice insurance group that Monks also worked for, as consultant and expert witness. It was how he and Larrabee had come to be friends and sometime partners.

"Dr. Rostanov, you don't know specifically how to interpret that document?" Larrabee said. "Or who the people are?"

"No. It's all in codes, and I don't have a key." Martine was sitting in a chair, typing on her notebook computer. Her hands looked thin and bloodless. So did her face.

Monks sat beside her, watching the screen. It showed only columns of numbers.

"Then, if you'll excuse my asking," Larrabee said, "how'd you figure out what it means?"

Her fingers stopped moving and her shoulders sagged.

"I helped set up the format," she said.

She looked at Monks, apologetic, a little teary-eyed. The well of information that she had not been forthcoming about was getting deeper.

"Certain genes have been singled out," Martine said, her finger reaching to the computer screen to underscore a number highlighted in bold type. "I think they're sex-linked. Passed on through the X and Y chromosomes."

Monks watched the screen, scrolling slowly. The document was divided into segments of several pages. Each segment began with an identification number and a date, then was followed by columns of multidigit numbers. There was no printed information, nothing but the complex numerical codes.

What they represented, according to Martine, were REGIS gene scans, over one hundred of them, which had been performed on real human beings. The columns of numbers represented the genes, for each person, that REGIS had identified as potentially troublesome.

"Look here," she said. Her finger touched an identification number, 103. "The one just means female, a woman. The zero three is her personal number."

Martine scrolled on several more pages, to another segment's beginning. "And here," she said. This number was two zero six. "A man, number six."

The screen moved on farther this time, to a segment beginning with a much longer identification number: 103206–201. "It's a combination of those two base numbers, with a suffix," she said. "Two for a male. The zero one—I think it means firstborn. In other words, those two parents, one zero three and two zero six, had a baby boy, their first child."

Monks said incredulously, "These are *pedigrees*?"

"As near as I can tell, there were fourteen women and nine men. Not monogamous couples—more like random mating. All together, they had one hundred thirty-seven pregnancies, in about four years."

Larrabee ran his hand over his hair, a gesture that signaled unusual agitation. "That's impossible," he said. "Isn't it?"

"I said pregnancies. Not children."

Monks was starting to get a queasy feeling.

"I'm sorry to be dense, Doctor, but I don't know zilch about science," Larrabee said. "Spell it out, please."

Her shoulders moved in a sort of shrug, a gesture of being overwhelmed. "It's like a reverse eugenics program. Breeding different combinations of parents who carried disease-linked genes and tracking how the genes were passed on.

"That's why some of the pregnancies are only a few months apart."

Monks pushed his chair back and walked to a window.

What it meant was that most, if not all, of the fetuses had been aborted. But the pregnancies were not accidental.

It was just the opposite. The fetuses had been bred so that their genomes could be scanned, and the hereditary aspects tracked. Then they had been discarded, with a high turnover to maximize efficiency.

The results would be a gold mine of information. Instead of the gargantuan task that legitimate researchers faced, of trying to track

inherited genes through a vast population of parents, here a very
few genomes could be manipulated in known combinations, the
genes charted easily—and quickly. Monks tried to imagine the mind
that had designed the research. A mind that had no concern for
human life, or was able to justify using life casually, in the name of
science.

Monks said, "Tell us how you helped set this up."

"Not *this*," Martine said. "My god, please don't think that. I just
worked on a theoretical model. I never dreamed somebody would use
it like this."

She looked away from them, hands folded tensely, shoulders trem-
bling a little. Monks felt pity for her, but that was not quite the right
word. It was as if her intense unhappiness had spilled over into him.
He wanted to touch her, to try to soothe her. But he was worried, too
worried that once again she was not telling him everything.

She was silent for another half minute, breathing deeply. Then she
began to speak. "A man named Walker Ostrand was sent to talk to me
by the personnel office, about five years ago. He was a physician, he'd
been in the military. Aesir hired him for translating theoretical aspects
of REGIS into actual medical applications. I'd been working on that
all along. I gave him what I had."

"This setup?" Monks said, touching the computer screen.

She nodded. "A very rough prototype. It was just a way of corre-
lating the genes that REGIS identified, with actual diseases. Of
course, there were other people working on the same thing, and I
gave it to them too. It was never meant to be used. It was just a tool,
a basic step. Much more sophisticated programs have been developed by now.

"After that, I forgot about Ostrand. I didn't see him for years. He
was a subcontractor, like a lot of the others, so he wasn't around the
offices. Then one night a few months ago he showed up at my house.
He was drunk, in a vicious mood. I was scared. There was something
scary about him anyway. A coldness, a vacuum."

"I don't have any trouble believing that," Larrabee muttered.

"He was in a disagreement with somebody at Aesir," she said. "He wouldn't say who. He felt he was being cheated out of a lot of money—but he had information that could destroy people, and if he didn't get the money, he would.

"Then he started into this slimy innuendo that I was in it with him somehow. That my model had been used for something highly unethical. And I had better help him—or I was going to be destroyed too. I finally got him to leave, with some vague promises that I'd do what I could. It shook me, but I put it down to his being drunk.

"Two days later, that computer disk came in the mail. Plain envelope, no note, no return address. I spent the next day trying to figure it out. I don't think I'd have known what it was if he hadn't come by earlier. When it started to sink in, I couldn't believe it. I tried to call him. That's when I found out he was dead. He'd fallen into a swimming pool with just a few inches of water in it. Knocked himself unconscious and drowned."

"Was there any flap about the death?" Larrabee asked. "Suspicion, investigation?"

"No, it was ruled accidental. I think he drank a lot."

But the coincidence of the death with the threat of blackmail was hard to ignore.

"Any idea who he was dealing with at Aesir?"

Martine shook her head. "I fished around in the company computer records," she said. "Ostrand just showed up as a subcontractor, doing data analysis. No specifics, not a hint about who hired him. I even drove to his office address, in an industrial park in south San Francisco. It was already rerented. The manager said somebody came and cleaned it out right after he died."

It was a good bet that the "somebody" had covered tracks in other ways.

"Did Lex Rittenour know about this research?"

"Yes. I showed it to him."

"*You* did?" Larrabee said. "You knew him that well?"

"All my life. Our families were friends. I'm four years older, I grew up taking care of him. Never really stopped. We had a bond, we were both geeks. He was a genius. I had this." She touched the brace on her leg.

"When did you do show it to him, Doctor?"

"Five days ago."

"How did he react?"

"He was devastated. He'd been wavering about REGIS anyway: that it wasn't ready yet, the IPO was premature. This pushed him to a decision. The press conference that was scheduled for today? He was going to get up there and publicly withdraw his support for REGIS. Knock the pins out from under the IPO."

Larrabee said, "Jesus wept." He paced, passing his hand over his hair.

You could fill a big graveyard with people who had been killed for less.

"Did he tell anybody else he was going to do that?" Larrabee said.

"He didn't plan to," she said. "He was going to drop the bomb, then take off, go someplace obscure for a while. But then he started doing drugs again. I don't know what he might have said or done since."

"Again?"

"I've gotten him off it twice. But when the pressure starts building, he goes back."

So: The man who was arguably the world's greatest software genius—like a Mozart, orchestrating the infinitely complex symphony of the human genome—was an addict. It was precedented; there had been a number of famous visionary narcotics users.

And other unfinished masterpieces which might or might not ever be successfully performed.

"Dr. Rostanov, I can see why you didn't tell anybody else about the research," Larrabee said. "But why'd you tell Lex?"

"I couldn't just not do anything. But I was scared. If I went public, they could hush it all up and get rid of me. Aesir's got tentacles everywhere: police, government, an incredible information system. I convinced myself that Lex was too important to get rid of. So I let him take the risk. God, I used to *baby-sit* him." She rocked forward, hands rising to cover her face.

This time, Monks stepped behind her and lightly put his fingers on her shoulders. Larrabee's eyebrows rose.

"I was up most of last night," she said into her hands. "Hoping he'd show."

Larrabee said, "The smartest thing you could do, Doctor? Flush that disk down the toilet, now. I'll help you cut it up. Then *you* go someplace obscure for a while. Come back with amnesia."

She sat without moving, as if she had not heard. Monks was touched again by the sense of her deep aloneness.

"I hated lying to you," she finally said, turning to Monks. "But I did it. I hate being a coward, but I am. But I can't let this go now, not with Lex gone. I have to do something. Please, help me decide what."

Monks waited. This sort of thing was Larrabee's side of the street.

"If this research could be verified, it would blow up like a hydrogen bomb," Larrabee said. "But right now, Doctor, all you've got is a bunch of numbers that only you can interpret. It might even be a fraud, something Ostrand cooked up to try to gouge money. If you come forward, but you're not able to prove anything solid—" Larrabee shrugged. "You've attracted very undesirable attention."

The kind of attention, Monks thought, that might have gotten at least one man killed.

"You could try leaking it to the media anonymously," Larrabee said.

"Like Deep Throat?" she said.

Larrabee smiled. "Yeah."

She looked intrigued. "I could use a new self-image."

"But I doubt the anonymity would hold up for long," Larrabee said. "You're too connected."

Everybody moved a little, physically; absorbing what had happened, thinking about what came next.

"Let's look at ways to *get* to whoever it is at Aesir," Larrabee said. "Who are the women who were having the abortions? If we had names to put to those numbers—then I'd feel confident about going public."

She shook her head again, this time wearily. "I'm sorry to be so helpless, but I have no idea. I wouldn't know where to start."

Monks had been considering possibilities for the research group—hospitals, schools, the military, prisons—but none seemed to fit. It had to be relatively stable; the same women and men had to have been available for a period of years. It was probably in the San Francisco area. Had the women known what was happening? Were they paid for silence? Was it forced? A religious group, perhaps, a cult or sect?

"If you want, then, I'll take it on," Larrabee said. She nodded.

"Carroll? Are you in?"

Monks had gotten pretty good at ignoring things. Stephanie was right: Too good. But children bred and destroyed like laboratory animals. Possible murder. This was no longer a matter of the abstract wrong that REGIS might do to the world, but individual people who had been harmed, and more who might be. Including Martine Rostanov. It was like a giant python of circumstances which Monks had hoped would go away, but which kept tightening around him.

She was watching him anxiously. He nodded, and was rewarded by her look of relief and perhaps even happiness.

"No guarantees," Larrabee said. "If we don't get something real soon—I think you're going to have to go to the authorities and take your chances. You should be thinking in terms of getting out of sight."

"Oh, I have been," she said, with unconcealed irony. "Most of last night."

Monks had thought about that contingency too. Some form of witness protection or guarded house arrest. Saying good-bye to the life you had built. Spending every minute after that wondering how long you had before a computer hacker pierced your disguise, or somebody on your own side slipped up or sold out.

"My guess is that Lex is okay, he just bolted," Larrabee said. "Wasn't ready to give up the drugs, or he got scared. But if he told somebody, you might be at risk."

She looked away unhappily. "I can't believe he wouldn't contact me if he was okay."

"Why don't you call in sick?"

"With all that's going on? I'd have to be dying."

"Fake it."

"They'd check up on me, believe me. If I left the area, or they couldn't find me, that would cause a stir."

"I'd prefer to operate without red-flagging them," Larrabee admitted. "But we're talking about your safety."

"I think—I need to be there. Something might come along about Lex. Some way I can help." She looked from one to the other of the two men, stubborn now. "Nobody's going to hurt me in the Bank of America Building."

"Then take a couple of precautions." Larrabee walked to his office safe, an antique black steel box the size of a refrigerator, and started turning the dial. "Stay around groups of people. Spend the nights at a hotel, don't tell anybody where. No parking garages, and check your car before you get in. Keep this in the glove box or your purse."

He took out a .38 caliber Smith & Wesson Airweight, a pistol not much bigger than a pack of cards, along with a handful of short thick bullets.

"It's got a shrouded hammer so it won't get caught," he said. "There's no safety and you don't need to cock it. If you have to use it, forget everything you ever heard or saw on TV. Just leave it in your purse. Point it at the middle of the other person's body as close range as you can get, and pull the trigger five times."

Aghast, Monks decided, was the correct word for her expression.

"I don't think I could," she said in a subdued voice.

"Then it's better not to have it."

"This is so unreal. I keep thinking I can just go on as if nothing's happened."

"You need to *act* that way, Dr. Rostanov," Larrabee said. "But think like a target." He offered Martine the pistol. She shook her head.

"Okay," he said, and returned it to the safe. "Give me a little while on the computer. I'll start a background check on Dr. Ostrand."

"Come on, Martine," Monks said. "I'll walk you to your car." She glanced at him swiftly, perhaps realizing that it was the first time he had called her by her given name.

They walked down the wide, silent old hallway. Its musty smell and worn tiled floor touched Monks with the memory of the Chicago apartment building where his maiden Irish aunt had lived.

"I didn't realize you were close, you and Lex," Monks said.

"I was the good girl, the straight big sister. I'd come visit him in Berkeley after he dropped out of college. He and a couple of his computer buddies were living in this sort of burrow, a big old garage they'd rented. A few mattresses on the floor, full of junk-food wrappers and electronic gear. They didn't know if it was day or night and they didn't care. Computers were their whole universe.

"It was wonderful at first. We were the good guys—the cutting edge of this huge great development. But it changed, and he changed. Drugs and a wild life. That sweet boy's still in there, but I've seen him less and less."

They reached the silver Volvo. Monks took her keys from her hand and opened the car door. She surprised him by touching his face with her fingers, the way she had done with Stephanie last night.

"I haven't told you how much it means to me, your doing this," she said. Her breath was warm and pleasantly scented. "You could have just told me to go away, on the phone."

"There's nothing hard about what I'm doing," Monks said. "You're the one looking at consequences."

"When I came into the emergency room last night—realized who you were—I thought, this was meant. He's going to help." She tried to laugh. "I don't even believe in things like that."

Driving away, she raised a hand. Monks waved awkwardly back, and watched the Volvo disappear into traffic.

NINE

Monks had discovered that his best way to correlate information in a situation like this was to sit down and write out what he knew. He listed the major points as brief notes on index cards—

Lex Rittenour comes into ER with OD
Walker Ostrand mails computer disk to Martine Rostanov
Walker Ostrand found dead
Lex Rittenour disappears

—then began arranging them in a sort of tarot reading, shifting them and pondering different combinations in an attempt to read the past. Questions, contradictions, and lapses would stand out, and a part of his brain below the surface of consciousness would worry at them until the knots started to dissolve.

Monks did this and made several phone calls, while Larrabee ran an initial computer scan on Walker Ostrand. When Larrabee was done, they got in the Bronco and drove north on Highway 101, crossing the Golden Gate Bridge into Marin County. Here, the fog began to clear and the road took on the air of a festive caravan, crowded with expensive SUVs and pretty women in sleek foreign-made convertibles, their hair blowing in the wind and gold glimmering at wrists, throats, and ears. The Bronco drove stolidly just at the speed limit, like a great rock in the slithering stream of nimbler vehicles that edged up behind and slipped around, but rarely came close. It was 11:42 A.M.

"The hard part," Larrabee said, "is going to be making this slimer look good."

The need to make Ostrand look good involved what they were about to try: getting information out of his family. Blood ties were strong, even—especially—with slimers, and it usually paid to start off friendly.

Monks did not care for deception, but in investigation work it went with the turf. It was easier for him to stomach when the target was an unpleasant individual. He had dealt with quite a few of those—usually physicians whose negligence tended to go hand in hand with arrogance, and, occasionally, outright criminals—but someone capable of doing what Ostrand had apparently done was unprecedented on his scale.

What they had put together so far was this.

Walker Ostrand had graduated from University of Illinois medical school in 1974, joined the army in 1975, and served until 1993. He had been in Special Operations, which meant that details were classified. His discharge was honorable, but it struck Monks as odd that a lifer would quit just two years short of putting in his twenty for retirement. In 1995, Ostrand had acquired a California medical license. This was about the time when he had hooked up with Aesir Corporation, and had come to Martine Rostanov for help.

Ostrand came to her again five years later, and this time hinted at the truth of why he had been hired: to conduct the illegal research. Now he wanted money from Aesir. He intended to threaten or blackmail the company with the report, and he tried to intimidate Martine into joining forces with him.

Two days later, Ostrand had been found "accidentally" dead.

Three months after that—five days ago—Martine had confided the story to Lex Rittenour. Outraged, Lex vowed to publicly denounce his own brainchild, REGIS, and undermine the IPO.

Now Lex was missing.

Ostrand was a physician and had probably done the fieldwork for the research: drawn the blood samples—perhaps performed the abortions. The blood analysis would have required sophisticated equipment; he had probably farmed that out to a laboratory, with a pretext for the intended use.

But someone at Aesir Corporation had to have been in on it too—to have commissioned and funded it. This was the person or people whom Ostrand had threatened—and who faced ruin and prison if discovered.

It was a strong guess that they had killed Ostrand to shut him up, and it was possible that they had killed Lex Rittenour too. They had covered tracks carefully and successfully. But a clandestine investigation just might turn up some piece of information that would give the research report an undeniable reality. Then it could be handed over to the media and authorities.

Larrabee's preferred method in a situation like this was to find someone who had a grudge: an ex-husband or wife, a jilted lover, a cheated business partner.

Or a stepchild.

Walker Ostrand's marital history showed a first marriage ending in divorce, back in Maryland in 1984—too long ago to be of help now.

But he had married a new Mrs. Ostrand just five years ago, about the same time he had been hired by Aesir. She had been married before too and had a teenage daughter.

Ostrand might have been one of those who could carry out a years-long intimate deception: ruthless and even criminal in his work, and a loving father at home. But there were not many who could sustain that kind of thing without at least occasional slips, and children were perceptive—particularly in a situation where they felt protective toward a natural parent, and disliked the new spouse.

But they had not been able to find an address for the daughter. So the second Mrs. Ostrand, the widow, was the first stop on the list.

*   *   *

Monks exited the freeway at Mill Valley and followed the directions to
Mrs. Ostrand's house, into the foothills to the west. The streets and
shops of the town gave way to ranch-type houses cut into the slopes,
spaced well apart. It was an affluent area—but the driveway into the
Ostrand residence was crowded with neglected vegetation. The only
visible car was several years old, American-made, nondescript. It could
have used washing.

The swimming pool's deep end was puddled from rain and matted
with leaves and duff. Here was where Walker Ostrand had fallen,
bashed his head, and drowned. It did not look like the pool was going
to see more use any time soon.

They rang the bell, waited a full minute, rang again. The second
minute was almost up, with the unhappy feeling coming that they had
wasted the trip, when a curtain moved.

A disheveled woman who might have been fifty, but looked older,
peered out. Larrabee gave her his best apologetic smile.

"Mrs. Ostrand?" he said, loudly enough to be heard through the
glass. "We're sorry to disturb you."

He held up a business card that identified him, under a false name,
as a claims adjuster for the Commonwealth Insurance Group. This
was also a false name, which Larrabee had chosen because it was non-
specific and yet had a certain grandeur, with a hint of a British connection. If anyone decided to check it out, the number would ring a
machine in his office which informed callers that they had reached
the Commonwealth Insurance Group and invited them to leave a
message.

The door opened. Clara Ostrand was wearing a housecoat over a
nightgown, and slippers. It was past noon. Her reddish hair was
permed but touseled, and her thick makeup, flaked and streaked. The
pupils of her eyes were somewhat dilated. Painkillers, Monks decided,
Percodan or codeine.

"We know you recently lost your husband," Larrabee said, handing her the card. "We'd like to offer our condolences."

"Is this about the settlement?" she said anxiously.

"Ah, no, ma'am. That's another company."

Her relief was evident. Presumably, she was satisfied at what she had received. Whether she was suffering any grief was harder to read.

"We represent a medical group that's in a very unusual situation," Larrabee said. "They have a cancer patient who was part of a study. He says your husband recommended treatment, but his advice was ignored. That was several years ago. Now the patient's dying, and there aren't any records."

Her expression segued into bewilderment. "I don't—know about anything like that." Then, abruptly, it went to fear. "My god, are we going to be sued?"

"We're working *for* you, Mrs. Ostrand," Larrabee said, soothingly. "Your husband did the right thing—but the records are gone." He leaned confidentially closer. "Anything you could do to help us would be to all of our benefit."

Monks stoically maintained his concerned look, aware of guilt at beating up on a befuddled, recently widowed woman.

She pressed her palms to the sides of her head. "Let me think."

"It was a research study, ma'am," Larrabee emphasized. "Did he talk about anything like that? Any group or institution he visited regularly?"

"Walker was gone a lot," she said. "He worked for himself. I don't really know much about it."

"Did he talk about working for Aesir Corporation?"

"No?" she said, drawing it out into a question. "I don't think I ever heard of them."

"How about anybody else in your family, Mrs. Ostrand? Am I right, you have a daughter?"

"Yes. I don't know if she'd be any help. She and Walker—didn't get along very well."

Larrabee's teeth just showed at the corners of his mouth. "I'm sorry to hear that. Could we talk to her?"

"She's living in San Francisco," Clara Ostrand said, doubtfully.

That was where matters stood, when another car swung into the drive—a small, canary yellow, projectile-shaped Mustang GT—moving fast and pulsing with the heavy beat of rap music. It was new and very clean. A young man got out. He was in his twenties, wearing a baseball cap, a T-shirt that came down well past his waist, and baggy shorts. His mouth was ringed by a smudgelike goatee.

"What's going on?" the young man said. Monks interpreted it as a greeting rather than a literal question, but there was a definite tone of challenge.

"We're working on an insurance case involving Dr. Ostrand," Larrabee said.

"Talk to our lawyer, dude."

"We've already talked to a lot of lawyers," Larrabee said. "That's why we're here. Trying to keep you folks from having to do the same."

"It's not about the death, Billy," Mrs. Ostrand said. "It's about research Walker was doing."

Billy's gaze shifted quickly from Larrabee to Monks and back, clearly not liking what he saw. "Yeah, well, we don't know anything about that. Why don't you go on inside, Clara."

"About what?" Larrabee said.

"Whatever you said, man. Now if you don't mind, we'd like to be left in private."

"Sure," Larrabee said. "Sorry for the trouble. But hey, could I take a look at your car? I was thinking about buying one just about like that for my daughter." He moved toward it, gazing at it admiringly. Larrabee did not have any children. "I'm a little worried it might be too much for her to handle," he said.

"Are you kidding?" Billy said. "A chick? *I* can hardly handle it. I pop the clutch, the front wheels want to come off the ground."

"Wow. What'd you pay for it?"

"Fourteen five."

Larrabee whistled in affected surprise. "Sweet deal."

"It's only three-forty a month, man." Billy was walking with him toward the car now.

"Stereo come with it?"

"I had it customized. Quad twenty-watt speakers and surround sound."

They drifted away: Larrabee plying his trade.

Monks turned to Mrs. Ostrand. "I understand your husband was in the military. I was too, probably about the same time."

"Walker was very proud of his service."

"Rightly so," Monks said. "Did he leave any records of any kind? Files, computer disks?"

She shook her head doubtfully. "He kept all that at his office."

"No storage space, safety deposit box, anything like that?"

"There was a deposit box with some valuables," Mrs. Ostrand said. "Jewelry and such. Besides that, just his personal things. I have a scrapbook I made when we were married. Would you like to see it?"

"Please."

The inside of the house was depressingly disheveled, as Monks had expected. Ashtrays overflowed, and it smelled of stale smoke. A glimpse into the kitchen showed a sink crammed with gummy dishes. A new-looking wide-screen TV was playing a daytime talk show and the couch in front of it had several pillows and a couple of bunched-up blankets. It looked like she spent a lot of time here.

"I'm sorry," she said, flustered, as if just now realizing the state of the place. "I just haven't had time to clean."

"Not at all," Monks said soothingly. "You should see *my* place."

She went down a hallway and came back with an old-fashioned scrapbook. There were several wedding photos of Clara Ostrand with a large, bland-faced man in his fifties. They had the slick, perfunctory look of having been taken as part of a wedding chapel package deal. She looked quite pretty and much more than five years younger.

It was quickly clear that the scrapbook was not going to reveal anything. Monks paged on, trying to look appreciative, through various family tableaux. Most featured Mrs. Ostrand, many with a girl at various ages—presumably her daughter. Walker Ostrand showed up in a few of the later ones, and in a couple of formal military portraits taken when he was younger. His face was always the same bland mask.

But toward the end, Monks stopped and looked closely at one. This was a black-and-white, showing three American soldiers in fatigues, standing outside a large, windowless cinder-block building on a muddy square of ground.

One of them was Walker Ostrand, with a major's insignia on his collar. This time, the camera—in spite of the unsophisticated setup, or maybe because of it—had caught something in his face that none of the other photos had.

Monks recognized that something instantly, his body reacting with a jolt, as if he had realized he was about to step on a rattlesnake. He had only seen it a couple of times before in his life: the sense of an *other*, a being of chilling inhumanness, living just behind the surface of the eyes. It was not insanity. That was the trouble.

A deuce-and-a-half truck with a red cross on it was parked nearby, suggesting that the Americans were medical personnel. Several Asian men in civilian clothes, a couple of them wearing white lab coats, stood with them. A sign on the building was written in the distinctive letters of the Korean alphabet. The place looked like a regional health center. Presumably, the Americans were there to give technical support: a goodwill mission.

Monks had visited a similar place during his own brief stay in Korea. Its functions were severely limited, with only a few beds and a lab that was largely devoted to combating the country's epidemic tuberculosis. The equipment—a couple of cheap old monocular microscopes, crude-gas Bunsen burners, hand-washed glassware—was half a century behind. All lab testing was done by laborious, obsolete methods, and the stock of medicines was almost nonexistent.

He remembered stepping outside the building, a young, healthy American officer in a clean uniform, uncomfortable under the gazes of the sick and weary Koreans waiting for treatment. Then an old woman broke from their ranks and hurried toward him, talking fiercely, shaking her hands for his attention. Her fingers were rotted away almost to stumps, and Monks had realized that he was looking at leprosy. The old lady talked on, her eyes both pleading and angry, and he had had to turn away and go back inside, unable to communicate with her, or to bear the sight of a horror he could do nothing about.

When Monks refocused his gaze on the photo, Walker Ostrand's face only seemed bland. Monks was left to wonder if he had imagined that look in the eyes, perhaps conjuring it up from an eerie association with that long-gone moment when the old woman had thrust her wretched hands in his face.

He handed the book back to Clara Ostrand.

"Was there anybody he was having difficulties with?" Monks said.

"No. What does that have to do with some person having cancer?"

"We'd like to know if there's anybody who might try to distort the situation."

She shook her head.

"Thanks, Mrs. Ostrand," Monks said. "We'd still like to talk to your daughter."

Clara Ostrand had to look up the address. Apparently, communication was not frequent.

At the door, she said, "Will you call me if there's going to be any trouble about this?"

Monks wanted to reassure her, but could not. "You'll be contacted," he said.

Outside, he walked over to join Larrabee and Billy. Larrabee looked as if he had run out of things to admire about the car. Monks gave him a slight nod: The interview was over. Larrabee's teeth showed again.

No more Mr. Nice Guy.

"So how do you figure into this, Billy?" Larrabee said. "Are you family?"

Billy looked surprised by the sudden shift from cozy car talk. "Walker wasn't around much," he said. "Clara hired me to take care of the place."

"He went, you stayed?" Larrabee said with an irony that was almost tender.

"She needed somebody," Billy said defensively.

"None of my business, but the place does look like it could use some work."

So could Mrs. Ostrand, Monks thought.

"I'm getting around to it, man. And you're right, it's none of your business."

Larrabee laid an avuncular hand on Billy's shoulder. But thumb and forefinger tightened suddenly on the deltoid muscle, high up, toward the neck. Billy's mouth opened in shock, and his feet made a little shuffling motion, as if he were about to kick.

"Hey, *fuck*, man, let go," he yelped, pawing ineffectively at Larrabee's hand.

"I've always wondered what's the deal with wearing the cap like that?" Larrabee said. "You get to turn it around frontward when you start growing pubic hair?"

Driving out, Monks glanced in the Bronco's rearview mirror and saw Billy flip them off, hot-eyed and prancing with rage.

"It looks like young Billy made himself a pretty soft landing," Larrabee said. "Mrs. Ostrand's paying for the car."

"Did it occur to you that he's the one who helped Walker fall into the pool?"

"Possible," Larrabee said. "But my gut feeling is, that's giving him too much credit. I think he was just at the right place at the right time to move in on her, and he doesn't want anybody rocking his boat."

It was Monks's feeling too. More to the point, finding out who might have killed Walker Ostrand was not of interest to them if it did not involve their case.

"Did you get the daughter's address?" Larrabee said.

Monks held up the slip of paper bearing Clara Ostrand's cramped handwriting.

The old Haight-Ashbury district had seen its ups and downs, from the flower children and Summer of Love in '66, to iron-grated storefronts and hard drugs flooding the streets ten years later. These days, as near as Monks could tell, it was somewhere in between, a mix of hip, gentrified, and dangerous.

He stood with Larrabee on the stoop of a three-story Victorian on Frederick Street. This building and its immediate neighbors had not shared in any high-grade upkeep. The window in the foyer door was grilled too; most of the mailboxes had several names, scrawled or taped on or half torn off.

Larrabee rang the buzzer of apartment six. Monks was a little surprised that it worked. After a moment, a scratchy voice came through. It was female and spoke a single syllable of query that he could not quite catch.

"I'd like to speak to Trish Roberson," Larrabee said.

"Who's 'I'?"

"A friend of her mom's."

"Not here. Sorry."

"Any idea where she is?"

"Nope." The static stopped. Monks realized that the communication was ended.

Larrabee rang again.

"Could I come in for just a minute? Leave a note asking her to call?"

"What's this about?" the voice said.

"Her mom's got a problem."

"I can believe *that*. How do I know you're who you say you are?"

"How would I know she's called Trish?" Larrabee countered. "I'd say Patty, or Patricia."

"Are you a cop?"

"No."

"You can't be, after you tell me that, right? I mean, that would be entrapment."

The two men exchanged glances: a law degree from TV University.

"Right," Larrabee said.

The door buzzer sounded.

They walked in, past a cardboard box of unclaimed mail with several ominous "Final Notice" embossments highly visible, and climbed the dim, creaky stairway. The balustrade was scarred from generations of moving furniture and god knew what else. Paint peeled in patches from the walls. The thump of heavy bass music came from somewhere, like the pulse of a huge, overcharged heart.

The door of apartment six was open just enough to give a glimpse of a female face under a shock of black hair, and a whiff of marijuana smoke. There were several locks, and on the inside, a chain stretched taut.

"You didn't say there was two of you," she said.

"Sorry."

"You *look* like cops."

"I'll take that as a compliment," Larrabee said. He grinned, with a boyish look that could take him a long way. "Are you Trish?"

"Maybe."

"That's a pretty name."

Her tone got a notch friendlier. "What kind of trouble's Mom in?"

"I didn't say she was in trouble. I said she had a problem."

"Same thing," she said, but apparently it swayed her. "Hang on." The door closed, then opened again, this time all the way. Trish was about twenty, with a thinness that hinted at anorexia, enhanced by her tight vest and jeans. Monks had never seen anything as black as her hair. If black was the absence of color, this was the absence of the absence. Several tattoos and piercings which were visible led to speculation about others which were not. The overall package was not unattractive, but it took him some getting used to.

The room had another occupant attached to a pair of leather sandals with feet in them, dangling over the arm of an old couch pulled up in front of a TV which played a *Star Trek* rerun. Their owner's face rose into sight, looked them over incuriously, and disappeared again.

"Is there a place we could talk in private?" Larrabee nodded toward a bamboo curtain screening off another door, the hallway to the interior, the portal to another world.

She hesitated, then said, "Okay."

Trish led them down a hallway to a room where the furniture seemed to consist mainly of cushions. A coffee table sprouted candle stubs solidified into pools of wax, with a couple of incense burners amidst them. The walls were plastered with film and rock music posters. The floor was a pile of clothes.

"This is like a flashback to a Dennis Hopper movie," Larrabee muttered.

"What do these kids *do*?"

"Work in shops and restaurants. Deal dope. Maybe a check from home here and there. It's probably fun for a while."

And then, Monks thought, they were thirty.

She turned to them when they stepped inside, hands behind her back. Her tongue wet her lips nervously, gaze flicking around at the two men and the room.

"You both coming in at once?"

"Is that a problem?" Larrabee said.

"I guess not. Who told you about me?"

"Your mother, Trish."

"No, really, who? I don't do this that much."

The dawn began to break in Monks's mind as to why Trish Roberson might be nervous about callers she did not know. Cops, for instance. Larrabee, ahead of him as usual, was already taking out his wallet.

"We're not here for what you think," Larrabee said. "But thanks anyway." He handed her a fifty-dollar bill.

She took it, looking relieved if perhaps slightly disappointed. "So, what do you want?"

"To talk about Walker Ostrand."

"Wow." She stepped back, almost jumping. "Major creep."

"Is that why you moved away from home?"

"Mostly."

"How long did you live there with him?"

"I was, like, fifteen when Mom and him got married. At first it seemed great, we were living in this dump in San Mateo, and he moved us to Mill Valley. He had money, he seemed like a nice guy. Then it got to where I couldn't stand being home. It was like—you ever see one of those ant farms? Where you can watch them through the glass? It was like living in one of those."

"Was he, ah, if you'll excuse me being personal, a voyeur?" Larrabee said.

"Nothing that obvious. Things he'd do that seemed accidental, but they bugged you. Then you'd start thinking, that's *why* he did it, he's pushing buttons."

"Like what, Trish?"

"The worst was my mom. He started her on Vicodin for some little pain. When she was hooked, the bastard cut her off. Then, after she was good and strung out, he'd start her up again. It was always, like, what was "good" for her, but I finally saw what he was doing. She's a mess, man. At least she got some money when he died."

Monks added some grains of salt for the anger of a hostile step-daughter, but it had an uncomfortable ring of truth.

"What did he do at work, Trish?"

She shrugged. "Some kind of soft money deal, consulting, like that. He was a doctor, but he didn't have any patients. No big surprise, he had to leave the army because of something. If *they'll* kick you out, you've really got to be fucked up."

It did not necessarily follow, but Monks conceded that it was rarely a gold star.

"Your mom said he was proud of his military service," Monks said.

"Yeah, well, Mom was zonked most of the time. She didn't know much about what was going on."

"Did he ever give you any idea why he left the army?"

"A couple times when he was drunk, he'd start bragging that he'd been in on these top-secret experiments," she said. "*That's* what he was proud of—figuring out how to make disease-bombs that would kill zillions of people. Then some general got in trouble, and they cleaned house; got rid of everybody underneath, to get the general off the hook. I didn't know whether to believe it or not."

Monks recalled Ostrand's "Special Operations" classification. The reason he gave for the discharge might have been self-serving, but the possibility that he had been involved in biological warfare was real.

"We have information that he was involved in a research experiment these past few years," Monks said. "A group of people, maybe twenty-some adults—" Monks was about to add, *and some children*, but caught himself. "He'd have seen them pretty frequently. You know anything about that?"

"Nope. He never said a word about work, and I didn't ask."

Monks was starting to feel the closeness of the room, a sign that another interview had dead-ended. Larrabee was starting to fidget too.

"Anything else you can think of, Trish?" Larrabee said. He was gazing past her at a wall, the question perfunctory, his mind on where to take this next. "Anybody he was arguing with? Anybody who might know something about this?"

"Well, you could try Gloria. I don't know if she'd help. She's not good people."

Larrabee was watching her again, his interest quickened. "Not good people" were just what he wanted. "Who's Gloria?"

"She worked for him, doing secretarial stuff. Worked *on* him too."

"What do you mean?"

"Walker brought her around the house a few times. No reason, I think he just wanted us to see him with a younger babe. Twist Mom a little more."

"And?" Larrabee prompted.

"One night, after I moved out, I had a fight with my boyfriend and went home," Trish said. "It was late—Mom was passed out—but I could just see through the living room curtains, something moving up and down. Like a basketball being dribbled. It was Gloria's head, bouncing in his lap. I couldn't believe it, couldn't believe she'd do it. She's maybe twenty-eight. I got out of there. Slept in the car."

Monks wondered if Clara Ostrand had forgotten to mention Gloria— or if she had known more about what was going on than Trish seemed to think, and did not want it coming to light.

"Did she have any medical training?" Monks said.

"I don't think so. She was an army brat. That's how Walker knew her, he'd been in Korea with her dad."

"Why did you say she's not good people, Trish?"

"She's nice on the outside, but you can tell. Like Walker."

"Do you know her last name?" Larrabee said. "Where we could find her?"

"Gloria Sharpe. She's opening a shop in SoMa."

Larrabee's eyebrows rose. "Oh, really?" Monks was impressed too. SoMa was a trendy little neighborhood.

"Yeah. She had the nerve to give Mom as a reference for the lease."

"What kind of shop?"

"Stuff. Antiques, jewelry, like that. I think she does feng shui too."

Larrabee handed Trish another fifty, along with one of the Commonwealth Insurance business cards.

"You want to give me your phone number, Trish?"

"It got cut off."

"Okay," Larrabee said. "Call if you think of anything else. Otherwise, you never heard of us, huh?"

Abruptly, she sat on the unmade bed, leaning back on her hands, knees spilling a little apart. Naughty, Monks decided, was the word for her expression.

"You going to tell me who I never heard of?" she said.

"I'm afraid that's not an option."

"Oh. So you know me, but I don't know you?"

"For now."

She smiled saucily. "I thought you guys were weird at first. But this is kind of cool. You should come back."

They returned through the gloomy hallway. The volume of music from somewhere in the building rose with each step.

Monks said, "How about you, Trish? Have you got plans?"

She shrugged, looking suddenly despondent. "I'm working at a video parlor. It sucks." She swept her hand to take in the apartment. "*This* sucks."

"Maybe your mom could use some help. You could go back to school, something like that."

"Yeah, well, first there was Walker, and now there's Billy," she said. "I think that's just how Mom is."

They reached the door. The feet hanging over the couch arm had gone limp, their owner no longer even at a minimal level of awareness.

Larrabee said, "You'd better be careful, doing—what you're doing."

"I can take care of myself," she said, but the defiance was forced.

Outside, the streets were a tapestry of movement, cars threading along the narrow patched pavement, strolling pedestrians finding their way to the bars and cafés. It all seemed relaxed and peaceful, and yet Monks imagined a covert sharpness in the gazes he met, the sense that this was a place where people carried secrets with hard edges.

"Feng shui in SoMa," Larrabee said. "Interesting career change for a secretary. I'd hate to suggest that when you've got a young lady blowing her employer who's twice her age, it's more likely to be for money than true love."

While his wife, addicted by him to prescription narcotics, slumbered in the same house. So far, it was no surprise that Walker Ostrand did not seem to have left much grief behind him.

"Let's go back to the office and do some thinking about how to hit Gloria Sharpe," Larrabee said. "This one's going to have to be a better class of lie."

Larrabee's computer scan and some phone calls yielded a sketch of information on Gloria Sharpe: vehicle registrations, employment at a couple of secretarial temp agencies, several overdue bills listed on credit reports—and most recently, an application for a city business license. She had moved out of her last known address, an apartment in Millbrae, three months earlier—a time that coincided with Walker Ostrand's death. There were no marriages and no indication that she ever had been associated with Ostrand.

It was possible—especially since she appeared to have no medical training—that she was, if not exactly an innocent, unaware of what Ostrand had been doing: that she had been simply a secretary or book-keeper having an affair with her older employer.

But it was a strong assumption that she *had* been involved, and she knew that if the research were made public, she was looking at prison.

One bit of information, Monks kept thinking, was all it would take to lead them to that group of research subjects. Even a single individual's name might be enough. Gloria Sharpe might have it, and might let it drop without realizing its importance.

But Larrabee was probably right. Getting it was going to require a better class of lie.

*   *   *

Gloria Sharpe's shop was located in a warren of small byways off Fifteenth Street just east of the 101 skyway, an old industrial area in the borderland between South of Market and the Mission. Tendrils of upscaling in the neighborhood were evident; several of the old stone and brick buildings had been sandblasted, with freshly painted signs advertising antiques and art galleries. The front window of Gloria's shop was papered over; a glimpse into the open doorway showed that the place was in the process of being redecorated.

Monks and Larrabee picked their way inside through ladders, buckets, a tangle of extension cords and tools, and several men in worn jeans and T-shirts moving purposefully. The main room was a good twenty feet wide by thirty deep, with twelve-foot ceilings and brick walls that had been exposed and sandblasted. The old hardwood floor was in the process of being repaired and finished too. It was evidence of good taste—

And money. A lot more than most secretaries made. It appeared that Walker Ostrand had paid her well for her services.

"She just left," an electrician told them through a hefty chew of tobacco. "Goes to walk her dogs. Sometimes she comes back. Sometimes she doesn't." He shrugged and spat in a trash can. That was the way life was.

Larrabee grimaced. "Any way to find her?"

The electrician pointed eastward down the street. "This dead-ends in a couple blocks, at the SP tracks. If she's there, you'll see her car. It's a new Chevy SUV, arrest-me red."

"What kind of dogs?" Larrabee said.

"Dobermans." The electrician spat again. "They take up some space."

Monks got into the Bronco, leaving Larrabee at the shop in case she came back.

He drove through fog dampening to mist until he came to the dead end at the Southern Pacific tracks. There were no dwellings or shops here, and the red SUV was easy to spot, parked alone at the curb. He parked behind it and got out.

A chain-link fence separated the street from the tracks and the stretch of vacant turf beyond, but it was torn and battered. He had no trouble finding a hole to step through. He walked with hands in pockets and head bowed into the wet wind that stung his eyes, the smell of the sea, as always, touching his memory.

A few hundred yards east, he could see the narrow channel of the Mission Creek Marina coming in from China Basin, with its small fleet of sailboats anchored against the bank. But the area in between was deserted, a blighted no-man's-land of old concrete and rusty iron and weeds, the kind of place where a woman alone might not have felt safe.

Unless, like the woman who was walking down by the channel's end, she was flanked by two rangy, whip-lean Dobermans.

"Ms. Sharpe?" he called. "Gloria?"

She turned to watch him approach. She was thin, even from a distance, giving an impression of wiry hardness, like the dogs. They were watching him too. He saw with relief that they were on leashes.

Monks raised a hand and worked on looking friendly.

He filled in details as he got closer. She was neither pretty nor not. Her dark curly hair had highlights of henna; her face was suntanned over an unclear complexion. She had either been on vacation or had worked on the tan under a lamp. The dogs fidgeted, pulling at their leashes, but not to nose up to Monks the way that most dogs would. They were restless because of him, and yet ignoring him. It made them more unnerving.

"The guys working at your shop said you came here," Monks said. "I thought I might get lucky and catch you." He handed her one of the phony business cards. "Jim Gallagher, Commonwealth Insurance."

She accepted the card dubiously. "What's this about?"

"It's good news, Gloria. You're the beneficiary of an insurance policy. It just showed up on our quarterly audit."

"Really?" she said, very much more friendly. "Who from?"

"Dr. Walker Ostrand."

Monks thought he saw her draw back slightly.

"Walker's death was a terrible shock," she said. The line sounded like she had learned it from a soap opera.

"I'm sure," Monks said consolingly.

"How much money?"

"What's left could come to about eleven thousand dollars, if everything works out all right."

Larrabee and he had sweated over deciding the sum—enough to entice, not so much as to cause suspicion; an odd dollar amount, to disarm.

Apparently, it hit. Gloria's lips parted slightly, the tip of her tongue appearing for a second before they closed again.

"What do you mean, 'if everything works out all right?' " she said.

Monks almost smiled.

"This is a medical *re*insurance policy," he said. "It's an investment, it earns interest at a high rate. But it also insures us, the insurers, against any outstanding claims."

"O—kay," she said slowly.

"Look, it's complicated and boring," he said. "But it's how insurance companies work. Other companies come to us with claims: insurance, unpaid bills, that sort of thing. We verify them or deny them. With Dr. Ostrand, there's only a couple of minor ones, but we have to settle anything outstanding before we can pass the money on to you."

Abruptly, he pulled a small leather address book from his pocket, opened it, stared, and snapped it shut again.

"Sorry, I just realized I'm going to be late for another appointment," he said wearily. "It's already been a long day."

"So?" she said. "Is there a problem?"

Monks lifted his outspread palms. "We can't verify the claims because we don't have Dr. Ostrand's records. Do you know what happened to them?"

"No," she said quickly. "I was just a secretary. When he died, I got my personal things from the office. That was it."

Monks exhaled. "I'm afraid that's going to hang this up."

"Can't you just go ahead and pay the bills, if I tell you to?" she said, anxious now. "I mean, it's my money."

"It's not that simple," Monks said. "You're only paying the insurance premiums. *We're* paying the actual claims. I'm sorry, Gloria, but we just can't do that unless we're sure they're valid."

"There has to be a way around this." She was starting to get angry.

Monks thrust his hands into his pants pockets and spent ten seconds gazing out to sea, as if making a decision.

"Okay," he said. "I'd like to get it off the books. Give me a quick rundown of where he worked, who he dealt with. If it checks out, I'll try to punch it through."

"He was a consultant," she said. "He worked out of his office."

Monks had the sense of walking along a narrowing trail cut into a sheer cliffside, with an abyss on the other side. He decided to take a chance.

"I think there was at least one bill from a laboratory," he said. "For blood sample analyses."

She was looking at him hard now. He had the sudden unsettling sense that her pupils had actually contracted.

She spoke a single quiet word: "Baron."

The larger of the dogs fixed on Monks. There was no more fidgeting; it was motionless as a statue. The other whined, looking nervously at its mistress. Monks's testicles tightened. There were hundreds of cars roaring by overhead on the freeways in plain sight, but in that lonely twilight, those dogs could reduce him to butcher's meat within seconds. There were times when he carried a pistol, but he had not dreamed that this situation might call for it.

"Look, I'm just a claims adjustor," he said. He stepped carefully back. "I didn't mean to upset you, I'm trying to get you some money. What's the problem?"

She did not answer. Her mouth was a tight, thin line.

"Okay," Monks said. "Sorry."

He walked away with less careful steps, stomach in a queasy knot and shoulders hunched against a sudden rush of motion behind him, teeth ripping into him and dragging him down.

But he made it to the fence and scrambled clumsily through, panting, armpits wet. He risked a wary glance back, expecting that she had fallen behind. He saw with unpleasant shock that she had kept pace with him and was coming through the fence too, the dogs tugging eagerly at their leashes. He hurried on to the Bronco.

She surprised him again by calling, "I'll try to remember, okay?"

Monks paused with one foot inside the big sturdy vehicle's door, feeling much better.

"My number's on the card," he called back. He backed the Bronco around in a quick three-point, aware of an absurd fear that the dogs might chew the tires off. A glance in the rearview mirror showed her still standing there, watching him.

Monks drove grimly back to pick up Larrabee, with mist smearing his windshield, blurring the oncoming headlights. Whether Gloria Sharpe would contact them, and what she might tell them if she did, was going to come down to some unguessable trade-off between caution and avarice.

Monks had started carrying a cell phone of his own for investigation work. He disapproved of them in principle, but in practice they were damned convenient. He was sitting in Larrabee's office, refining his tarot deck of information, when it rang.

"Dr. Monks? This is Martine Rostanov. We met last night?"

Monks was surprised by the formality, but then realized that she might not be alone.

"Of course, I remember," he said.

"I'm awfully sorry to bother you. We have someone injured up here at Aesir Corporation offices. I'd like to get an emergency physician's opinion."

Monks was surprised again. "You don't think you should get them to a hospital?"

"I don't *think* it's that serious, and he'd rather not go to a hospital if he doesn't have to, with all the hubbub right now. It's Pete Hazeldon. You met him last night too."

Monks remembered him: the boyish-looking research and development head.

"What kind of injury?" Monks said.

"He got his hand caught in some sort of machinery. I dressed it and gave him a tetanus shot. I don't think there's anything broken, but I'm worried about infection."

"Any red streaks on his forearm?"

"Not that I can see. But I'm not completely sure of myself."

"Do you have penicillin?" Monks said.

"Yes, I've got a full set of standard medical supplies."

Monks looked over to where Larrabee was slumped in front of his computer monitor, trying to cast a wider net around Walker Ostrand.

"Any problem if I take off for an hour?" he said to Larrabee.

Larrabee signified no with a headshake and grunt.

"All right," Monks said into the phone. "It shouldn't take me long to get there."

"I'll wait for you at the front desk," she said.

Larrabee's gaze was a shade acerbic. "Seems like those Aesir people are getting to like you."

Monks walked out to the Bronco just after dusk. The late rush hour traffic was winding down. He could see the top of the brightly lit, towering citadel of the Bank of America Building: an impregnable fortress where the tapestry of the world's destiny was being embroidered on, high above the ken of common people.

It was going to feel pretty strange walking in there—like an ant that was trying to chew the feet out from under a giant, paying him a visit and hoping he wouldn't figure it out.

Martine was waiting at the desk, as promised. This time the security guards allowed her to be Monk's escort.

Walking across the lobby to the elevators, she said very quietly, "There's bugs and cameras all over this place."

"Call me later from a safe phone," Monks said. In a normal tone, he said, "How did Pete Hazeldon get injured?"

"He's been working on the company boat. The one in the press conference?"

"I saw it on TV," Monks said.

"Wiring it for a communications system, something like that."

"They can't afford to hire an electrician?"

"Pete says it relaxes him. But I don't think he'll be doing any more of it for a while."

The Aesir offices seemed even busier than they had been last night. Martine led him down the main hall to a room that was outfitted as a physician's examination room, with adjustable bed, sink, scale, blood pressure cuff, and all the other standard appurtenances. Aesir executives did not have to wait in doctors' offices for minor medical attention.

"I know it must seem extravagant," she said apologetically, catching Monk's wry expression. "Please wait, I'll get Pete."

Monks stood inside the doorway, unobtrusively watching the bustle up and down the hall, with the steady background noise of ringing phones and office machinery. The IPO was only about forty hours away now.

Then he realized that a woman walking toward him was Audrey Cabot. Today she was wearing slim black flannel slacks with an ivory silk blouse, and a single strand of lustrous opalescent pearls. The ensemble was tastefully casual, and probably would have put a down payment on Monks's house. He expected that Audrey would pass by without recognizing him, but she paused, turning to him with a poise that suggested a model on a runway.

"I see some doctors still make house calls," she said.

"Under special circumstances."

"I'll keep that in mind if I feel special." She smiled faintly and walked on.

Martine and Pete Hazeldon were coming down the hall from the other direction. Audrey Cabot ignored them, perhaps pointedly, as she passed by.

"This had to happen now, of all times," Hazeldon muttered. His left hand was bandaged from the wrist to the first joints of the fingers. His frizzy hair and skin were damp with sweat, and he looked shaken, perhaps feverish. "I can't believe how goddamned stupid I was. I was fish-ing a wire through the anchor cable housing. I must have tripped something. All of a sudden, *whammo*. I could hardly pull my hand out."

There was probably a product liability lawsuit in it, Monks thought.

He sat Hazeldon on the bed and pulled up his sleeve. "How long ago did it happen?"

"An hour. I came straight here."

An hour was too early for the red streaking of blood poisoning to show. Monks unpeeled the bandage. The inside layers were soaked through with blood that had started to crust. He worked the gauze free carefully, but felt Hazeldon's winces.

"He won't take anything stronger than ibuprofen for the pain," Martine explained.

"I've got to stay clearheaded," Hazeldon said stubbornly.

Monks dropped the clump of bloody gauze in the trash and turned the hand, examining it. It was swollen to almost twice its normal size, and deep purple with bruises. There were several bloody ragged tears on both palm and back. It looked like it had been stuck into a big electric pencil sharpener.

"Can you move those fingers?" Monks said.

Hazeldon waggled them feebly.

"Okay," Monks said. "Watch the forearm closely for red streaking. Start penicillin immediately if it shows. Get the hand examined tomorrow by an orthopedic surgeon. You need to make sure there's no damage to tendon and nerve functions."

"I want the penicillin now," Hazeldon said. The stubborn tone was more pronounced. Monks was mildly surprised. Most people were relieved to avoid shots, at least the kind that did not provide any pleasurable payoff.

"You probably don't need it," Monks said. "The wound's been well cleaned. Machinery's not the sort of thing that's likely to cause infection."

"I can't afford to take any chances."

Monks started to point out that there were no chances involved, as long as precautions were duly observed. But it was not his emergency room, and not worth arguing about.

"Ever had any allergic reactions, anything like that?" Monks said.

"Nothing."

Monks looked at Martine. "Doctor? Any objections?"

She shook her head. "I haven't given one of these in a while."

"One point two million units, ProPen G," Monks said.

She opened a cabinet and got out the penicillin and syringe. Pete Hazeldon, with his good hand, started rolling his other sleeve up to his shoulder.

"I'm afraid this one has to go in the rump, Pete," Martine said.

Hazeldon glanced swiftly at her. His face was flushed and startled.

"You think that's funny, making me drop my pants?" he said. The words rushed out in an angry burst.

"Of course not," she said soothingly. "It's just a fact. A dose this massive needs a bigger muscle."

"I'll give it, if you'd be more comfortable with that," Monks said.

Hazeldon looked away, then nodded curtly.

Martine gave Monks the filled syringe, looking apologetic again, and stepped out of the room, closing the door behind her. Hazeldon turned his back to Monks and pushed his trousers down, revealing thin, tensed buttocks.

"Why don't you lean over the cot and put your weight on your elbows," Monks said. "This will be easier for both of us if that muscle's relaxed."

Hazeldon did as he was told. His breathing was quick and shallow, and his flesh jerked at the needle's bite. It was an undeniably awkward situation, but one that Monks had faced daily, in some variation, over many years. Unless there was real pain or fear involved, it had all the emotional impact to him of a mechanic changing spark plugs.

"Okay," Monks said, withdrawing the needle. "You can zip up. We'll give you a course of oral Pen Vee for follow-up."

Hazeldon turned, buckling his belt, his face still tense. But then it relaxed into an odd pleased grin—the look of a man who had been through an ordeal, with the worst over.

"Thanks, Doctor," he said. "I owe you one."

Monks opened the door for Martine. "He's ready to bandage up again."

"I'm sure you'd like to get going," she said. "If you don't mind, Pete, I'll just walk Dr. Monks out."

They rode the elevator down in silence, conscious of hidden ears that might be listening. This time, walking across the lobby, she whispered, "I'll get to a pay phone in a few minutes."

At the main doors, she offered her hand. Monks shook it.

"Thanks," she said. "Don't forget to send us a bill."

"I won't forget," Monks said.

Monks had crossed Market Street and was driving through the quieter blocks of the old industrial district when his cell phone rang.

"It's me," Martine said. Her voice was breathy, as if she had been walking fast. "I've left the building."

"Were you okay today?"

"Nobody paid any attention to me," she said. "They're all wrapped up with everything else that's going on."

"Any word on Lex?"

"Not about where he is. Plenty about him not being here. They've got security people combing the globe. How about you? Did you find anything?"

"Not much," Monks said unhappily. "Can you make it another day?"

"I don't see why not."

"You're going to a hotel tonight, like Stover said?"

"Yes. I haven't picked one yet. But I have my cell phone." She hesitated, then said, "You want to have a drink some time? When this is over?"

"I want ten drinks, right now," Monks said. "But, yes."

"I'll stock up. Tell me what."

"Vodka," Monks said. "Finlandia, preferably. Does that work for you?"

"Are you kidding? With a name like Rostanov?"

"It's exotic," he said. "The name."

"Mongrel, more like it. A great-grandfather who was a fur trader from Smolensk. He married a woman who was Scottish, Mexican, and Pomo Indian, as far as she knew, and it went from there. But the vodka stayed."

Monks said, "Keep in mind that one of those Aesir people might be a killer."

"I know," she said in a smaller voice. "It's hard. I've worked with them for years."

"I'll call you soon," he said.

His phone rang again almost immediately. He said, "Hello," thinking it was probably Martine, calling back to tell him something she had forgotten.

But it was a man's voice, crisp and friendly. "Dr. Monks? My name's Ed Towry. I'm an independent fire inspector, working for Pacific Insurance. How are you today, sir?"

Monks's first thought was that this was a sales pitch, and wondered how the hell they had gotten his cell phone number. Then he remembered that Pacific Insurance was the conglomerate that handled Mercy Hospital's accounts.

"What can I do for you?"

"Doctor, you were present at the incident at Mercy Hospital last night? A fire and some damage?"

"I was there, yes," Monks said warily, already sensing that this was going to cost him time and trouble.

"I'm wondering if there's any chance you could drop by the hospital and we could go over a few details," Towry said.

Monks had been starting to think in terms of dinner. There was a Chinese take-out joint that Larrabee called the Mongol Horde, not far from the office, which offered a bloodcurdling fireworks shrimp.

"Now?" Monks said.

"If it's not too inconvenient, sir, we'd like to get it wrapped up. It should only take a few minutes." The tone was importunate, almost wheedling.

Monks exhaled: best to get it over with before he got settled again. "Okay."

"Thank you, Doctor. I won't keep you long."

Monks turned the Bronco west toward Mercy Hospital. He *did* want ten drinks. He tried to imagine what might develop with Martine Rostanov after this was over—whether he could fit in with her seven-figure house and lovely things, her society of the wealthy, influential, scientific world-shakers.

The answer was easy. He could not. And the momentum of that sparkling torrent would be hard for her to pull away from, even if she wanted to.

Still, he had to speak sternly to a part of his mind that was phrasing a phone call to her. It began: *Tell me where you're staying tonight. Let's get together for just one.*

THIRTEEN

It was full night, foggy and damp, when Monks crossed Nineteenth Avenue into the Sunset. There was almost no traffic on the dozen blocks from there to Vallerga Street, a one-way that led toward Mercy Hospital's parking lot. He had been driving on automatic pilot, mentally reconstructing the events of the fire, trying to make sure he would not slip and link them with John Smith.

Then, a parked car without headlights pulled out from the curb to his left just as he came alongside.

Monks slammed on his brakes and veered right, narrowly avoiding the collision. He glared, waiting for the vehicle to pull out of the way. It was a beater, a lowslung, early 80's Chrysler or GM sedan, sporting scraped greenish paint and several dents. Clearly there had been more than one wreck already. The windows were smoked, probably with the film you could buy at auto parts stores.

But the front passenger window was opening. The face inside was turned to him. Monks just had time to register the impression that it was wearing a ski mask.

A light popped like a flashbulb. The glass beside Monks's head split open, with pellets spraying his skin.

He lunged to the right and down, face-first across the passenger seat. Two more shots smashed through glass; then came a metallic *whunk* as the next one, moving downward to follow him, hit the door. A wasplike buzz of sound passed inches above his head.

He grabbed the steering wheel with his left hand and stomped on the accelerator, his body still splayed across the seat.

The Bronco smashed into the side of the sedan, throwing Monks forward, wedging him etween the dash and the floor. He fought himself free and stomped the gas again in surges, rocking the other car. He thought he heard more shots, but could not be sure over the sound of his own shrieking breath.

Monks fumbled the floor shift into reverse and jammed down again on the gas pedal. The Bronco peeled backward and slammed into something. He dropped the shift into low and bucked forward, jerking the steering wheel farther to the right, trying to get clear. His left front fender caught again. But this time the other car yielded, moving with him.

The Bronco's windshield burst into a glassy shower.

Monks jammed down on the gas again and again, rocking forward a few inches at a time, the Bronco's big 351 and truck drive train dragging the other vehicle along.

Then, with a rending scream of metal, he was free.

He careened down the narrow street, feeling the Bronco sideswiping parked cars. After a few seconds, he pulled himself up and risked a glance back. The sedan's bumper was locked with a parked vehicle that the Bronco had rammed it into, tires spinning as it bucked to pull free.

There was cross traffic on Thirty-ninth Avenue but Monks floored it, lunging through veering cars and blaring horns. Halfway down the next block, he looked back again. There was no one following. He could not be certain in the dark, but he thought the sedan was gone.

He drove on for several more blocks, checkerboarding, watching the streets intently for a sign of the vehicle that had attacked him. Gradually, he slowed, then pulled into an alley and stopped behind a Dumpster. He sat there for two or three minutes, trying to calm his body, while the outrage of what had just happened mushroomed in his mind. What he felt was far beyond anger or shock. He *marveled* that it was possible, this act of unchallenged savagery in the midst of civilization.

The floor and seats were covered with beaded glass. Three spider-web patterns in the windshield radiated out in ragged spokes from quarter-sized holes. Most of the window beside his head was gone, with shards clinging in the frame. The glass on the passenger side was honeycombed with exiting rounds. There was another hole in the door panel to his left, the shot he had heard pass above his head.

But the real miracle had happened with the very first one, which had come point-blank from a few feet away. He had not escaped by getting out of the way in time. He had seen the muzzle flash. It could only have been deflected, just enough, by the thick original glass.

Monks spent a moment in something like prayer, thanking this grand old horse of a vehicle for the armor that had protected him, and the power that had freed him.

The rearview mirror was intact, an almost comic touch. He twisted it and examined his face. He was bloody, but it looked worse than it felt. The Bronco was still idling quietly, with no obvious leaking fluids. The passenger-side headlight still worked. With his breath slowed, Monks thought he heard sirens.

He drove back toward the scene, this time pausing for the cross traffic on 39th. Vallerga Street was already a kaleidoscope of flashing blue and red lights. Uniformed police had cordoned off the area and were holding back the growing crowd of bystanders. Monks watched, with an eerie, disembodied sense coming over him, a sort of floating. It occurred to him that perhaps he had died after all, that this was like a movie with his ghost trying to carry on, unaware that its bullet-riddled body was cooling and still.

He got out of the Bronco and started toward the police to identify himself.

Then he stopped again. There was a green Jaguar convertible parked just outside the cordon—identical to the one driven by Ronald Tygard, that Monks had seen parked in Martine's driveway last night.

Monks stepped into shadow and waited.

Three or four minutes later, a black and white SFPD patrol car pulled up to the scene. A rear door opened and a man got out. He was white-haired, powerfully built, wearing an overcoat and necktie. He was moving fast and looked angry.

He was the same man Monks had seen last night in Aesir Corporation's offices, talking to Ronald Tygard, with his shoulder holster exposed.

The white-haired man glared toward the Jaguar and made a quick, lifting gesture with his chin. Then he strode into the scene with lowered head, his coat flaring around him. The uniforms melted out of his way, a couple touching their caps in salute.

The Jag pulled away from the curb and left.

Monks trotted back to the Bronco and crept away with his lights turned off. Several blocks farther, he pulled into another alley. He punched Stephanie's number on his cell phone and closed his eyes in relief when she answered.

"Get out of your place, right now," he said.

"What—"

"Grab your purse and *go. Now*, this second. Call Stover when you get someplace safe."

He always carried extra supplies in the Bronco: clothes, tools, camping gear. He changed quickly into jeans, a sweatshirt, and running shoes. Then he took his Beretta pistol from a safety deposit box concealed under the console and slipped it into his pocket. It was a Model 82 light, not much bigger than his wallet. He was not going to be without it again.

Monks started walking, cleaning his face unobtrusively with a handkerchief and saliva, wary of cruising black-and-whites. When he was a couple of blocks clear, he took out his phone again and punched Larrabee's number.

"Somebody tried to take me out," he said. "Shot up the Bronco."

"*Christ*."

"You better come pick me up."

"What do you mean, pick you up? Aren't there cops there?"

"I don't think I'll be talking to them just yet," Monks said.

Monks waited at a bus stop on Taraval, hanging in the shadows of a nearby storefront until Larrabee drove up in a gray Taurus, a car he favored for its inconspicuousness.

Monks gripped the windowsill and said, "Did Stephanie call?"

"She's at a restaurant on Irving Street. Get in, somebody's going to think you're peddling your ass."

Monks swung himself in and described what had happened, while Larrabee drove. A police scanner in the car punctuated his terse words, squawking static-laden commands, codes, and comments.

"Nice driving," Larrabee said.

"Lucky, Stover. Lucky they used a handgun. A shotgun or full auto—"

"They'll get it right next time." Larrabee's finger tapped the radio. "They've been referring to an attempted carjacking in the Sunset."

"*Car*jacking. A twenty-five-year-old beater truck?"

"Crackheads." He glanced at Monks's outraged face and shrugged. "Fuckers are crazy, they'll steal anything. That's how it'll get put down."

Monks slumped back in the seat. "Any arrests?"

"Doesn't sound like it. You're sure that cop's the same guy you saw at Aesir?"

"Pretty sure. Late fifties, stocky, white hair. Walked in jaw first, like he was getting into a ring."

"Could be Mickey Hearne. A captain in the western division. A guy you don't want to fuck with."

"How did they know what we're trying to do?" Monks said. "For Christ's sake, I've patched together two of their executives in the past twenty-four hours."

"I've been thinking about that. My guess is, Gloria Sharpe. That she called somebody at Aesir and told them you'd been to see her."

"I gave her a phony card," Monks said.

"Did she see your vehicle? Close enough to get the license number?"

Monks remembered his last glimpse of her in the rearview mirror, standing behind him, flanked by her dogs.

"Yeah. But—" he started to say that tracing a plate would take more time.

Not for somebody inside Aesir.

The enormity of it was growing swiftly, astounding him with the realization that if a competent organization really wanted you dead, there was almost no way to stop it. The protection you grew up taking for granted, from government and law enforcement, could only go so far. The fact was that an organization like Aesir had unlimited resources: billions of dollars, an incredible information network, and, clearly, not an instant's hesitation to shoot him down on sight.

Larrabee said, "You still got that blood sample?"

Monks nodded. "At home, in my refrigerator."

Larrabee grinned unpleasantly. "Sorry. That shouldn't be funny. I think you better get it. It's proof that that was Lex Rittenour in your ER. That will add a lot of weight to your story."

"We have Martine's testimony on that."

Larrabee turned east on Lincoln, skirting the Golden Gate park panhandle.

"I don't thing I'd stake too much there, Carroll," Larrabee said. "Sorry, but I've seen a lot of times when somebody made a noble decision, then got cold feet."

"What are you saying?"

"I'm saying that's another possibility for why you got nailed. Maybe she went back there to Aesir and started thinking about all she had to lose. Broke down and told somebody about her talk with us."

"Jesus, Stover. I can't believe she'd be that coldblooded. I just *saw* her."

"I don't mean she did it on purpose, or even realized it. Just maybe opened the door for somebody else."

Monks pressed the heels of his hands into his closed eyes, trying to comprehend the turn this had taken.

"Don't let that blood sample out of your hands," Larrabee said. "Not around here, anyway. Too easy for it to get lost or switched. You're going to take it to FBI headquarters yourself. Fly to D.C. and walk in. Kick up a fuss, insist they take it straight to the lab and you go with it. By then there'll be a lot of people paying attention."

Larrabee pulled over to the curb. "You take this car. I'll get a cab and find Steffie. Don't worry, I'll take care of her." He got out and Monks slid into the driver's seat.

"They might send somebody around your place," Larrabee said through the window.

Monks's address was unlisted and the house was not easy to find, marked only by an unnamed mailbox and hidden in the woods a hundred yards up a dirt drive. But he had seen how fast these people could move.

"I'll go in the back way," he said.

"You better be ready to shoot, because they will be."

Monks nodded.

"In case it makes you feel better," Larrabee said. "If we weren't on to something, they wouldn't have tried to kill you."

Monks drove carefully toward the Golden Gate Bridge, staying at the speed limit. The thought came to him that he was on a pilgrimage, to recover the Precious Blood of Saint Lex: a relic now called upon to perform a true miracle—saving his life.

FOURTEEN

Northwest of San Rafael, on the back roads he knew well, Monks stepped harder on the gas. Traffic had dropped off to nothing by the time he got to Tocqueville Road. He pulled into a turnout a half mile short of his driveway and eased the car behind a screen of brush. From here, he knew the terrain well.

He stepped through the wire fence along the road and stood unmoving for three or four minutes, tuning his eyes and ears to the night. Crickets chirped in steady rhythm. A tree frog sang its heart out, trying to win a ladylove. Farther away, an owl hooted. The smooth sinuous trunks of the madrones glistened with the damp and moved with the night breeze, seeming to twist like huge snakes.

Monks began to walk, following a deer trail down to the creek that ran behind his place, then picking his way along its rocks. The creek was dry most of the year, but right now it was running swiftly from spring rains. In years past, he had spent many hours down here, sitting with a book while the kids played, until they were old enough to handle the dangers of fast water in floods and the occasional rattlesnake. Not much had changed.

He found the path back up the bank that would take him onto his own property. When the woods began to thin, he moved one slow step at a time.

Ahead through the foliage, he spotted a glimmer of light.

Monks checked his location and placed the light carefully, grasping at the thought that he might be turned around and it was a neighbor's. But it had to be from his own house.

He was certain that he had not left any lights on.

He stood motionless for a full minute, grappling with consequences. Smart money was to turn back.

But this had gone past smart money. He took out the Beretta and walked on in careful silence. When he reached the edge of the woods, he saw a car parked in the drive, a newish, midsized sedan. He had never seen it before.

What kind of assassin would advertise his presence?

Monks listened hard through the surrounding woods, fearful now that the display was intended to lull him, that someone else was waiting hidden. The night creatures' sounds continued, reassuring but no guarantee.

Then a hard *thunk* and a blur of motion dropped him to a crouch, the pistol rising. Breath stopped, he waited.

There was more movement: Someone on the deck was rising awkwardly from a chair, body pulling itself up with what sounded like labored cursing. A man stood and lumbered toward the kitchen, letting out a wedge of light as he opened the door. Something glimmered on the deck railing, and Monks realized that that was what had thunked:

A beer bottle, set down hard.

Monks heard the refrigerator open and close. The man reappeared in the house doorway. He was good-sized, well dressed but disheveled, and was holding a fresh bottle of Monks's private stock of Moretti beer.

Monks's scalp bristled with mystical awe.

It was Saint Lex himself, risen from the dead.

FIFTEEN

Monks said quietly, "Don't panic."

Lex Rittenour, aka John Smith, wheeled at the sound of the voice. He moved his head back and forth, staring into the darkness with his nose raised, like a bear sniffing for food.

"Are you alone?" Monks said.

"Yeah." Lex was wearing the kind of leather jacket that cost a great deal of money to look distressed. But otherwise, his clothes were the same ones he had had on in the ER, and his hair was greasy and matted. He looked like he had been living in the car.

Monks stepped out of the shadows and edged forward, wary of other movement.

"Hey, it's *you*," Lex said. His teeth showed in a ragged grin. "Where the hell have you been? I didn't think you were ever going to show up."

"Where have *I* been? The whole world's wondering where *you* are."

Lex raised a hand in deprecation. "Let them wonder."

Monks walked to the sedan and opened the passenger door. "Get in," Monks said. "I'm taking you home."

"Fuck home. I could have gone home myself." Lex raised the beer bottle and swilled, glaring.

"You can't just wander around loose," Monks said.

"Why not? Hey, calm down. I'll get you a beer."

"A lot of people think you're dead, is why not."

"They were almost right."

"Yeah, I was there, remember?" Monks said impatiently. "Come on, get in."

"I'm not going back. Somebody tried to kill me."

I don't need your cooperation, Monks was starting to say, trying to visualize pulling a gun on a world-ranking celebrity. Then this new byte of information hit. He spent several seconds absorbing it. Off in the woods, the tree frog chirped hopefully.

"Who did?" Monks said.

"I don't know. Whoever set up that overdose."

"Whoa, slow down. You think it was deliberate?"

"Don't look so surprised," Lex said. "*You're* the one who told me."

Monks tried to peer back through the maelstrom of the past twenty-four hours. "When did I do that?"

"When I was leaving the emergency room. You said, 'Be careful what you put in your arm, this happens because it's purer than what you're used to.' "

Monks vaguely recalled issuing the warning, but he had intended it for future, not past.

"Tell me how it happened," Monks said. "The overdose."

Lex shrugged, as if it should have been self-explanatory. "I came into SFO last night on one of the company jets. There was a limo waiting, with that driver and the girl, the ones that brought me to the hospital."

So much for the "taxi-driver-passing-by" story, Monks thought.

"She had a vial of pharmaceutical Demerol, exactly the same I'd been using," Lex said. "It was a welcome-home present—a blow job and a shot. Well, when she finished with the first, I thought, why wait for the second? So I went ahead and did up, there in the car. One milliliter, same as always.

"But it was way too strong. I knew it the second it hit. She panicked and started screaming. Kicked me out of the car. That's the last thing I remember until I opened my eyes and I was looking at you."

An overdose of street heroin could easily be accidental. But with pharmaceutical Demerol, that was highly unlikely.

"You didn't ask her who sent her?" Monks said.

"I didn't *care* who sent her. Pretty girl with a hot mouth and a bottle of high. I wanted them. Besides, she didn't speak English."

So: Martine Rostanov was right. Somebody wanted to kill Lex.

And Lex was not just avoiding the public eye; he was on the run.

Too.

"Why," Monks said, "with all the places in the world to hide out, did you come here?"

"I want to hire you."

Monks closed his eyes. He had been invalided out of Vietnam for malaria. The attacks had decreased in frequency over the years until he had almost forgotten about them. But once in a while, a situation would arise that was so surreal, he would fear that he was slipping into another feverish nightmare.

He opened his eyes. Lex was still standing there on the deck.

"Hire me for what?" Monks said.

"To find out who gave me that dope, what do you think? You're an investigator, right?"

Monks was increasingly aware that minutes were passing, and that there might be men from Aesir coming this way. He tried to weigh it all, short-term risks and long-term consequences on the one hand—

And payoff on the other. Having Saint Lex in the flesh opened up a whole new avenue of possibility.

"We can talk," Monks said. "Right now we've got to move."

"Name your price."

"My family."

"What do you mean?"

Monks climbed the stairs onto the deck and pulled open the kitchen door, turning in the light to display the crusted blood on his own face.

"They tried to take me out too," he said.

"No kidding?" Lex's expression changed to what Monks could only interpret as boyish wonder. "What did *you* do to piss them off?"

"Made your acquaintance."

"Hey, that gives us a bond!"

"Yell if you hear anybody coming," Monks said, and stepped inside.

"You got a needle in there?" Lex called after him.

"I'm not a pharmacy."

"Get off your fucking pulpit, will you? I've got my own stuff; just no spike."

Monks exhaled in contained anger.

"Come on," Lex said coaxingly. "I'll quit, but now's not the time."

Monks strode through the house, flanked by nervous cats darting around, and threw things into a duffel: several thousand dollars cash from the safe, a medical kit, his twelve-gauge shotgun. He added his address book and pulled the tape from his message machine, in case there was something traceable from Stephanie. He ripped open a twenty-pound sack of dry cat food and left it on the floor.

"You guys are going to have to rough it for a while," he said to the accusing stares. "Catch some critters."

Then he pulled open the refrigerator and palmed the tube of blood. The sense of unreality hit him again: These few milliliters of liquid had been all-important, worth risking his life for, and now their source was standing on the deck outside. Still, Larrabee was right: It remained the only hard evidence that that particular man had been in Mercy Hospital that particular night.

But Monks admitted the deeper truth: He was operating on superstition, the sense that the Blood of Saint Lex had carried him this far.

He wrapped it in a towel and stowed it carefully in his bag.

*   *   *

Monks eased the sedan down his driveway without lights, and cut the engine to coast the last fifty yards. His head was out the window, listening. There were no sounds but the crunching of the tires on the gravel, the faint night wind, the distant murmur of the creek. He waited half a minute, tensed for the possibility of a shape or sound shattering the peaceful darkness.

Then he realized that Lex, in the passenger seat, had rolled up his left sleeve and was wrapping his belt around his forearm.

"Knock that off," Monks said angrily.

"It will only take a minute."

"First we get someplace I'm not going to get shot at again."

Lex watched him with a look Monks remembered from the ER: a bit wounded, a bit petulant, a bit arrogant—a look that was used to getting what it wanted. Monks was starting to grasp that this was a quality to Lex's persona that lent it power, the ability to morph back and forth with lightning speed from haughty genius to sly charmer or vulnerable boy—all genuine.

"We'll be stopping in a few minutes," Monks said. "You can do it then."

He started the engine and pulled out fast, still without headlights, accelerating westward into the coastal mountains. Anyone approaching his house would probably be coming from the other direction, behind them. Probably.

"Where are we going?" Lex said.

"To an old friend of mine. We need to gear up."

When Monks had first bought his place, there was not much occasion to get to know the scattered, reclusive neighbors. Then one spring, a series of torrential storms washed sections of Tocqueville Road down the mountainside. For two days, before county crews could make repairs, Monks's house and a couple of dozen others were cut off from town. Soon after that, the power went out.

It was not a serious crisis for his family—they had plenty of food and a wood stove—and even an adventure for the kids. Then, late the second evening, a gunmetal gray pickup truck that Monks had never seen before came rumbling up the drive. It looked like it had been welded together out of battleship plates.

A powerfully built man, whom Monks had never seen either, got out. He walked to the house through the still-pounding rain, carrying a frightened, weeping little girl. Inside, he informed Monks that his name was Emil Zukich, he lived up the road, and he had heard there was a doctor living here. A fly had crawled into his granddaughter's ear.

By candlelight, with Monks's own children watching breathlessly, and Emil glowering over his massive folded forearms, Monks soothed the girl and extracted the insect.

Emil offered cash. Monks refused. A vodka was drunk and a few words of grim thanks muttered.

Monks heard nothing more from Emil for the next months, but he heard a few things about him: that he was a good friend and a bad enemy, and a legendary mechanic who could bring machines to life and weld the crack of dawn.

That next May, with the sun back and the road repaired, Emil pulled into the drive again one afternoon, this time in a rebuilt '74 Ford Bronco. He informed Monks that it was his for one hundred dollars, no more and no less. Monks agreed, more to humor the grizzled Hunkie than because he wanted it. But it did not take him long to realize what he had been given. Monks had owned other cars since then, but the Bronco was the one he kept.

"What if this friend recognizes me?" Lex said suspiciously. "Decides to rat us off."

Monks almost smiled at the idea of Emil Zukich ratting someone off.

"He'd wonder what I was doing hanging around with somebody like you," Monks said. "But he'd be too polite to say so."

Lex reared back. "Fuck you."

"How'd you know I was an investigator? How'd you *find* my place?"

Lex's pique dissolved in a sort of cackling sound that might have been laughter.

"Give me a little credit," he said. "I design information systems."

Fog was creeping up the gullies, covering the road in patches. Monks decided to flip on the headlights.

"Fill me in on how you got from the ER to here," Monks said.

"They took me to Ken Bouldin's house and put me to bed," Lex said. "Everybody was oh-so-concerned. But any one of them could have been the one who sent that dope. Maybe *all* of them. I kept my mouth shut and figured I'd get out of there as fast as I could.

"Except Ron Tygard stayed outside my door. Supposedly in case I had trouble. But maybe he was going to come in and put a pillow over my face. I laid there like a little kid, terrified of a monster under the bed. I was still feeling like shit. But then—"

Monks glanced over at the change in Lex's voice.

"Something came over me," Lex said. "Are you into Zen?"

Monks was unprepared for the direction this was taking. "I don't know much about it."

"It was like this little flash of satori," Lex said. "Like a samurai stepped inside my head. All of a sudden it was just *there* in me. I got a bottle of Perrier and wrapped it in a towel, and hid behind the door. I started moaning, like I was in pain. Tygard came walking in and I admit, I was so scared I almost pissed my pants.

"But I did it. *Boom* across the back of the head, both hands, like Mark McGwire crushing one into deep center."

So that was what had caused the bruise on Ronald Tygard's head: a bottle of deluxe sparkling water.

"I snuck outside and found a car with keys in it, one of the help's," Lex said. "Hauled ass out of there."

"Why didn't you go to the police?" Monks said.

Lex snorted. "Companies like Aesir *are* the police. Except they operate all over the world, they don't owe shit to anybody, and they don't have to play by any rules. Governments kiss their ass. *They* dictate policy, not the other way around. They want me dead, and they'll destroy evidence, suborn witnesses, spend millions on lawyers to dissect every molecule and stall every move. And gain plenty of time for another shot at me."

Ahead, Monks saw the water tank, made of a section of galvanized iron culvert, that marked Emil Zukich's place.

He slowed and swung the sedan in.

Emil's house, like Monks's, was secluded, a good quarter mile up a steep and rutted dirt drive. The sedan bucked feebly up the climb, wheels spinning and the low chassis scraping.

"Next time, steal a better car, will you?" Monks said, teeth chattering with the jolts.

"Hey, I didn't know we'd be running the Baja 500, okay?"

Monks exhaled in relief as they topped the rise onto level ground.

"How about that shot?" Lex said.

They were still in the woods. Monks cut the engine and lights, then broke out a plastic-wrapped syringe from his medical kit and handed it over. He had administered thousands of shots and taken his share, but never for pleasure.

Lex wrapped the belt tight around his forearm, swelling the antecubital veins, and held up a clear glass vial of pharmaceutical Demerol: twenty milliliters at one hundred milligram strength. It was almost full—enough to last a moderate user a few days.

"You're sure this stuff's okay?" Monks said.

Lex nodded. "This is my own supply." He drew clear liquid into the syringe, and stopped with a practiced touch at the 1 ml mark. Monks could just see a dark flower of blood appear in the syringe as Lex probed his flesh with the needle. Then it disappeared again as he eased the plunger down.

He settled back in the seat with a soft exhalation, gaze going unfocused. Monks watched tensely for another minute, still fearing that Lex was wrong and this vial also might be tampered with. But Lex looked just fine.

Monks drove the final fifty yards to the house, aware that by now
Emil would be standing inside his door, watching. Monks left the
headlights on and stepped into their beam.

The front door opened and Emil Zukich came out. He was in his
sixties, not tall and not fat. The word to describe him was *thick*, from
his bristly gray hair down to his ankles.

Monks spoke without any preliminary politeness. "I need a big
favor, Emil. Rent that RV of yours a while."

Emil rubbed his ear pensively. "Can't rent it. Borrow it, sure."

Monks followed him to the compound that was Emil's real home—
a salvaged World War II quonset hut filled with tools and equipment
of every kind, and surrounded by what might have been the planet's
neatest junkyard. Car hulks and stacks of scrap metal were arranged
with the precision of hors d'oeuvres on a French waiter's tray. The
RV, a midsized Pace Arrow, was kept in its own shed like a stallion in
a stable.

"Two gas tanks, switch on the dash," Emil said, pointing. "Should
be enough in there now to get you four, five hundred miles. There's
water and canned food. Need anything else? Guns?"

"I'm covered there."

"If you do, call. I'll look in on your cats."

Monks hesitated. He disliked leaving the cats alone, but did not
want to put a neighbor at risk either.

"There might be somebody around my place who shouldn't be,
Emil."

"Guessed maybe something like that. Your face don't look too
good."

"The Bronco saved my ass," Monks said. "I'm afraid she's in pretty
bad shape."

Emil's countenance darkened, as if he had just learned that someone
had roughed up his wife.

The RV started at the touch of the key, settling into a smooth,
throaty idle. Lex got out of the sedan at its approach. From somewhere, he had produced a dark blue San Francisco Giants baseball cap.

It was creased and pulled low over his face, giving more the impression of the junkie Monks had first seen than a computer genius.

Lex opened the car's trunk and dragged out a grip about the same size as Monks's, but made of fine leather. Apparently it was heavy; Lex seemed to be struggling. Monks stepped in to help, but Lex pulled it away.

"You keep your hands off it," Lex said hotly. He managed to heave the bag into the RV, and climbed in after it.

Emil watched all this dubiously, then walked with Monks to the driver's side and leaned his heavy forearms on the windowsill. On one was a faded tattoo of a marine corps serial number over a dagger. Monks remembered that Emil had been at Pork Chop Hill in the Korean War, remembered accounts of that action he had heard from veterans during his own navy service. With the end of the war looming, the Communists had attacked in wave after impossible wave, having been told that they would keep every yard of territory gained.

"You bring her back when this is over," Emil said.

Monks gripped the thick forearm in thanks. "I'll be in touch."

He eased the RV back toward the steep drive, getting the feel. It was awkward on the dirt, but he knew it would stabilize on the open road.

"Who's 'her'?" Lex demanded.

"My Bronco. The one that got shot up. Emil sold it to me."

"That's a car? A Bronco?"

"Like a pickup truck, but closed in."

They reached the end of the drive and turned onto Tocqueville Road again. They had not yet passed another vehicle. The night was dark and still.

"Where we going now?" Lex said.

"I don't know," Monks admitted. He had been concentrating on *away*.

"Let's hit a store. I need something sweet."

Monks's first reaction was irritation. But he had not eaten since morning himself, and fatigue was setting in. He knew a National Seashore campground on Tomales Bay where an RV could park for the night.

"Okay," he said.

Lex settled back, obviously in a better mood. "That place," Lex said, nodding his head back toward Emil's. "That's a different world from mine. I never really thought about guys like him being out there."

"They're out there," Monks said.

SIXTEEN

They drove into Point Reyes Station just before nine P.M. and found a grocery store that was still open. Monks went in alone and bought bread, sausage, cheese, several types of sweet bakery goods, and a sackful of chocolate bars. He walked back to the RV and handed the candy through the window. Lex tore a wrapper off greedily and crammed the bar into his mouth, like a child with a candy Easter egg.

Monks walked a few yards farther away, took out his cell phone, and punched Larrabee's number. Larrabee answered on the first ring.

"Steffie's here with me," Larrabee said immediately, at the sound of Monks's voice. "Not real happy about it, but otherwise, fine. You?"

"I scored," Monks said.

"That's a relief. I was getting nervous. What's your situation?"

"Secure and mobile. There's been a slight change in plans." Monks was about to explain, when he saw the RV's door open. Lex hopped out and made a beeline for the store.

"God *damn* it, get back here," Monks called furiously, but it was too late: Lex was inside.

"Who are you talking to?" Larrabee said.

Monks exhaled. "The man who disappeared. He's back from the dead."

There came a longish pause. Larrabee said, "Are you saying what I think you are?"

"Yeah."

"He came and found *you*?"

"Nobody's more surprised than me," Monks said. "Believe me."

"That does put a different spin on things."

"Somebody tried to kill him, all right," Monks said. "The overdose was deliberate. At least that's what he thinks."

"So what now?"

"He wants us to help him find out who."

"Jesus, Mary, and Joseph," Larrabee said. Monks could picture him passing his hand over his hair. "I guess we should be flattered. I can't remember the last time I was so much in demand."

"I want to get him settled down," Monks said. "I'll call you early."

"Don't lose him," Larrabee warned. "He weighs a ton."

Lex came out of the store a minute later, clutching a paper sack of his own.

"That checkout lady asked if you and me had been in a fight," Lex said. "We must both look pretty beat up." He seemed quite pleased at the idea.

"*That's* how you're going to get recognized, walking into a place like that," Monks said angrily.

"Are you kidding? With what those fluorescent lights do to people's faces? It's like *Night of the Living Dead* in there."

Lex climbed back into the RV and pulled a bottle from the bag, with the flare of a magician producing a rabbit from a hat. It was Finlandia vodka.

"Your brand, isn't it?" Lex said. His face had gone sly.

Startled, Monks said, "How the hell—"

"I told you, give me some credit."

Lex lifted out a lemon, rolling it in his palm. After that came a sack of ice. It was oddly, annoyingly touching.

"This is no time for juicing," Monks said, shoving the vehicle in gear.

"Nobody's going to find us tonight," Lex said, then cackled. "This must be driving them nuts, whoever tried to zap us. Both of us disappeared."

The road from here on was darker, dipping in and out of the brush-clogged gullies that leaked water from the small coastal mountains, down into the sea. Monks turned into the campground, a paved stretch along the beach that gave way to a graveled loop lined with isolated parking slips. There were only a few other vehicles. He pulled into a spot at the far end.

Lex opened the passenger door and leaned out. "Not bad," he said, and stepped down to the ground.

"Don't go far," Monks said sternly.

"Just a little fresh air. Hey, come on out. This is great."

Monks went to the rear of the vehicle and found a cup in a storage cupboard. He filled it with ice, then with vodka, and carved a slice out of the lemon with his pocketknife. The first one went down fast, in three long swallows. He poured a second, full to the brim, then stepped out into the night, with the mist cool and soothing against his face.

The waxing moon over Tomales Bay was a suggestion of glow in the southern sky, behind the dark silvery veil of fog. Swells broke easily on the sheltered coast, crests streaking in phosphorescent shimmers, masses of kelp rising and falling like a vast undine shaking out her hair. The air was cool and sticky, redolent of brine and eucalyptus from a nearby grove. It was a picture-perfect spot for a campout.

"You should have seen Tygard go down," Lex Rittenour said, hopping along the edge of the bluff, fingers curled as if gripping a baseball bat and eyes alight with glee. "Hit the carpet face first and started crawling. I blasted him again, just to make sure." Lex slapped a fist into his other palm. "*Boom!*

"When I got out of there, I was still terrified. But then I started getting high on it. Me, Mr. Whitebread Computer Guy, acting like

James fucking Bond. You have any idea how that felt? I thought, I don't *have* to walk back into that cage. I can take care of this on my own."

Monks wondered how much of the infused courage might have come from drugs, not to mention sheer desperation. But that was academic. It had worked.

"I met some of your colleagues," Monks said. "Bouldin, Hazeldon. Audrey Cabot. Give me a rundown."

"Bouldin's a businessman. What you see is what you get. Pete's a computer geek; not the genius he wants to think he is, but good enough. Audrey—the other two, at least they've got blood in their veins, but she runs on antifreeze. She likes younger guys. Sucks them dry and throws away the husks."

Monks supposed he should have been more flattered at Audrey Cabot's remark about house calls. But she probably had just been keeping in practice. He was not exactly a younger guy.

"Tygard?" Monks said.

"An errand boy, but dangerous. Thinks he's some kind of corporate commando."

"Did any of them know you were about to withdraw support from REGIS?"

Lex shook his head. "I didn't tell anybody. Except Martine."

Monks stayed silent, recalling what Larrabee had said earlier: *I've seen a lot of times when somebody made a noble decision, then got cold feet.*

The vodka bottle was nearing the one-third empty mark. Monks poured another drink.

"Did she tell you how the research was done?" Lex said. "With fetuses?" He was looking out to sea.

"Yes," Monks said.

"You think I'm to blame?"

Monks shook his head. "People can misuse any technology."

"I designed the REGIS prototype," Lex said. "What happened after that, I didn't know about. I was doing other things."

"Your spiritual phase? Ashrams in India? Or was it Zen?"

Lex glared at him. "I tried some of both. The press made a big deal of it."

"There were some other episodes too, weren't there?" Monks said, recalling the tabloid headlines and the paternity suit. "A little more earthy?"

"I tuned out for a few years," Lex admitted. "Then, all of a sudden, the company executives told me they're going to put REGIS on the market. I told them, there's no way it's ready. They told me, 'Thanks for the opinion, Lex. Now stay out of the way and speak your lines for the press.' "

Lex lurched to his feet. A haggard look had come across his face.

"I should have done something then," he said. "But I didn't. Then Martine came to me with that research. I thought, 'Okay, Lex, this is it: your chance to show some balls. You're going to stand up in front of those microphones and tell the truth about what you think.' " He snorted. "But it wasn't balls. It was dope. I was on a cloud. When I almost got my ass killed, I woke up."

Lex stepped clumsily to a nearby clump of rocks and urinated. He said something over his shoulder, words that were muffled by the surf.

"I didn't catch that," Monks said.

Lex turned, feet planted wide apart. He was swaying noticeably. Monks realized that the shot was wearing off.

"I said, I should have spent more time *out there*. Like your friend Emil." His tone was perplexed, even aggrieved. He made his way back to the RV, moving heavily now, like a windup doll that had been briefly charged with life, running down.

Monks decided that he was definitely done drinking and poured one more. The mist was turning to rain, a fine spray against his skin. He had not been to sea in twenty-five years, but there were times when the smell of salt air would bring back, with sudden fierce intensity, that drive to sail onward into a freedom that lured like the sirens, but remained always just out of reach. He had chased it with alcohol too, a fool's game, seeming to put it within your grasp and then slamming you down.

But there were times when drinking could illuminate things that lurked under the surface of consciousness, twisting uncomfortably but refusing to show themselves. One of those lights was flickering on.

Who you were and what you would become—your destiny—was once thought to be written in the stars. Now, it was known to be largely written in the genes. But the stars were beyond control. Genes were quickly coming within reach.

It was John Calvin, the sixteenth-century Swiss reformer, who had solidified the doctrine of the elect. These were the lucky few predestined for heaven. The damned, a much greater majority, were doomed to hell. There was nothing an individual could do to change this: How you lived your life, whether with saintlike virtues or steeped in greed and murder, was not what mattered. Your status as elect or damned was ordained by divine will.

The Vikings had seen it very differently. To them, deeds were everything.

Cattle die, kin die, the man dies too.
One thing I know that never dies.
The good name of the dead.

In theory, it was impossible to tell the elect from the damned. Only God knew which were which. But this was where human ingenuity had stepped in and applied a very simple criterion. It was obvious that the wealthy—privileged, successful—were looked upon favorably by heaven. The poor, the simple-minded, the halt and the lame, were not.

And, the thinking went, both classes deserved to be treated accordingly. The elect, as rightful masters, should enjoy the earthly fruits of their holiness. The damned were to be downtrodden, as a help to God in punishing them for their sins.

The strict interpretation of that doctrine had been watered down over the centuries since, and the modern sects that had descended from Calvinism would have reacted with horror to be accused of any such thing.

But in recent years, Monks had sensed a burgeoning of what he thought of as neo-Calvinism, an undercurrent that was not spoken of, but was tacitly understood. It had nothing to do with any church: Unlike the original, it had no religious justification. But the thinking was the same. Prosperity meant superiority, with all the privileges thereof. Those who were under life's boot heel deserved to stay there.

Up until this point in history, the elect had possessed no clearcut way to identify themselves. But that was changing fast. Monks was pretty sure that neo-Calvinism was about to take the next jump; that the future elect would be not just self-declared, but self-creating, translating divine will into genetic reality. Lineages could be established, with health, intelligence, beauty, and maybe even immortality, available to the few—and withheld from the many. It was exactly the sort of thing that Walker Ostrand's research had been moving toward:

Genetic manipulation of sex cells, to determine the effect on the embryos. A huge—and hugely illicit—head start on the new market in high-performance human beings.

Rationally, Monks could not find any fault with neo-Calvinism. The world was shaped by the best and brightest. But in his heart, he belonged to the losers, the damned, who either never had a chance to begin with—were condemned to act out the predestined flaws in their genes—or blew what chance they had.

He got to his feet and walked back to the RV.

Lex Rittenour was curled up on one of the mattresses, eyes not quite closed. His right hand clasped his left forearm, thumb laid caressingly over the vein where the needle had bit again to quell the invasion of reality for a few more hours—the strike of the healing snake-god Asclepius.

"You ever try this stuff?" Lex said.

"A few times, for pain."

Lex's eyes opened, cold and far away. "But you're *above* it, huh? Well, I need it. Do you have any idea what's going on in here?" His finger rose to tap his temple. "Boolean algebra. Algorithms. I don't apply math, I *create* it. My mind's like a racehorse. It takes off and won't stop running."

Monks said, "I'm humbled."

"Fuck you. It drives me nuts. It gets exhausted, starts going in circles and slamming into walls. That's what the Zen and all that was about. I was trying to calm it. But it doesn't want to be calm."

Lex's gaze took on a defensive, wounded look. "You think that's bullshit, don't you?"

"No," Monks said. "That's why it scares me."

Lex closed his eyes again and settled back. "I trust you, you know that?" he murmured.

Monks draped a blanket over the creator of REGIS, the perfect monster that had turned on its master, and lay down on the other bunk.

SEVENTEEN

Monks brewed coffee blearily on the propane stove, listening to the offensively cheerful patter from a San Francisco morning show on the RV's small television. Whether you woke up in your own bed after a Saturday night bash, or sprawled on a foam pad in a mobile hideout, a hangover was a hangover. It was just dawn, damp and cool with the sea's freshness. Most of the other campers were still quiet; a few stirred, beginning the day's recreation or packing to move on.

He shaved quickly, a ritual he could not face the day without, then tried the coffee. It was from a can, bitter and flat, not the good French roast he was used to. Lex apparently did not notice or care; he stirred a copious amount of sugar and condensed milk into his, then dunked in pieces of sweet roll. He seemed in good spirits; Monks surmised that he had already taken his morning fix. For the first time in his life, Monks felt a touch of envy that he could not do the same.

"Take a look at this," Lex said.

Monks stepped over to view the TV. The screen showed San Francisco's Bank of America plaza, with the fifty-story black monolith towering in the background.

"Lex Rittenour's failure to appear at a press conference yesterday has sparked rumors that all might not be well behind the scenes at

Aesir Corporation," the announcer said. "To counter these, Aesir has released a video of Rittenour, made last week."

The scene shifted to the outside balcony of a luxury house, overlooking a body of water. Silver champagne buckets rested on a white-clothed table, along with open bottles of Veuve Clicquot. The small crowd included several faces Monks was getting to know: CEO Kenneth Bouldin, COO Audrey Cabot, and research and development chief Pete Hazeldon. Ronald Tygard stood off to one side and behind the others, like a sentry. They were dressed informally, drinking champagne.

On-screen, Lex looked somewhat glazed, much like the real Lex right now. He had probably just shot up then too, Monks thought.

Kenneth Bouldin held up his champagne flute and said, "To ten years of hard work from a great group of people." Then he stepped over to Lex and gripped his upper arm in a manful gesture of comradeship. "And to the genius of one."

The group raised their glasses in a toast. Monks thought he perceived Lex hesitate slightly before joining them.

The television screen cut back to the Bank of America Building.

"Aesir Corporation stresses that the video was informal, not intended for public viewing," the announcer voiced over. "The REGIS IPO, potentially valued at more than a billion dollars, will begin when Wall Street opens tomorrow morning, less than twenty-four hours from now."

"Those lying fucks," Lex said. "That tape was made two months ago." He seemed more amused than angry. "I've got to hand it to Ken. Either he thinks I *am* dead or he's running a hell of a bluff."

Monks dumped the rest of his coffee in the sink and started the RV's engine.

"Where are we going?" Lex said.

"To hook up with my partner," Monks said. "A private detective. Then we're going to go looking for that girl who gave you the bad dope."

"You have a way to find her?"

Monks had remembered that before the young Korean woman fled from the emergency room, she had been in intense conversation with Mrs. Hak. It was possible that she had given Mrs. Hak some bit of information that would help to identify her.

"Maybe a place to start," Monks said.

The going was difficult for the RV down Highway 1, with its tight, steep curves and close-hanging fog. Lex started to fidget. He opened the console and rummaged around, then took out a plastic multicassette holder.

"Well, what do we have here?" he said. He pried the cassette holder open and examined Emil Zukich's music collection. "Hank Snow. Bob Wills and the Texas Playboys. Kitty Wells. I never heard of any of them."

"Look on that last one," Monks said. "Is there a song called 'It Wasn't God That Made Honkytonk Angels'?"

"Yeah. You *know* this stuff?"

"Call it a nodding acquaintance."

"It's, like, country-western, right? I didn't know you grew up in the country."

"I didn't," Monks said. "In Chicago, when I was a kid, there were a lot of people up from Appalachia, to work in the factories. A couple of the radio stations would play country on Sunday nights. I didn't even know what I was listening to."

But he remembered it vividly, coming over a crystal radio he had made with copper wire wrapped around a toilet paper roll, and an antenna strung to a tree in the yard.

"I was into punk and heavy metal," Lex said. "Messing with computers, down in my basement."

"Dr. Rostanov said she grew up with you."

"She was the good girl. Got thrown by a horse when she was nine.

Most of a year there, she couldn't walk, poor kid. I think she turned all that pain into her studies."

"And into you?"

Lex gave him a glance that was swift and hard, but then softened.

"Maybe so," he said.

Lex pulled a tape free and examined it. "It's the first song on here," he said. "That one you asked about, 'It Wasn't God That Made Honkytonk Angels.' " He punched it into the cassette player.

In a few seconds, the clear, plaintive lilt of Kitty Wells's voice melded with country fiddle and guitar, singing to the generations of working people who turned to a barstool and a jukebox for a few hours of warmth in their hard-edged lives. Lex's fingers started tapping time on the dash. His head was turned to look out the window toward the fog-shrouded Pacific.

"Martine's the one who got me thinking about medical applications for software," he said suddenly. "The genome's a lot like a program: a bunch of either-or commands, a handful of three-letter combinations repeated a couple billion times. I started working on how to translate from one to the other. Got to where I was seeing huge flocks of them flying around in my mind—CAG, AGT, like those monkey-things in *The Wizard of Oz.*"

"I don't have a clue how you can arrange that so you can tap a keyboard and it comes up on a screen."

"The mechanics?" Lex waved a hand, as if it were nothing. "There's plenty of people who can do that. Plenty working on genetics software. Maybe a few who even thought of a model like REGIS.

"But I *see* it. That's my gift. I can't explain how I do it. I just do."

The song ended. Lex leaned forward, punched the rewind button, and started it again.

"I need some clothes," he said. He gestured down at his soiled outfit, a sort of flipping motion of his hands as if he were throwing something to obliterate it. "I can't go around like this."

"We don't want anybody to see you, Lex."

"That doesn't mean I have to look like shit."

Monks admitted that he could use some cleaning up. "We can stop up ahead, on 101. There are a couple of malls."

Lex shot him a sly glance. "Find a place that has cowboy, okay?"

The fog lightened as they drove inland, and by the time they reached Highway 101, there were patches of sunlight. Monks pulled into a shopping center south of Marin City. Western apparel was not prominently featured in this urban mall, but Sears carried a reasonable facsimile. Monks came out ten minutes later carrying half a dozen pairs of blue jeans with varying waist sizes 36–40 and lengths 34–38, several long-sleeved cotton shirts, packets of underwear and socks, and a pair of tooled lizard-skin Justin boots, size 12D.

He waited behind the RV's wheel, sipping a cold Coke, while Lex tried on outfits in the back. There was a fair amount of banging around, mumbled cursing, and clothes being tossed, but eventually Lex emerged, looking like a rough draft of the Marlboro Man. His turquoise ring and bracelet added a rhinestone cowboy feel.

"I've got to have a hat to go with these," he said, pointing to the boots. "A Stetson. Seven and three-quarter, black." Monks trudged back to the store.

When he came out this time, Lex was out of the RV: crouched beside the window of a small, newish car, talking earnestly with its passenger. Monks walked faster, and stepped it up again when he realized the car's two occupants were teenage girls.

Abruptly, the car peeled away. The girls were laughing, one covering her face with embarrassment.

"What was that all about?" Monks demanded.

Lex was grinning. "I told her I'd give her a thousand dollars to watch her take a bath."

"Are you fucking *crazy?* Those girls are sixteen." Monks grabbed Lex by the arm and jerked him toward the RV, realizing that he had almost never in his life before now used the word "fuck."

"Hey, take it easy." Lex tried to struggle. "I wasn't going to touch her."

"I'm going to keep you on a leash from now on."

Monks shoved Lex into the RV door and drove hurriedly back toward 101, with a wary eye for flashing lights and grim-faced cops eager to take down a pair of perverts.

Lex turned the hat by the brim, scowling. It was a sort of faux snakeskin with plastic scales, definitely not a Stetson, but more or less black.

"What the hell do you call this?"

"It's all they had."

Lex tried it on, angling it various ways. "We have to get a real one," he said, but it stayed on his head, tipped back. The baseball cap lay on the console. Monks eyed it, thinking about disguise, and put it on.

They passed through the rainbow-striped Waldo Tunnel and down to the Golden Gate Bridge, through streamers of mist flowing around the huge red towers. It was a tourist Mecca, with strings of sightseers, joggers, and bicyclists lining the walkways. To the east, ferries steamed back and forth from the Wharf to the stark gray walls of Alcatraz, conducting pilgrims through that shrine where the infamous had lived and died. The Bay was dotted with triangular white sails, the faithful undiscouraged even by the cool weather.

"This being 'out there' isn't all that bad," Lex murmured.

Monks felt that odd touch again, as if they were two old enemies thrown together by trouble, realizing they had more in common with each other than with the rest of the world.

It would have made for a fine road trip, stocked up with their drugs of choice, to just keep on driving.

Stover Larrabee was waiting in a turnout parking lot above Point Lobos at the north end of Ocean Beach, the miles-long stretch of sand at the city's western edge. Monks had no trouble spotting Larrabee's van, a beaten blue Dodge that he used for surveillance. It had a rack on top with lengths of copper and PVC pipe, and a sign that read ON THE SPOT PLUMBING. The inside was equipped for sophisticated surveillance but there was also a full stock of tools. There were times when that provided a good cloak of invisibility.

Monks pulled in beside it and got out. They were overlooking a brushy cliff that sloped down to the shore. Below, the concrete outlines of the old Sutro Natatorium were still visible. Seals dove and cavorted on the offshore rocks. It was a grand view, breathtaking, yet all but deserted this time of year, the ocean a bleak gray-green beneath the lighter gray of the sky.

Larrabee was getting out of the van. Monks just had time to register that there was someone else in the passenger seat, when that door flew open. Monks tensed, but realized in the next instant that it was Stephanie, running to him. She threw her arms around him, propelling him backward a couple of steps.

"You almost got *killed*."

"I'm fine," he said, stroking her hair awkwardly. "You're supposed to be stashed."

"I want to help." She pulled away from him, and started around to the RV's passenger door with what could only be described as a flounce.

Then she stopped, staring through the windshield at Lex Rittenour. Lex grinned and raised a hand in greeting.

Stephanie turned accusingly to Larrabee. "You didn't tell me about this."

"I work on a need-to-know basis," Larrabee said.

"What's he *doing* here?"

"He almost got killed too," Monks said. "Honey, the biggest help you can be is to stay someplace safe."

"*Stop* treating me like I'm ten."

"Okay, okay," he said. He put his arm around her and led her a few steps away. "Tell you what," he said quietly. "You keep Mr. Smith-

Rittenour company. Play cards, watch TV, whatever—just don't let him go anywhere." Monks thought he saw a determined look come into her eyes. She nodded, accepting the mission.

Stephanie climbed into the RV and offered her hand shyly to Lex, like a teenage girl in the presence of a rock star.

"A pleasure, ma'am," Lex said, tipping his hat.

"We actually sort of met," she said. "You probably don't remember."

You had an Ambu-bag over your face most of the time, Monks started to add helpfully, but thought better of it.

"Stephanie's going to hang here with you, while Stover and I check some things out," Monks said. "We can keep in touch by phone."

"You going to make friends and influence people?" Lex said.

"Maybe."

Lex dragged his leather grip out from under a seat and opened it. Inside, stuffed together carelessly like pairs of socks, were banded packets of one-hunded-dollar bills.

Monks felt like he had been hit very hard and was coming out of it light-headed.

He said, "We've been carrying a bale of cash around?"

"I never go anywhere without a little mad money."

"How much is that?"

"Not quite three hundred grand," Lex said. He handed Monks several of the packets. "Best way *I've* ever found to make friends."

Stephanie was transfixed by the sight. It occurred to Monks that he was witnessing a career change.

Monks descended the RV's steps back down to the outside world. Stephanie followed.

"Is he still using drugs?" she whispered.

"Demerol," Monks said.

"That's creepy," she said, but her eyes were afire. "I can't believe I'm going to be alone with Lex Rittenour and a quarter of a million dollars!"

"Stephanie," Monks said sternly. "Don't accept any offers that involve bathing."

"Ex*cuse* me?"

"Just do as I say. After all, I'm your father." He kissed her quickly on the cheek and got into Larrabee's van.

"What was that all about?" Larrabee said.

Monks exhaled. "Hygiene."

EIGHTEEN

Mrs. Hak's apartment was on Anza Street near Sixteenth Avenue, the second floor of a small row house with a garage at ground level, virtually identical to the others that lined the block: pleasant, sheltered, the kind of place where you could live a lifetime without meeting or even seeing your neighbors. Monks rang the bell, conscious that she worked evenings and might be sleeping. But he felt a very faint response, as of the quiet footsteps of someone walking inside. The door had a tiny peephole, like a glass eye. He took off Lex Rittenour's cap and sunglasses and stood directly in front of it, doing his best to appear affable.

The door opened just enough to reveal her. She looked very small.

"Docta Monksa-shi," she said. She did not seem surprised, but then, she never did.

Monks said, "I need your help, Mrs. Hak."

She opened the door the rest of the way. Monks followed her into the apartment.

The inside was antiseptically clean, with modern American decor in subdued, tasteful colors. But everywhere, there were hints of Asia: an intricately carved wooden ship; a Korean-lettered calendar featuring woman wearing a kimono-advertising a brand of kimchee; a collection of fine porcelain dolls, lords and ladies, lean peasants and rotund monks, appearing as they must have centuries ago. There was only one photograph that suggested family—a portrait of a gaunt-faced Asian man wearing a cheap suit and tie, smiling broadly.

"Your husband?" Monks asked.

She nodded. "He die, eight year ago."

"I'm sorry."

"Me too. You like tea?"

"No. Thanks."

She gestured to a chair, then sat on the couch facing him. Her back was very straight, knees together and hands clasped in her lap, face attentive.

"I can't explain this too well," he said. "Those two Korean people who came into the emergency room, night before last—I need to talk to them."

"Gone," she said firmly. "No names."

"Is there any possibility of finding them?" Monks said. "Anything you remember? Someone you know in the community?"

She shook her head.

"You said you thought he might have been a soldier."

"Many soljas," she said.

"Were they illegals?"

"Maybe. Some Koreans smuggled in, sure. Chinese too. Mexicans too."

"I'm not making a judgment, Mrs. Hak. Not trying to get anybody deported."

"Why you want them?"

"That man they brought into the ER—the overdose was deliberate," Monks said. "It was a murder attempt. That girl gave him the drug. I need to find out who gave it to her."

Monks imagined just a glimmer of yielding in Mrs. Hak's facade, that maybe she held some bit of information after all. He hesitated, sensing that she was waiting for him to offer something that mattered, and that neither money nor fear would tip the scale. This woman owned herself.

He said, "Somebody tried to kill me last night."

Her eyes widened.

"You might have been working when it happened," he said. "It was right outside the hospital."

"Ahhh." Her finger rose to point at him. "*You?*"

"Me. They called it a carjacking, but it wasn't. I'm hiding out right now. My daughter too. It could ruin her life. She might have to go into witness protection."

Monks took twenty thousand dollars from his pocket and laid it on the coffee table.

"If this would help somehow," he said.

Mrs. Hak gazed at the packets of bills for some time. Then she rose in a swift, graceful motion, and walked to a window, hands still clasped before her.

"Smugglers Korean army. Very dangerous, treat people very bad. Somebody complain, get hurt. Maybe disappear."

The words opened a glimpse to Monks of the risk he was asking her to take.

"I'll do my best to keep anyone from getting hurt," he said. "But I can't promise."

"You good man." The words had a decisive tone.

Mrs. Hak picked up a telephone and punched numbers quickly; more than seven, to a long-distance exchange. Monks listened with utter incomprehension while she spoke in Korean, with the decisiveness still in her voice. The sense was that she was commanding, rather than persuading, someone to do something.

She put the receiver back in its cradle. "You know Ferry Building?"

"Yes, of course," Monks said.

"Meet in front. Two hour."

"How will I find you, Mrs. Hak?"

"You walk. I find you." She waved at the money, still lying on the table. "Bring with you."

Monks was on his way down the outside stairs when she called, "Docta Monksa-shi."

He stopped and looked back up at her, standing in the doorway. Her neutral gaze had returned.

"No witness protection in Korea," she said.

The words followed Monks as he walked, hunched under the baseball cap, back to where Larrabee waited in the van.

Monks had been thinking a lot about Gloria Sharpe, she with the two Dobermans and the shop in SoMa—she who had probably identified his license plate and almost gotten him killed. They were on their way to her shop when the van's speaker phone rang.

The caller was Stephanie, sounding concerned. "Everything's okay. But Lex insisted on going out and walking around."

"Dumb bastard," Larrabee growled. He braked and veered into the right-hand lane to turn back the way they had come.

"I tried to talk him out of it," Steffie said. "But—it's like he thinks this is a party. He's got some *great* stories."

"Don't let him out of your sight," Monks ordered. "We'll be there in a few minutes."

They headed west on Geary, making most of the lights. Monks saw with relief, when they pulled into the turnout, that the RV was the only vehicle there. Stephanie was standing at the edge of the cliff, watching something below. She turned at the sound of the van's approach and waved at them anxiously.

Monks and Larrabee got out and hurried to her.

"He's getting into a fight," she told them breathlessly. "This guy was beating up his girlfriend, and Lex went down to help her."

Halfway down the cliff, at the edge of the park that extended to the north, Lex Rittenour faced a young man wearing huge baggy pants, a black T-shirt, and several chains hanging from his belt. Lex had his fists clenched in a clumsy boxer's stance, while the kid was crouched, talking and gesturing in threat or obscenity or both, hands and feet weaving in unimpressive karate-type chops.

Monks just caught a glimpse of another figure, small, slight—and wearing Lex's distressed leather jacket—disappearing into the thickly wooded park.

"*Hey*, dipshit!" Larrabee yelled at the young man. He looked up and saw them. Quick as a ferret, he was gone into the bushes too.

Lex lowered his fists and turned around. Even from that distance, he looked bewildered.

"Looks like Lex just bought somebody a jacket," Larrabee said quietly.

Lex's faux snakeskin hat had fallen off his head. He put it on and trudged up the slope, slipping in his clumsy new slick-soled cowboy boots. It was a painful sight. Monks braced himself at the cliff's crest and reached down to grip Lex's hand, helping him up the last few feet.

"That guy was slapping a girl around," Lex panted. "I went down there and told him to quit. He starts yelling he's going to kick my ass. She ran over to me and said, 'Please mister, he tore my blouse, can I put on your coat a minute?' "

"Your heart's in the right place, Lex," Monks said soothingly.

But his jacket was not. That seemed to be coming home to Lex; he was patting pockets that were no longer on him.

"We've got to catch them," he said urgently.

"Forget it, Lex," Larrabee said. "They've got bicycles. They're a mile away by now."

Lex's eyes widened and his tone escalated to panic. "My *stash* was in it."

Monks closed his eyes, took the bridge of his nose between his thumb and forefinger, and squeezed for long seconds. It provided an odd relief.

Lex pawed in supplication at his shoulder. "You've got to help me," he said woefully.

Monks opened his eyes. Larrabee was gazing out to sea. Stephanie had her hands clasped in front of her, looking apprehensive.

"I can't walk into a pharmacy and buy narcotics any more than you can, Lex," Monks said.

"Then take me some place I can score on the street."

"That's a great idea," Monks agreed. "If you don't get busted, you can try for another O.D."

"What am I going to do? I'm going to need a shot in a couple hours."

Larrabee turned back to them. "Let me talk to somebody," he said.

"How long's this going to take?" Lex demanded.

"As long as it takes," Larrabee said harshly. "We've got other priorities. Now for Christ's sake, this time, stay inside like we told you."

"You try to do the right thing and you get screwed," Lex said bitterly.

"It goes with the turf of being out there, Lex," Monks said, putting an arm around his shoulders and steering him toward the RV.

In the van again, Monks and Larrabee drove back into the city.

"I know a million people who deal dope, everything illegal you ever heard of," Larrabee said. "But the *legal* stuff—that's hard to get."

"You have somebody in mind?"

"A respectable gentleman who got into an ugly situation with a young stud hustler, a couple years ago. I helped make it go away."

The respectable gentleman happened to be a dentist with a very tasteful, upscale office in the Noe Valley. Larrabee went inside and Monks waited in the van, while the first drug deal he had ever been party to went down.

Larrabee returned with an envelope containing four small white tablets. Monks recognized them as oxycodone, a synthetic opiate. They were time-release painkillers, and would not provide the quick sweet high of Demerol.

"He swore that's all he could spare," Larrabee said. "I didn't have time to push it."

"I'll make him pace it," Monks said. "Maybe it will get him through this."

"Maybe," Larrabee said.

*   *   *

Gloria Sharpe's shop presented a different picture than it had yesterday. There were no tradesmen's vehicles parked out front, no signs of activity, no light showing through the papered window or closed door.

Monks waited in the van, concealed by the door panel, while Larrabee knocked. No one answered. Larrabee walked to the art gallery next door and disappeared briefly inside. A minute later, a middle-aged woman returned with him to the sidewalk, talking and gesturing at Gloria's shop in a way that did not look happy.

"Gloria's got some people pissed off," Larrabee said, getting back into the van. "The neighbors think she's been living here illegally. Sometimes she leaves the dogs, they bark and drive everybody crazy. But this morning, she didn't show. The workmen couldn't get in."

"Are the dogs in there now?"

Larrabee shook his head. "All quiet."

It came as no surprise. Gloria Sharpe had plenty of reason to take a sudden vacation.

It was 1:38 P.M.—getting to be time for the meeting with Mrs. Hak. Larrabee started the van toward the Ferry Building. Both of them were aware that their list of options was getting slimmer.

Monks walked the pavement in front of the Ferry Building, moving unobtrusively with the crowd of commuters and sightseers, his cap pulled low and sunglasses on in spite of the foggy afternoon. On the Bay, the gray sky hazed into the choppy water with no visible horizon, bringing a premature sense of twilight. Pigeons trotted around with the nervous, fussy manner of elderly ladies. Gulls kited past, squawking and fighting over bits of refuse. A few prosperous-looking pelicans squatted on nearby piers. The bird community, Monks thought, were survivors.

After a couple of minutes, he became aware of two women walking toward him. Both were wearing scarves and large sunglasses that almost hid their faces. One was Mrs. Hak.

Then, with fierce elation, he realized that the other was the girl who had come into the ER. She was pretty, full-faced, not heavy but strong. Built like Stephanie, Monks found himself thinking, and about the same age. She stood with eyes downcast, hands clasped tensely.

"This Miss Lee," Mrs. Hak said. "Not real name."

Miss Lee bowed shyly, eyes still down. Monks bowed back.

"We walk?" Mrs. Hak asked.

"Yes," Monks said.

They paced along the Embarcadero, Monks keeping a covert eye on surrounding pedestrians, accusing himself of paranoia but doing it anyway. Larrabee was following behind, watching too.

"She talk to me in hospital and beg to hide," Mrs. Hak said. "Forgive please not tell you right away."

"She's staying with you?" Monks said, astonished.

"I send her to friend in Oakland. Try to decide where she go next."

"Is she illegal?"

Mrs. Hak nodded and pointed toward a huge tanker moored at a pier to the south. "Come on ship like that. Fifteen people, bucket for toilet. Twelve day. Hidden in room." She held her hands up, palms close together. "Between—like walls. How you say?"

"The hulls," Monks said, fighting off the claustrophobic vision of human beings crammed into a narrow steel chamber for days or even weeks, to escape into a new life—of menial labor or prostitution, never able to pay their ever-increasing debts.

"Men find her, send her back Korea," Mrs. Hak said. "Slave in hawhouse." She watched calmly while Monks absorbed this comment on several thousand years of civilization. "You see, Docta, why I help her? How I grow up in Seoul. Husband buy me, bring me here."

Mrs. Hak patted his arm, as if she were the one consoling him, perhaps because of the look on his face.

"You bring money?" she asked briskly, all business now.

"Yes."

She opened her purse casually, as if looking for something inside. Monks glanced around again, making sure no one was watching, then placed the packets in. Miss Lee stared at the money, then, fearfully, at him.

Mrs. Hak spoke crisply in Korean. The girl threw her arms around Monks, burying her face in his chest. He tried to disentangle himself but she clung, sobbing.

"She run away now," Mrs. Hak said.

"Tell her it's from the man she brought to the hospital."

Mrs. Hak looked puzzled, but spoke again. Miss Lee let go of Monks and backed away, bowing and gasping out words.

"She sorry she kick him. Very scared."

"He forgives her. If she knows where the driver is, who was with her that night—there's money for him too."

"He leave her at hospital. Not see again. They find him, he dead." It was not clear whether this was what would happen, or it already had. Monks decided to let it stay that way.

Mrs. Hak was waiting, watching him with polite inquiry.

"Ask her who gave her the bottle with the drug in it," he said.

Miss Lee lowered her eyes again. When she spoke, he could hardly hear her voice.

"Name Kwon," Mrs. Hak said. "Very tough solja. Girls belong him."

"Were there Americans involved? People he associates with? Does she know who hired her and the car?"

Mrs. Hak translated again. Miss Lee shook her head timidly.

Monks grimaced in disappointment; he had been hoping against all reason that this would identify one of the Aesir crew or someone with an obvious link, that it would be the key they needed.

Miss Lee spoke anxiously.

"Afraid she not tell you what you want," Mrs. Hak said.

He did not have the heart to confirm that she was right. "Can she take me to Kwon?"

"Scared he see," Mrs. Hak translated.

"He won't. We'll keep her hidden. All she has to do is point him out."

The two women talked quickly, with Mrs. Hak taking a firm tone. She shook her purse emphatically, perhaps to remind Miss Lee of the money.

"Okay," Mrs. Hak said to Monks. "Place on Inez Street, she show you where. Kwon come and go. Okay?"

"Yes," Monks said. "Thanks, Mrs. Hak. We'll keep her safe."

Monks escorted the fearful Miss Lee to the van. He and Larrabee settled her in the back as comfortably as they could.

They drove south, into a part of the city Monks was not very familiar with. Mostly, he came down here only on the rare occasions when he had reason to go to San Francisco General Hospital. The neighborhood shops displayed an ethnic spectrum of signs—Hispanic, Chinese, Thai, Vietnamese, and some that Monks recognized as Korean. In spite of the cool weather, plenty of people were hanging out on the streets and in the couple of parks they passed: young men with the trappings of gangs and drugs, older men drinking in front of corner stores, the homeless sleeping and the aimless wandering and a few short-skirted women on the corners, calling saucy invitations to passing cars.

Inez was a side street off Army near Twenty-Fifth, lined with boxy, nondescript three- and four-story commerical buildings, neither new nor old, that could have housed anything. The one Miss Lee pointed out—with words Monks could not understand but a whispered tension that was all too clear—sported a partly lit neon sign of a tipped martini glass with the word COCKTAILS underneath. An old painted sign below that read HOTEL INEZ. There were more signs in Korean. The windows of the glassed-in lobby were painted different bright opaque colors, shielding clients from being seen.

This was where Kwon's stable of prostitutes worked, and where, according to Miss Lee, he would show up soon. They parked down the street, with a view of the hotel's entrance.

"Some of those girls probably aren't much older than ten," Larrabee said. "Wonder if Lex Rittenour would have been so hot to trot with Miss Lee if he'd known she was working out of a place like this."

Then he glanced back quickly at her. "I hope she didn't understand that," he muttered. To her, he said, "Can you see okay, honey?" He made circles with his thumbs and forefingers and held them to his eyes like goggles. "Okay?" he said again.

She smiled timidly, nodded, and returned to watching out of the van's rear window.

The minutes passed, with a trickle of clients—all male and mostly Asian—going into the Hotel Inez. Monks watched tensely, with a little flare of hope rising and dying out with each arrival. Miss Lee remained silent and still.

Then, at last, she clapped her hands and jabbed her finger ferociously at a stocky man getting out of a car.

"Kwon," she said.

Kwon was wearing sunglasses, a short-sleeved polyester shirt loose at the waist over slacks, and a gold flex-band wristwatch. His black hair was carefully combed back and shiny with oil. He walked into the Hotel Inez with an unhesitating stride that suggested power.

"He got the pimp-car *make* right," Larrabee said. It was a black Cadillac Eldorado, a shortened new model. "Just not quite the look."

Miss Lee scuttled forward on her knees and crouched behind the front seats.

"I go now?" she whispered, the first knowledge of English she had betrayed. Her face was turned up, pleading like a child's.

Larrabee nodded. "I'll drive you where he can't see you," he said, and tried to convey the meaning with gestures. He pulled around the corner. Monks opened the van's side door for her. Miss Lee hurried away at a near-trot, without a backward glance.

Larrabee drove on around the block quickly and parked several spaces behind Kwon's car, facing the same way as it. They did not want Kwon to be seen talking to them if they could help it. Their best bet for getting the information was to bribe him, and he was more likely to cooperate if his own people did not know about it.

They had been watching for several more minutes when Monks's cell phone rang. He answered warily, remembering that the last call had come from the phony fire inspector, setting up the assault.

"Is this an okay time to talk?" With a little shock, he recognized Martine Rostanov's voice. She had been a steady presence in his mind, there every time he dropped his guard—a tormenting enigma he could neither trust nor discard.

"Yes," he said.

"I've been hiding in corners at Aesir, being a mouse," she said, with quiet excitement. "I may have something interesting. I overheard Ron Tygard talking to somebody, I don't know who, but he was very secretive, very nervous. He said, 'For Christ's sake, that's crazy.' And then, 'All right, I'll meet you there by six.' Like he gave in. Can you follow him?"

Monks did not answer. Apparently, she did not even know about the shooting. It was impossible for him to believe that she was capable of pretending otherwise.

Almost impossible.

He finally said, "It depends."

"I could try it," she said uncertainly. "I'm afraid I wouldn't be very good at it."

"Any idea when he'll go home?"

"There's an executive meeting at four in Aesir's offices," she said. "It should be over about five. Then there's that gala ball tonight in Marin. The big shots are sailing over on the Viking boat."

"Does that include you?"

"No," she said emphatically. "I *am* going to be sick for that."

The Hotel Inez's door opened. Kwon came striding out, moving toward the Cadillac. He was alone. Larrabee turned the key in the van's ignition.

"Call me when Tygard's leaving the building," Monks said into the phone. "I'll try to be somewhere near." He punched disconnect without saying good-bye.

"You've got a short memory, Carroll," Larrabee said, cutting the steering wheel to pull out.

When Kwon reached his car, Larrabee drove up alongside him and stopped. Kwon turned with wary swiftness. One hand went inside his loose shirt, no doubt for a gun.

Monks, in the open passenger window, held up a sheaf of hundred-dollar bills, fanned like cards.

"All we want is a name," Monks said to Kwon. "Ten thousand dollars."

Kwon glanced around. There was no one nearby.

"One name," Monks said. "Then we're gone, we never heard of you."

Kwon looked around again—a quick but intense sweeping glance, like a soldier surveying terrain.

"You follow," Kwon said, and got into his car.

Larrabee pulled over and let the Cadillac pass. They drove several more blocks to the parking lot of an industrial building, deserted on this damp and darkening afternoon. Kwon pulled over and Larrabee brought the van abreast again.

Kwon watched them stonily through the obsidian insect eyes of his sunglasses. His right hand was back inside his shirt. Now Monks could see the bulge of an unholstered pistol in his waistband.

"What name you want?" Kwon said. His accent was thicker than Mrs. Hak's, his speech, like his body, blunt and forceful.

"The night before last, you sent a girl to a man, with drugs," Monks said. "Who told you to do it?"

"You give money." He thrust out his left hand. It was short-fingered, square, oddly plump. Monks gave him five thousand dollars.

"All money," Kwon insisted.

"The name first."

"*Meekook*," Kwon said. "American. Okay?" The chubby fingers waggled in impatient demand.

"The *name*."

"Don't got name. Phone numba at home."

"You have his phone number?"

"Neh, neh, neh," Kwon said, head nodding yes.

"What did he look like?"

"You follow. Get phone numba, draw pitcha." Kwon jammed the car into gear and pulled away.

"*Mother*fucker," Larrabee said, and took off after him.

Kwon led them west, driving frenetically, lunging ahead and suddenly braking with no apparent reason for either. Turns did not appear to be premeditated. Larrabee kept cursing but stayed with him.

In a few more minutes, they were deep in the Mission. The buildings were run-down, the sidewalks cracked and gummy, strewn with broken glass. Accordion grilles covered the windows of the small corner grocery-liquor stores, and painted graffiti was rife—symbols that Monks could not interpret but which he assumed were gang-turf markings. He recalled that some gangs required a killing—say, of a convenient stranger—in order for a member to be made.

Kwon swerved to the curb, skinning a tire, in front of one of the small stores. Its sign was in Korean. No one was standing in front of this one. He got out of the Cadillac and strode inside without looking at them, but once in, he turned and beckoned, waving them toward him, with his fingers pointed down.

The store was empty of customers when they stepped warily inside. Kwon was at the rear, talking rapidly to a middle-aged Asian woman. She stared at the two Anglo men, her mouth a small O. Kwon kept beckoning to them with his downward wave.

Monks and Larrabee made their way through shelves stacked with a melting pot of goods—oriental delicacies, brightly labeled cans of refritos and chiles, a rack of *Penthouse* and *Hustler* magazines. A locked, glassed-in case behind the counter offered half-pints of liquor and sweet wine. They stepped cautiously past the woman, following Kwon through a curtain into the back room.

It was warm and dank, the air pungent with the eye-watering smell of kim chee. An elderly man in loose-fitting pajamas was sitting at a table, spooning sugar onto a plate of sliced tomatoes. He stared at them too, his spoon paused in midair. Kwon snapped quick words at him in Korean. The old man rose with jerky haste and disappeared through a farther door.

"You wait here," Kwon said to Monks and Larrabee. "Back two minute." He left through the same door as the old man.

The two minutes passed, and then two more. Sounds from the street came through the walls, but inside, it was still.

Larrabee stepped to the curtain and twitched it aside to peer through.

"They cut the lights," he said quietly. "We're out of here."

They strode back through the darkened store toward the street. Monks shoved the door, fearing that it was locked. His stomach unknotted a little when it swung out. They walked fast to the van.

They had almost reached it, when a voice said, "How's it going, man?"

The sound was thin, hard, edged with menace. The accent was faintly Hispanic. Monks could barely make out two human figures, one lean and one much larger, in the building's shadow.

"Good," Monks said. He and Larrabee kept walking. The two men in the shadows stepped out, blocking their path to the van.

"You fixing some pipes?" the same voice said.

The speaker was thin, olive-skinned, wearing a denim jacket with the sleeves cut out and a dark stocking cap pulled over his hair. He had a faintly reptilian cast and the cold, hollow eyes of a real junkie. His companion was taller and built like a bullet: shaved rounded head, neck that sloped outward from below his ears, chest as thick as his shoulders were wide, with no delineation of waist or hips. His left hand hung open beside a thigh the size of a fire hydant. His right was hidden behind his leg.

The lean man moved toward them with a nervous, fidgety grace, like a cat working its way closer to a bird.

"You in our place, man," he said. "You got to pay a toll. Throw down your wallets and shit, we let you go."

Monks hitched his thumbs in his belt behind his waist, fingertips brushing the butt of the Beretta in his back pocket. He had never fired a weapon at a human being. He tried to swallow but could not. His heart was beating very hard.

Larrabee said, "Walk into that store. Go on, do it."

The lean man smiled with the contempt of an adult condescending to a child.

"Hey, sure, man, *no petho*." There came a click, a glimmer, and he was holding an open double-bladed butterfly knife. The bigger man's right hand was visible now, gripping what he had been holding behind his back: a shortened baseball bat.

Monks eased the pistol butt out, curling his fingers around it.

Headlights appeared, turning the corner three blocks down. For just a second, the light was in the other men's faces. Monks was aware of a blur of motion to his left.

It was Larrabee, lunging forward and side-arming something across the lean man's face, a sudden vicious lash. There came a *crack*, like a dry stick being sharply snapped. The lean man doubled over in agony, hands flying to his mouth, the knife skittering across the sidewalk. Blood spilled through his fingers and onto the pavement. The thick pillar of flesh jumped back with a sort of *huh*, baseball bat rising.

Larrabee was holding a pistol pointed between the two men at gut height.

"I'm about to shoot you both in the stomach," Larrabee said. "Get in the store. *Move*."

They moved, the big man in a clumsy trot, the lean one burbling sounds that might have been weeping or threats or both, into the darkened store.

"You stick your fucking heads out, I'll blow them off!" Larrabee yelled in after them.

He and Monks sprinted to the van. Larrabee wheeled it around the corner and gunned it, checkerboarding through the next dozen blocks, finally turning north on Van Ness and resuming a more sedate pace.

"I haven't done anything like that in a long time," Larrabee said. He seemed to be bristling with energy. "You can bet Kwon's on his way back to that store, with help. It'll be a sweet little surprise, having those two inside. Asshole versus asshole, let them cancel each other out. I know it ain't P.C., but it felt pretty fucking good."

Monks was starting to breathe more easily, but he was still hearing that *crack*.

"Where did that gun come from?" he asked.

"Spring-loaded holster, up my sleeve. Nice light piece with a six-inch barrel. It works dandy as a sap." Larrabee bumped his forearm against the steering wheel and showed Monks the pistol dropping down into his palm: a .22 magnum AMT Automag, lightweight and powerful.

He turned off Van Ness onto Fourteenth Street and pulled over. The fact was that they were no closer to the information they needed—the name of the American who had given Kwon the tampered-with Demerol, or the women who had been the subjects of Walker Ostrand's research—no closer to whoever, at Aesir, had engineered murder. Nothing else had offered itself. The search had been a series of defeats, and the list of options had dwindled again.

Larrabee punched numbers on the speaker phone to check messages from his office. The digital recording informed him that there was only one.

The voice was a woman's, young and hesitant. "Have I got the right number?" she said. "This is Trish Roberson." It took Monks a few seconds to place the name: Clara Ostrand's daughter, the ink-black-haired young woman in the Haight-Ashbury apartment.

"I remembered something about Gloria Sharpe," Trish said. "Just thought you might want to know." The last words were spoken in a sort of teasing lilt. The connection ended without further information: no phone number, but then, Monks recalled, there was no phone.

"Ten to one it's bullshit," Larrabee said. "She's angling for another fifty bucks. But—"

Monks checked his watch: 4:27 P.M.

"I need to get downtown if I'm going to follow Tygard," he said.

Larrabee nodded. "We'll split."

"What are we going to do for another vehicle?" Monks said.

"I'll borrow one." Larrabee started driving again, cruising slowly into a wasteland of concrete and scrubby vacant lots under the skyway. There were no pedestrians but a lot of parked cars in this area, many of them older models. Monks realized that Larrabee was driving slowly because he was looking them over. It was just dusk.

"Borrow?" Monks said nervously.

"I haven't done any repos in a while either, but it's like riding a bicycle." Larrabee pulled the van over behind a late seventies Ford sedan. "This should do. Hand me that red box back there, will you?"

Monks reached into the back and got a battered metal Milwaukee Hole Hawg carrying case. Inside lay an assortment of lock picks and other tools you would not find in a suburban homeowner's garage.

"Maybe this isn't such a good idea," Monks said.

"Take it easy. I'll call the owner and tell them where to find it. Leave them some money for their trouble."

Monks started to say that it was not the owner he was worried about, but Larrabee was out, slipping a slimjim down between window and frame. The door lock popped immediately. He slid into the driver's seat and fit an instrument that looked like a ratchet over the ignition.

Monks watched the stream of traffic overhead on the freeway roaring by, the lines of headlights crowding along the main streets only a couple of blocks away, and marveled again at how you could get away with just about anything. He envied people who could pull it off. Whenever he tried something even slightly illicit, he felt like he was wearing a neon T-shirt.

The car rocked to life with an uncertain rumble. Larrabee got back out and came to lean in the van's window.

"This is going to sound ugly, Carroll," Larrabee said. "Make Dr. Rostanov ride with you. Just in case there's somebody waiting again. Maybe that will give you some insurance. And if she hedges on coming along—maybe you better not go."

He walked back to the Ford, fingers rubbing his temple, where he carried a three-inch scar, still faintly purple, from his own encounter with Robby Vandenard. Monks knew the gesture was not intended as a reproach, but he winced anyway. It was not his fault, but it had happened because of him.

Monks started the van toward downtown.

TWENTY

Monks waited, parked illegally on Montgomery Street, scanning the Bank of America Building's California Street exits with a pair of Larrabee's binoculars—powerful Leicas that would pick out details at several hundred yards, even in poor light.

He had talked to Martine again on the phone, arranging to meet her. She was due to come out soon, trying to keep just ahead of Ronald Tygard.

She had agreed, with apparent eagerness, to come with him.

It was after five now, and people were leaving the building in a steady flow, hurrying across the plaza and past the adamantine Banker's Heart, joining the crowds emptying the financial district. As the day shift ended, the night shift was coming on—the homeless, their ranks swelled astonishingly in the past couple of years, as if they had been put on buses in New York's cleanup of Times Square and shipped west. Some wandered with their garbage bag bundles; others staked out street corners, demanding tribute. Union Square had become a favorite place, with panhandlers mingling with the beautifully dressed elite who cruised the elegant shops.

Monks focused the binoculars on two men inside the BOA lobby, just coming out a door. Something about them struck him as familiar, not so much visual recognition of facial features as their bearing.

He realized that one was Kenneth Bouldin, Aesir's CEO—digni-fied, upright, impeccably dressed—and the other was Pete Hazeldon, the R&D chief. He looked rumpled, even from this distance, slouch-ing along with one hand thickly bandaged from his run-in with the Viking boat's anchor machinery, the hand held stiffly away from his side. Monks recalled that Hazeldon had refused pain medication. No doubt it hurt.

The two men walked together across the plaza, then parted at its edge. Bouldin walked on toward Nob Hill. Hazeldon raised his unin-jured hand in farewell, and stood there for several seconds, watching Bouldin's retreating back. It gave him a forlorn look. Then he turned and walked east, a slight, hunched figure who seemed to be almost scurrying against the wind.

Martine came out of the building a couple of minutes later, walking with quick, uneven steps. Her dress was of a soft fabric that swirled around her ankles. Monks watched with a bittersweet mix of pleasure and apprehension.

She climbed into the van, face flushed, breathless.

"Tygard was putting on his coat when I left," she said. "He'll be coming out of the parking garage."

Then, with sudden concern, she said, "My god, what happened to you?" She leaned close to him, fingertips touching the scabbed skin over his cheekbone.

"I took a header," Monks said. "Cat got between my feet. My own damned yard. My own damned *cat*."

"They're the ones that will get you."

Monks did not have time to sound out just how she meant that, because a green Jaguar convertible was pulling out of the parking garage exit.

"That's him," she said, pointing with one hand and gripping Monks's arm with the other, whispering as if she could be overheard.

Monks started after the Jag, glancing in the rearview mirror, just in case another pair of headlights was pulling out behind him.

Tygard drove several blocks east and then turned south, crossing

Market and merging onto Interstate 80. He jumped immediately to the left lane, impatiently tailgating the vehicle ahead. Monks floored the van to keep up, cutting dangerously in and out of traffic. Less than a mile later, Tygard swerved back to the right and exited at Fifth. He tore through two city blocks and climbed another freeway entrance, this time onto 280 south.

"You think he knows somebody's following and he's trying to shake us?" Martine said.

"I think he just likes to drive fast. Any guesses where he's going?"

She frowned. "Aesir has a warehouse down in Potrero. Computer equipment. But there's no reason for Ron to be going there."

Unless, Monks thought, Tygard had other business that a warehouse might be suitable for.

The bayside docks were another area of San Francisco where Monks rarely had reason to go—an industrial maze of viaducts, railroad sidings, dilapidated warehouses, sagging cyclone fences lined with wind-blown litter. Monks followed the Jaguar along Tennessee Street for several blocks, keeping well behind. It turned onto a side street. There was no other traffic here. Monks cut the van's lights.

Tygard drove three more blocks, then turned into an alley. It crossed a railroad track, and ended in an eight-foot-high chain-link gate topped with razor wire. Behind it stood a massive old three-story brick structure.

The windows were dark, the parking lot empty. In the argon lights, Monks could just make out a faded sign on the bricks that read GRANNELLI BROS. Beyond it was a railroad track, and past that, the dead gray concrete walls of a dock terminal.

Tygard had stopped the Jaguar and was standing at the gate, unlocking it. He drove through and locked it again behind him. Then he drove on around the building, out of their sight.

Monks glanced in the rearview mirror once more. He was pretty sure no one had followed them. It was still possible that someone was waiting.

"Can't you say something?" Martine whispered. "I hate to nag, but, *god*."

"Like what?"

"Like, you know, tell me what you're thinking."

"I'm nervous," he said. "That's what I'm thinking."

He drove on past the alley entrance and the warehouse's front. Then he saw that in its rear corner, to the south, a single top-story window was dimly lit.

The high razor-wire fence surrounded the building's concrete yard. There was no way to get closer. He took out the binoculars. The view through the iron-grated window gave only an oblique glimpse of a warehouse room stacked with cardboard boxes—probably computer equipment.

But then a figure passed by inside, moving quickly. It was only a blur, but that was enough for Monks to recognize Tygard.

"He's in there," Monks said. He was aware of her breathing beside him, a soft, anxious sound.

Tygard's upper body had been moving as he passed by; Monks thought he was shrugging off his coat. Monks watched for another minute, but Tygard did not reappear.

Monks started driving again, looking for a vantage point that would give a better angle. They passed two more alleys, both dead-ending at the fenced-off railroad tracks. But he could see that the next one crossed over them.

The crossing was posted with PRIVATE signs, but the buildings on the other side looked rundown and were dark. Monks eased the van over the tracks and drove tensely through the deserted trainyard. Cinders and broken glass crunched under the tires.

At the far northeast corner, he swung the van to face the building. Now the angle to the window was almost straight on. He lifted the binoculars again.

The interior vista was similar—cardboard computer boxes—but this time there was a human figure clearly visible: stationary, or almost. It was a woman sitting upright on a stack of the boxes, straddling something. A lacy black camisole was draped around her waist. Her breasts, medium-sized and firm, were bare, swaying as her buttocks, also firm and bare, undulated in a leisurely up and down rotation. Her eyes were open and her faint smile suggested the cool pleasure of control.

Monks had been right about Audrey Cabot. At almost fifty, she looked pretty damned good with her clothes off, too.

"Can you see Tygard?" Martine whispered.

"Part of him."

Abruptly, Audrey turned her head, staring directly at Monks. It was impossible that she could spot him, but his scalp still prickled.

"What's happening, dammit?" Martine said.

"We'd better go."

"Let me look."

"I don't think that's called for," Monks said, turning to set the binoculars down. She wrested them away from him and put them to her eyes.

Several seconds later, she handed them back into his chest with, it seemed to him, more force than was strictly necessary.

He turned the van around and drove back the way they had come.

Martine was leaning against the far door, arms tightly folded, looking straight ahead.

"Audrey's always looking for a new kick. I guess she's already done all the hotels in town," she said. "That slut."

Monks stayed on Third Street, driving north back into the city, skirting the dockside tracks and terminals. Martine Rostanov's gaze turned to him.

"Where are you taking me?" she demanded.

"To your car. So you can go to the party."

"I don't want to go to my car or to the party. I want to go with you."

"I can't do that," Monks said.

"Oh?" Her eyebrows rose, giving her the exotic expression he had noted before, and her voice took on a dangerously sweet tone. "Why not?"

Monks tried to phrase carefully what he did not want to say.

"Your connection with Aesir, Martine," he said.

"What about it?"

"I'm wondering if it's closer than I'd thought."

"I'll tell you how close it is," she said heatedly. "They'd kick me out the door this second if I didn't know Lex. I'm not pliable enough. I won't do things like write drug scripts for executives who whine about how stressed and overworked they are."

"What about Kenneth Bouldin?" Monks said.

"What about him?"

"I saw him put his hand on your arm that first night. Like he owned you."

She did not answer right away. They passed China Basin, back into a part of the city where it seemed that people actually lived. Monks could see the top of the Metreon now, lighting up once-seedy Mission Avenue like an electric-blue torch.

"Ken's the kind of man who won't leave a woman alone until he's had her, if that's what you mean," Martine said. "It's not even about sex. It's power."

"I probably shouldn't ask if you know that from experience."

"You probably shouldn't." She folded her arms tightly again. "So, is *that* what you want?"

"What do you mean, 'that?' " Monks said.

"What do you think I mean? Like Audrey just now."

Monks was startled into candor.

"Well—sometimes," he said.

"*All* right. Here."

She twisted with a swift, lissome movement, leaning forward, hands rising and falling over her body, as if she were caressing herself in some way he could not quite see. Then she pried open his fingers and stuffed something into his hand.

Monks realized that he was holding a small, filmy bit of nylon, pearl in color—warm, tantalizingly scented.

They drove on in silence, both gazing straight ahead, for another minute or so.

Then Monks said carefully, "No one's ever done that for me before."

"We're not kids. Does my brace turn you off?"

"No."

"On?"

"I don't know. I don't think so."

"Some men, it does. It's like they get to undress me another layer. *Jesus!*"

Monks slammed on the brakes, sending them both lurching forward in their seats, barely stopping short of a car that came hurtling across their path from the left. Its horn blared tardily as its taillights dwindled.

"I had the right of way," Monks pointed out.

"That's a big comfort."

They were back in the area where Larrabee had borrowed the car. It was busy all around and above, but quiet within. Monks turned off Third Street and pulled over along a darkened stretch of freeway underpass. Martine glanced around nervously, tongue quickly wetting her lips, but she made no move to retreat.

"I didn't trip over a cat," Monks said. "I got shot at, driving. Last night, after I talked to you."

She stared, her mouth opening in shock.

"Oh, god, I had no idea," she murmured. She reached out and touched his face again. Her eyes were intense with concern. "Who?"

"I don't know," Monks said. "But I saw Tygard's car at the scene afterward. And a police captain I'd seen at the Aesir offices."

"Why would anyone—?"

"I'm more interested in *how* they knew I was involved. Have you told any of this to anyone else?"

She pulled back from him, her eyes widening in outrage.

"You think it happened because of *me*?"

"Answer my question."

She slapped him, stingingly hard, then dropped her face into her hands and began to weep. He let her.

"I told you," she finally whispered. "I'm not brave and I've crossed lines I shouldn't have. But I haven't breathed a word of this to anyone. Believe me. Please."

She looked up, cheeks damp, eyes dark with pain and fear, waiting for him to pronounce sentence.

Monks put his hand lightly on her shoulder, conscious that his touch was an effort to overpower Kenneth Bouldin's, to eradicate whatever claim he or any other man might have.

"I believe you," he said.

She gripped his face in her hands and kissed him, bruisingly hard. It was the most wonderfully ferocious experience in his memory.

"I don't know what you saw, that first night," she said. "But what I saw was *you*."

A little dazed, Monks aimed the van down the street again. He considered that it would be gentlemanly to offer her her underwear back, but they were stuffed inside his shirt, comfortably warm against his skin, and she did not ask.

TWENTY-ONE

W ho is this woman?" Martine said, perhaps a trifle jealously.

"Her name's Gloria Sharpe," Monks said, piloting the van through the streets of SoMa. "She was Walker Ostrand's assistant. We think she might know about the research, but she wouldn't talk to us." The chances were slim that Gloria had returned to her shop, but it was close by. He had decided to check.

His attention focused sharply when he saw the gleam of red metal under the lights in the alley behind the shop. He drove slowly past the alley entrance. The gleam was coming from Gloria's red SUV, its color standing out against the dark grays and browns of the buildings. He was sure it had not been there earlier in the day.

Monks drove on around the corner. The storefronts along the block, including Gloria's, were dark. He got out of the van and tried her shop door cautiously. It was locked, the inside silent. He knocked loudly, bracing himself in case the Dobermans erupted. Nothing.

He got into the van again and said to Martine, "Let's take a look around the back."

The alley was narrow and poorly lit, lined with Dumpsters and bits of unclaimed debris and iron fire escapes zigzagging up the backs of the old buildings. But it was deserted, with none of the shelters and fire barrels of the homeless. Gentrification had gone that far.

The SUV was parked behind a loading dock, beside a steel garage-sized overhead door in a raised bay. There was a plain industrial man-door next to it, with two deadbolts. Monks got out and tried the knob.

It turned. The door opened inward at his push.

Monks leaned his head carefully into the shop. It was entirely dark. The air was warm and smelled stale. If there was an alarm, it was silent; the only sounds were the hums and whirs of an old heating system.

He walked back to the van. "Stay in here and lock the doors, just in case anybody comes along," he said, getting a flashlight.

"You're going inside?" Martine said.

"Just for a look. It will only take a minute."

She glanced around nervously, then shoved the van's door open and stepped out too.

"I'll wait in the doorway," she said. "If somebody does come along to rape me, I want you to hear me scream."

Monks stepped through the door that should not, no way, have been unlocked, shining the flashlight around. He was in a rear area, a utility room partitioned off from the main shop. A laundry-sized sink was mounted on one wall. Beside it, a partly open door revealed a toilet. The fixtures were old and hard-water-stained. The kitchen appliances were newer: refrigerator, microwave, and coffeemaker. Building materials for the remodel were stored inside the garage bay, a litter of electrician's boxes, wood trim, and fasteners. A dozen four-by-eight-foot sheets of gypsum drywall leaned against a wall.

Monks stepped through into the large, open main shop. The flash-light's beam scanned the inverted vee of a stepladder, wires hanging in loops from the ceiling, dropcloths and buckets in clusters. The unfinished hardwood floor was white with drywall dust and drips of eggshell paint.

Except for one patch of red, a touch of color as the beam of light swept by.

Monks turned the flashlight back to it.

The red was a sticky splash of blood, running out in streaks that looked like the long clutching fingers of a hand, collecting to pool in a low spot in the floor. It was just beginning to coagulate.

Monks flicked off the light and waited without moving for a full minute, barely breathing, listening. He could pick out the creaks of the old building readjusting its shape as the temperature dropped with the night, the whisking tires of a car passing on the damp pavement out front, the low hum of the mechanical system. But he was pretty sure there was nothing else living in that room.

He turned the flashlight back on and followed the blood trail until it picked out the lean dark body of a Doberman, lying on its side with one foreleg extended in an oddly puppyish way. Its rib cage had been torn open by an exit wound half the size of Monks's hand. A few feet away, the other dog lay sprawled less gracefully, with what looked like bloody dents in its muzzle and the left side of its head. The wall behind them was sprayed with blood.

Monks managed to swallow dryly. He kept walking, faster now, the beam sweeping the room. It paused at a black plastic dropcloth loosely rolled into a bundle that was several feet long and about eighteen inches thick.

He knelt and touched it. Through the layers of plastic, he felt the unmistakable yielding of flesh. He parted the folds at one end and shined the light in. It showed dark curls of human hair with the reddish tinge of henna. The plastic on the inside was slick with blood.

Monks backed away, still on his knees, trying to distance himself from the real or imagined smell.

A sharp whisper cut through the room:

"Carroll?"

He leaped up, fingers clawing for his pistol, grunting with the hot pain of twisting his knee in the sudden movement, before he realized that the whisper was Martine's.

He swung the flashlight beam to find her. She was in the doorway to the back room, holding the jamb, leaning forward tensely.

"Somebody's coming," she said. This time he heard the fear in her voice. "A truck. It stopped and turned off its lights."

Monks trotted past her to the rear door. He eased it open half an inch and put his eye to the crack. There was movement in the alley: the figure of a man in dark clothes, approaching in a stealthy crouch along the brick walls.

The man crept up behind the van and rose slowly to peer in the rear window. He was wearing a ski mask. His right hand held a pistol, barrel pointed up—a large, high-powered automatic. He stayed crouched there for several seconds, scanning the van's interior. Then he stepped out into the alley, and waved toward the entrance.

Now Monks could see the square front end of a delivery truck parked in the alley's entrance. Headlights out, it started moving forward.

Monks eased the door shut, breathing hard with mounting panic. In a second, he scanned and discarded possible places to hide or escape—main room too open, toilet too obvious, front door too far, and locked. There were at least two men coming, armed.

He looked again at the leaning stack of drywall.

He pulled Martine with him, shoved her to her knees, then headfirst ahead of him into the narrow space between the leaning stack's bottom and the wall. He crawled in on top of her and lay with his face pressed to her hair, suddenly and bizarrely aware of her perfume. He could feel her breathing, labored but controlled, through his own ribs. He became aware of a rumbling outside, the truck engine. It ceased abruptly.

Now there were quiet footsteps inside, and the glow of a flashlight. The steps moved into the main room as his own had done, squeaking a little: rubber-soled running shoes on a hardwood floor.

The footsteps returned, faster. A man's voice at the door spoke quietly, words that Monks could not make out. There came more footsteps, at least one other man. They went into the main room again.

This time, when they came back, they were dragging heavy objects.

The sounds moved outside, the thumps and shuffle of the bodies being loaded into the truck. Monks stretched forward enough to peer out the end of the drywall tunnel. After a moment, the flashlight glow returned. He saw a dark figure move by, carrying something: a square metal can.

There came the sound of sloshing liquid.

The figure came back into view, backing up, throwing liquid right and left. Monks could smell it now, not gasoline but some other kind of petrochemical. He cringed as a splash hit their protective gypsum wall, spilling out onto the cardboard boxes. The dousing moved to the wooden table beside the refrigerator.

The figure bent over it, gloved hands busy—

Doing something to the coffeemaker.

The hands piled paper napkins around the base and flipped the switch. The red "on" light glowed.

The figure stepped back toward the door and waited: ten, twenty, thirty seconds. Something else was starting to glow—a loop, like a strand of wire, around the coffeemaker's base. It was touching the paper napkins. Monks put his palm over Martine's mouth and pressed the side of her face against his chest.

A spurt of flame burst up and caught the napkins, then flickered, with the speed of a gunpowder fuse, down to the floor, separating into long tendrils to the main room.

Monks saw a flare, then another, as plastic drop cloths caught. The table was quickly becoming a bonfire, flames climbing the legs with a sound like a flapping sheet. Something popped close to his head, and another heap of flame leaped up among the cardboard boxes.

Monks pulled himself forward until he could see, dragging his body over hers, clenching his teeth against the heat beginning to sear his face. The man was gone, the outside door closed, the room a field of flame. He straddled her back with his knees and heaved upward, pushing out from the wall until the heavy stack of drywall sheets tipped and crashed to the floor.

He got hold of her arm and pulled her to her feet. They stood pressed back against the wall. The fallen sheets had smothered the flames directly around them, but they were cut off from any exit. Smoke was swirling thickly now, burning their eyes and lungs.

Coughing, Monks gripped the edge of the top sheet, raised it, and flipped it forward. It crashed down, stamping out another few feet of flames. He threw another, and another, building a bridge to the door. Then he grabbed Martine's hand, hooked her fingers in the back of his belt, and waded forward.

The knob was almost too hot to touch, but he got it turned. He pulled the door open, and they lunged through it into the night, thrown forward by a blast of mushrooming flames. They stumbled to the van, hacking out smoke and sucking in shrieking breaths of fresh air. He boosted Martine into the driver's side and crowded himself in after her. His hand shook as his burn-tender fingers forced the key into the ignition. The engine caught. He stomped on the gas pedal. Behind them, the open doorway to the shop diminished, a rectangle of leaping flames in a black and smoking backdrop, like a gateway into hell.

Blocks away, Monks pulled over. He rested his arms on the steering wheel and his head on his arms. Martine was huddled against the other door. Her dress was singed and her face smudged. The vehicle was permeated with the unsettling reek of burnt hair.

"I want to go live on the northwest coast of Ireland," Monks said. "Where my grandfather was born. Get a little place. Putter around a few hours in the morning, take a long walk on the beach, then stop into the pub. Couple pints with your mates. Fall asleep listening to the rain."

She shook her head slowly. "I'm trying to believe I'm really here." She was starting to shake, reminding Monks of one of his cats, as a kitten, trying to hide after almost being killed by a dog. He put his arm around her shoulders, trying to steady her.

"Who did that? *Why*?" she said.

Monks shook his head. He was pretty sure that Gloria Sharpe had tried to get money out of somebody before she left town, in return for her silence—probably the same somebody who had funded Walker Ostrand's research. But she had misjudged the stakes.

Monks saw no reason to tell Martine that the bundles dragged by the men had contained the bodies of Gloria and her two dogs, and the fire was probably intended to obscure evidence.

Set by a man wearing a ski mask, and started by a coffeemaker.

TWENTY-TWO

When Monks drove the van into the parking lot where the RV waited, he could see Stephanie sitting in the driver's seat, watching like a sentry. She jumped up when she saw the van coming and hurried out to meet it.

Her eyes went wide at the sight of Monks's singed hair and clothes, and wider when Martine stepped out of the van too.

Monks held out his hand palm first at Stephanie. "I'll explain later," he said.

Lex was lying on his bunk at the RV's rear, with cowboy boots crossed and the snakeskin hat tipped low over his eyes. He pushed it back and sat up at the sound of people arriving. He was not a pleasant sight. His face was taut and grayish with a sheen of greasy sweat, his beard sprouting in patches through the scab-encrusted skin, giving it a fungoid look. His eyes were feverish with anxiety and discomfort. They fixed Monks with a burning question: Did you score?

Monks nodded. Lex exhaled in relief and started to get up.

But he stopped when Martine pushed past Monks and gave Lex a razor-edged stare.

"How dare you let me think you were dead, you son of a bitch," she said.

Lex turned shakily back to Monks. "I can't believe you brought her here." His voice was dry and hoarse. "She can't keep her mouth shut, that's what started all this."

Martine shook her head wearily. "I'm not the rat, Lex. I've already been through that once tonight. Believe it if you want, but it's not true." Her hand patted his cowboy boot. "I'm like your mommy. Safe to blame."

Monks said, "Why don't you ladies give Lex and me a minute alone?"

Lex watched Monks with hungry eyes, rolling up his sleeve. "You know the best description I ever heard of a strung-out junkie?" Lex said. "He's on a street corner without a dime, the dealer's across the street wanting five hundred dollars. The junkie will have the money by the time he gets across the street. It wasn't that bad yet, but I was getting there."

"I'm afraid this isn't quite what you had in mind, Lex." Monks took the envelope from his pocket and shook out one of the oxycodone tablets onto the RV's table.

Lex glared at it in outrage, then turned the glare on Monks. "That is *it*?"

"It was safe and available," Monks said. "Take it or leave it."

Lex's expression turned calculating. "How many of those have you got?"

"Four."

"Let me have them."

"Uh-uh," Monks said. "They've got to last you."

"Two, then," Lex wheedled. "What are they, ten mg?"

"Yeah."

"One's not going to touch it, you know that. Come on."

Monks decided wearily that there was no point in arguing. Lex, happy, would be a lot less trouble than Lex pissed off. He took another tablet out of the envelope and set it beside the first one.

Lex was on his feet now, moving with swift efficiency, the antithesis of the listless husk he had been a couple of minutes earlier. He yanked open a cupboard and found a heavy china coffee cup, then knelt and started crushing the tablets with it, grinding them carefully to dust.

"What are you *doing*?" Monks said.

Lex ignored him. With the concentration of a surgeon, he scraped the powder carefully into the cup, then added about a teaspoon of water from the sink. He stirred the mixture with a spoon, covered the cup with a tissue, and strained it into a saucer.

Finally he looked up again, fingers fumbling to undo his belt.

"How about a syringe?" he said.

Monks broke one out from the medical kit, and watched the needle slide into Lex's raised vein. Lex's face eased, pained features melting into a near smile, as if the drug inflated him briefly with borrowed life.

"It isn't going to last long," Lex murmured. "Leave the rest with me, in case you have to go out again."

"I'll give you the rest in four hours."

Lex's eyes opened, his gaze sharp now. "I'm going to be miserable in four hours. What am I supposed to do?" The tone was petulant: the demanding rich kid again. It hit Monks's frayed nerves wrong.

"The same thing the rest of us are going to do," Monks snapped. "Quit whining and take our chances."

Monks walked back to the RV's front. Stephanie and Martine were talking in low tones. They stopped when he appeared.

"I'm going to start making phone calls," Monks said. "To the media and law enforcement agencies."

He climbed down the RV's steps into the night, then leaned back and pressed the heels of his hands against his closed eyes, seeing in his mind Gloria Sharpe's bloodied hair—

Imagining it as Stephanie's instead.

This was over. It was only a matter of time until the hidden killer at Aesir would track them down. The best course now was to make the story public, rely on government protection—and hope that evidence turned up to support it.

But their thin fabric of allegations remained unprovable, vulnerable to the power of big money to override and obscure. If that happened, it meant spending their lives in fear of a ruthless, hugely resourceful enemy.

Monks thought he felt the vehicle rock slightly, as if someone around the rear had shoved it. There were no cars parked nearby, no reason for pedestrians to come by here. Apprehensively, he walked around to the back.

The RV's rear door was hanging open.

His gaze picked up something moving, perhaps a hundred yards away. It was a human figure, hurrying furtively across the parking lot toward the Great Highway:

Lex Rittenour, clutching his Gucci bag of cash in both arms, looking for all the world like Mr. Toad of Toad Hall escaping with his ball and chain.

Lex had made it into Golden Gate Park past the old windmill and heading toward the golf course, when Monks and Martine caught up with him in the van. Monks slowed to creep alongside, while she leaned out the passenger window.

"Lex, have you gone nuts?" she hissed. "There could be muggers in here."

Lex hurried doggedly along, clutching the suitcase. "You just leave me alone," he panted. "I'm looking out for Lex from now on."

"*When* haven't I looked out for you? I did *not* tell anybody you were going to make that announcement, goddammit!"

"Don't pretend you cared about me. You always just wanted me to be what *you* wanted."

Martine slapped the van's windowsill in exasperation. "Name *one* time when I did that."

"What about Cindy Parmelou?"

"What about her?"

"You sabotaged the relationship."

"Lex, you were in ninth *grade*."

"I was in love with her."

"In lust, is more like it." She turned and explained to Monks, "Cindy had three kids by the time she was eighteen, all by different fathers." She spun back to Lex. "Yeah, okay, I said a few things to her. You never had a chance there anyway, she only hung out with losers."

"Oh, so now it's sweet talk," Lex said grimly.

Martine threw her head back, rolling her eyes. "Just think, a little thrashing around in the backseat, and you'd have spent the next twenty years dodging child support payments instead of getting rich and famous."

Lex clamped his jaw shut and stomped along, eyes straight ahead. The van was moving at a crawl, blocking the right-hand lane of traffic. Irritated drivers behind were sounding their horns, then cutting around it, some holding out upraised middle fingers.

"I thought you trusted me!" Monks yelled, leaning across Martine.

"That was before."

"Before what?"

"Before you let me down. No help finding out who tried to kill me and no drugs."

"Let you down?" Monks said, outraged. "You ungrateful bastard, I've been out there getting stomped while you've been lying around doing dope!"

They were passing one of the small lakes, getting into the neighborhood of the buffalo pen. Monks thought seriously about jumping out and trying to wrestle Lex inside, but that was fraught with peril. He was cannily staying in plain, well-lit view, and like Popeye infused with the spinach of narcotics, he could probably give Monks a pretty good fight.

"Lex, get *in*," Martine said. "Where do you think you're going to go?"

Lex hesitated. She reached back and got the van's side door open. Monks was poised to breathe a silent prayer of thanks.

Then, with a speed Monks would not have believed, Lex bounded through a hedge and disappeared.

Monks cut the van into the curb, jumped out amid more blaring horns, and ran after him. He forced his way through the scratchy brush, but all he faced on the other side was an empty expanse of darkness, with nothing moving except leaves twitching in the breeze. In less than thirty seconds, Lex had completely disappeared.

Monks turned and trudged back to the van, numb with the realization that Lex Rittenour's testimony—by far the strongest link in their chain—was gone.

They drove silently back to the RV. Monks climbed in and met Stephanie's questioning look with a shake of his head, like a doctor snuffing the hope of someone waiting to learn if a loved one had survived an operation. He dragged out his own grip and stuffed into it the rest of the cash that Lex Rittenour had given him earlier: twenty-some thousand dollars.

"There's a hotel about a mile down the Great Highway," he said, handing the grip to Stephanie. "Don't use your real names, and don't let this bag out of your sight. I'll call you soon."

"Get rid of the women and pull the wagons into a circle?" Martine said coolly, with raised eyebrows and folded arms.

"Don't worry," Monks said. "You're going to have plenty of chance to fight."

He hugged Stephanie and then Martine, an embrace that lingered just long enough to affirm that something had begun between them—if circumstances had not already ended it.

Monks got out. The RV pulled cautiously away, with Stephanie driving—the new guardian of the Precious Blood of Saint Lex, still hidden inside Monks's grip. At least it would prove that Lex Rittenour had been the John Smith in the emergency room, and lend weight to the rest of the story.

As to whether it might be doing anything more than that—working its protective power like a medieval relic as it passed from hand to hand—Monks confessed that he was losing his faith.

He got back into the plumber's van and punched Larrabee's cell number.

"We lost Lex," Monks said into the phone.

"I finally found Trish," Larrabee said. "It took me awhile, I had to hunt through a few bars." His voice was tense with excitement, and Monks realized that something seemed to have turned up.

"Remember," Larrabee said, "Gloria Sharpe didn't have any medical training? We figured Ostrand hired her because she was willing to fuck him?"

Monks searched back through the jumble of information that had accrued over the past days.

"Vaguely," he said.

"Well, Trish remembered something else. What Ostrand was looking for was somebody who spoke Korean. That's why he hired Gloria. She'd been an army brat, raised there. She'd picked up the language."

"Ostrand needed her as a translator?" Monks said.

"Yeah. Now think about those research women. A bunch of them getting pregnant by different men, and having two, three abortions a year. Authorities never hearing a word about it. How about a whorehouse? A Korean one?"

Monks slumped in his seat, letting his head fall back and his arms sag until his knuckles hit the floor, while a circuit of connections flashed in his brain.

The Hotel Inez. Run by Kwon, the ex-military pimp; the man who had sent the tampered-with Demerol to Lex Rittenour via Miss Lee.

Who had almost certainly been operating under instructions from someone at Aesir.

"Mrs. Hak will be working at Mercy's emergency room," Monks said. "I'll meet you there."

Wearing sunglasses and baseball cap pulled low, Monks walked into the lobby of his own emergency room at Mercy Hospital, and approached the desk where Mrs. Hak was sitting.

After a few seconds, she looked up with a polite smile. It changed to astonishment.

"*You*," she said.

"We need your help again, Mrs. Hak," Monks said quietly. "Whatever you have to do to get off work, do it. Tell them there's a family emergency. I'll be outside."

He walked back outside to wait with Larrabee in the van. He realized that his gaze kept returning, of its own accord, to a particular spot on the sidewalk only a few yards away. Then, he remembered that that was where Lex Rittenour had lain dying while Miss Lee ran into the emergency room, just forty-eight hours ago.

Mrs. Hak came hurrying out to the van a couple of minutes later. She looked apprehensive, and Monks felt the kick of guilt at drawing her further in. But he handed her his cell phone.

"I need you to talk to Miss Lee, right now," Monks said. "Ask her if any of Kwon's girls got pregnant often."

"Hah?" Mrs. Hak said, eyes widening.

"Not just an occasional accident. Again and again."

Monks decided that there was no doubt in Mrs. Hak's mind that he had gone insane. But she punched a phone number, then began speaking rapidly in Korean. There was a pause while Mrs. Hak listened to Miss Lee's probably startled reply.

"She say yes," Mrs. Hak said. "All girls take pill. Some not lucky."

"Was there an American doctor who treated them?"

Mrs. Hak talked and listened again, then nodded. "Miss Lee never see him. Only hear about little bit. Girls not supposed to talk."

"Are any of those girls still working there? Does she know their names?"

"Okay," Mrs. Hak said, after another exchange. "She know three, four name right now. Think of more later."

"Give me her address and tell her to stay there," Monks said to Mrs. Hak. "You go back to work. We'll get to her as soon as we can."

Monks and Larrabee had traveled less than three blocks from the hospital when bright headlights flared behind them, along with the quick pulse of blue.

"I've got a bad feeling this isn't coincidence," Larrabee said. He pulled over. The lights pulled over too, staying behind.

A man's voice spoke through a bullhorn: "Put your hands on the dash!"

Half-blinded by the glare, Monks could barely see crouched figures approaching, holding pistols in two-handed combat grips. He put his hands on the dash.

The van's doors were yanked open. "Get out and put your hands on the vehicle," the voice commanded.

Monks did as he was told. A foot kicked at his ankles, separating his legs. Hands patted him up and down, finding and removing wallet, Beretta, and cell phone.

"Wrists behind you."

For the first time in his life, Monks felt the cold bite of cuffs on his wrists, clicking tight enough to pinch his skin.

He could see better now. Larrabee had been cuffed too. His face was taut with anger. The car behind them was an SFPD black and white squad unit; the two blue-uniformed cops were athletic young men. One stood guard while the other talked on a phone.

The one with the phone returned it to his belt. He leaned into the squad car and turned off all the lights.

"Get in," he ordered, opening a back door.

It was awkward climbing into a car with your hands cuffed behind your back, Monks discovered, and quickly uncomfortable. The radio had been turned off, but the engine was running and the heater on, adding to the claustrophobia. The street was quiet, with little passing traffic and no pedestrians. The two cops waited outside.

Monks and Larrabee waited too.

Ten to fifteen minutes passed before another car pulled up, an unmarked sedan with a plainclothes driver. There was one passenger in the backseat. As he got out, the car's interior light gave a glimpse of him. He was white-haired and thick-bodied, Irish looking, wearing an overcoat and tie.

"That's the man I saw after the shooting," Monks said.

"Captain Mickey Hearne," Larrabee said.

One of the uniforms came back to the squad car and opened the door, ordering them to get in the other car. Monks and Larrabee clambered awkwardly out and walked to where Hearne stood waiting.

Larrabee said, "How's it going, Captain?"

Hearne turned a stare on him that was as hard a look as Monks had ever seen.

"I know you?" Hearne said.

"This is primed to blow up," Larrabee said quietly. "There are people out there ready to do it if they don't hear from us."

Hearne turned and made a clawing gesture with one hand toward the uniformed cops. They faded back out of earshot.

"This isn't your style, Captain," Larrabee said. "Let us go. We'll deal."

"You used to be a cop," Hearne said, staring at Larrabee again. His tone was blunt, accusing. "You shot an asshole, down by the Wharf. Years back."

"Eighty-six."

"The city treated you like shit."

"It left an impression," Larrabee agreed. The "asshole" was a vicious mugger who had preyed on tourists for months, often beating or slashing women after he had robbed them. Larrabee had shot him in the course of a running chase, but the mugger managed to ditch his pistol. It was never found, and defense attorneys established reasonable doubt as to his identity. Larrabee was suspended from the force, and quit in outrage, with only the satisfaction that his shot—considered by his fellow cops to be world-class, hitting a running target at night—had blown out the man's spleen. There were no more of those muggings.

"You should have killed him," Hearne said. "That was your mistake."

"I found that out too late."

Hearne kept the stare on him for seconds longer. Then he yanked open the car's rear door. Monks and Larrabee got in. Hearne climbed into the front. The driver, also wearing plain clothes, pulled away from the curb and turned north.

"How'd you know where we were?" Larrabee said. "Just out of curiosity."

"Don't push it," Hearne snapped.

Except for Hearne's terse directions to the driver, no one spoke again.

They crossed the Golden Gate Bridge and stayed on 101 north for several miles, then exited toward Tiburon. The driver took the coast road down the Belvedere side of the peninsula, passing the misted lights of the secluded luxury houses overlooking Richardson Bay. The car slowed toward the peninsula's end at an ornate black iron gate, manned by a security guard. He waved them through, talking on a phone.

The private road was lined with luxury cars and limos, many with drivers sitting inside or standing together, smoking and talking. The lights of a house came into view. It was huge, multileveled, faced with white stone that gave it a Mediterranean look. Figures moved inside and on the large balconies: scarlet-waistcoated waiters serving champagne from silver trays, men in dinner jackets and women in gowns, some sporting fur wraps. Their jewelry sparkled like tiny stars in the dense black night. Monks recognized it as the place where the video of Lex Rittenour had been made—and tonight, the scene of Aesir Corporation's gala party to kick off tomorrow's IPO.

Just off shore, he could see the dragon-prowed Viking boat that had brought the dignitaries here from San Francisco, rocking slowly with the sea's easy chop.

The car drove past the house, down a slope, around to the rear. First-story windows showed a professional kitchen inside, with white-jacketed staff busily preparing food on the long stainless-steel tables. Monks could hear music now, a jazzy live sound from the upper stories.

But that was where the party stopped. Here below, it was dark and deserted. A garage door set into the basement opened automatically. The car drove into a spacious parking area supported by concrete pilasters. The door closed behind them.

Hearne and the driver got out. The driver opened the door for Monks.

"You stay in the car," Hearne said to Larrabee. The driver waited too, taking up the watchful attitude of standing guard.

Hearne walked Monks into the house's basement, down a hall, and into a windowless room. Monks recognized the electronic panels, numbered by zone, of a sophisticated security system. A bank of video screens set into one wall showed what was happening in different areas of the property: the front gate, the entrance to the house itself, the kitchen, and several views of the party, with the elegant guests mingling, drinking champagne, and dancing to the music of the orchestra.

Monks was not surprised to find Kenneth Bouldin, in black tie and dinner jacket, standing in front of the video screens, waiting.

"Dr. Monks," Bouldin said. "You look like you've had a rough night."

Hearne unlocked Monks's cuffs. He flexed his hands, numb from constriction. Hearne stepped back and stood with hands on hips, coat unbuttoned—shoulder holster and pistol butt clearly visible.

Bouldin picked up a remote control and flicked on several video screens that had remained blank. These showed bed and bathrooms. Most were unoccupied. One offered a glimpse of a seated woman's high-heeled shoes and uncovered knees, poking primly out past a toilet partition.

And in one luxurious suite, Lex Rittenour, washed, shaved, and dressed in evening clothes, was standing with his hands at his sides like a little boy, while Audrey Cabot, severely beautiful in a long sleeveless gown, tied his tie.

"Lex is going to make a brief appearance tonight to quell those ugly rumors," Bouldin said. "He called us to come get him. He got scared, all alone out there in the big world. Realized he was going to be needing drugs. Then some homeless people kicked him down and took his money."

There was going to be a lot of screw-cap wine drunk in some San Francisco alley tonight, Monks thought. On the screen, Audrey stepped back, surveying Lex. He looked cowed. His rebellion and his adventure were over.

"He told me the whole story of what's been happening," Bouldin said. "The appalling research that was done. The murder attempts on

him, and on you. Dr. Monks, I give you my word. I did not know anything about any of it until tonight."

Monks said, "You can't seriously expect me to believe that."

Bouldin smiled thinly. "It confirmed something I've suspected. Bits
and pieces that have been adding up. You and I have an enemy in common: Ron Tygard. He's been playing some kind of Machiavellian
game. Corporate intrigue, triple-crosses, wheels within wheels, like on
TV. Thinks he's G. Gordon Liddy."

Monks recalled his glimpse of Tygard a few hours earlier, clasped in
the embrace of Audrey Cabot's silken thighs. Climbing the corporate
ladder, on an inside track.

And startlingly cold-blooded, if he had engineered Gloria Sharpe's
murder at just about that same time.

"He set up that assault on you, then called me to cover it," Hearne
said gruffly. "I wouldn't have allowed it."

Monks was familiar with the military thirty-second apology. He was
impressed: This one had taken less than half that.

"Things can be very simple when each of you has something the
other wants," Bouldin said. "Like with Lex and me tonight. So here's
what *you* want. I'll see to it that Tygard doesn't cause either of us any
more trouble. I'll guarantee your safety, and I'll send you home rich.
No quibbling from you this time."

"And I just let this all go away?"

"Essentially. Yes."

"But it's not simple at all," Monks said. "It's an atrocity. The outrage
will scorch the planet."

"Appalling," Bouldin said again. Monks got the sense that he was
studying the effect of his own voice. "I'd make reparation if it were
possible. But—you must understand, the legal implications prohibit
any such thing. It would be an admission of responsibility."

The apology and veneer of civility did not conceal the coldness far
back in his eyes. Monks realized that for Bouldin, this was not even
about money. It was about something Monks himself could not
fathom. Perhaps it did come close to the desire to be a god.

"You're leaving out the criminal element," Monks said. "I don't know if those abortions would be considered murder, but they're certainly in that court."

"I'll remind you, I had nothing to do with any of it," Bouldin said. "Neither did Aesir Corporation. It was Tygard and that doctor, Ostrand."

"They worked under your auspices," Monks said. "The Aesir gods are going down. And you'll be at the longboat's helm."

"It would be expensive for us, in the short term," Bouldin agreed. "It would stop the IPO. But then—" Bouldin raised a hand, the same gesture he had made from the deck of the Viking ship to dismiss the crowd of reporters. "The dust of that outrage would settle. The market for REGIS would be unchanged. Sharpened, if anything, by proof of a practical application. We'd drop back a little, quietly regroup, and bring it out under another name."

It was chilling. Mainly because it was true.

"So you see, Dr. Monks, you're contemplating a noble gesture that wouldn't do anyone any good. But, I'm afraid, would cause you grief. You, and—most regrettably—your daughter."

Monks stepped quickly toward him, hand rising to reach for his throat. But Hearne moved in between them like a boxing referee.

"My daughter is not to be a part of this in any way," Monks said.

"But she already is." Bouldin did not step back. "She knows about the research. Knows that someone shot at her father. And Lex says she's something of a crusader. Now, none of that's a problem. I have no intention of harming either of you. I just want to be sure that she doesn't do anything impulsive.

"Bring her here. Now."

Monks's rage flared, but with it came a jolt of elation, making him almost giddy. From the instant he had seen the flashing blue lights, he had feared that Martine, after all, had lost her nerve; had called Bouldin, and told him where Monks and Larrabee would be.

But then Bouldin would know that Stephanie was with her.

"You'll both stay here in comfort tonight," Bouldin said. "Tomorrow, after trading's closed, I'll send you home, with her medical education paid for and plenty besides."

"She stays out of this," Monks said harshly. "We're going to take it public. If what you've said is true, you won't go to jail."

Bouldin listened with the air of a school principal hearing a child's excuse.

"Let me give you a gesture of good faith," he said.

He half-bowed, politely gesturing Monks ahead. Monks walked warily to a heavy steel door, like a bank vault, at the far end of the room. Bouldin opened it and stepped aside.

It revealed a concrete-walled chamber with a drain in the center of the floor. Ronald Tygard, hog-tied and gagged with duct tape, was on his knees. He looked up at them, wild-eyed, and jerked at his bonds in a sort of hopping motion, trying to stand or flee.

Bouldin nodded to Hearne.

Hearne stepped into the room, drawing from inside his coat an old-fashioned .38 police special with worn bluing. He placed his right foot on Tygard's neck, forcing him face down on the floor. Then he leaned over, put the gun to the back of Tygard's head, and fired. The sharp blast of sound echoed from the dense walls, bringing Monks's feet right off the floor.

Tygard jerked forward, his face twisting like a cat's that Monks had once seen caught in a car fan. Hearne fired again.

Bouldin made the same polite bow, ushering Monks away.

"Our common enemy is gone," Bouldin said. "I don't want to harm you, or your daughter, Dr. Monks. But if I did—how long do you think you could hide?"

They walked back to the security room, with Hearne and his gun following. Bouldin handed Monks a phone.

"Call her," Bouldin said.

Monks punched Stephanie's cell phone number.

Her "Hello?" was cautious, apprehensive.

Monks said, "Steffie, start calling news desks. Tell them what we found out. Right now."

Hearne placed the gun barrel against the back of Monks's neck, a hard cold ring just below the foramen magnum. Bouldin pulled the phone out of his hand.

"If you do that, Miss Monks," Bouldin said. "I promise you, you won't be seeing your father again. Now tell me where you are."

Monks yelled, "No!"

Monks waited, through the slowest and clearest seconds of his life, for that tiny muscular contraction of Mickey Hearne's forefinger.

Bouldin grimaced and pushed Hearne's hand down.

"Let's negotiate," Bouldin said to Monks, the businessman again. "There's no point in both of us losing."

Monks took the phone back. This time, it was Martine's voice on the other end.

"Are you all right?" she demanded.

"So far."

"What *happened* to you?"

"They found us."

"Who's 'they?' "

"An old friend of yours."

"Oh, no. Ken?"

"Yes."

Voice charged with anger, she said, "Put him on."

Monks offered the phone to Bouldin. "Dr. Rostanov," Monks said. He had the grim satisfaction of seeing surprise, then wariness, come into Bouldin's eyes.

Bouldin jerked the phone from Monks's hand.

"What the hell do you think you're doing?" Bouldin said icily.

Her reply was loud enough for Monks to hear through the receiver. "I swear to god, Ken, if you hurt these people, I'm going to be a nightmare you can't imagine!"

"No one's going to get hurt if you behave sensibly," Bouldin said soothingly. "Where are you? I'll have someone pick you up."

"You think because you fucked me you *own* me? I'll rip your eyes out."

Bouldin winced again. "This can be overlooked, my dear. Think about all you'd be giving up," he said, but his voice was losing its confidence.

Monks caught Bouldin's wrist and clamped down hard. This time Hearne did not interfere. Monks twisted the phone free, still gripping Bouldin's struggling hand.

"Remember those lines you crossed," Monks said to Martine. "You have to hold this time. It's everything."

"I'm holding," she said fiercely. "I'm holding what I found."

"Get out of there and keep moving," Monks said. "If you don't hear from me in one hour, start making those calls."

For a few more seconds, Monks listened to the sound of her breathing.

Then he let go of Bouldin and side-armed the phone hard against the concrete wall. Its plastic case cracked and it skittered across the floor. Bouldin backed away, rubbing his wrist, with an ugly look on his face.

"She'll come back," Bouldin said. "Just like Lex."

"The stain's spread too wide already," Monks said. "Too many bodies to hide. How are *you* feeling, Captain?" he said, swiveling to face Hearne. "One woman murdered already. A couple more on the list. Along with a good cop."

Hearne shifted his shoulders, not in a shrug, but in the quick, angry movement of a man trying to shake off an intolerable truth.

Bouldin turned slowly, his head twisting so that he was half-looking at Monks over his shoulder. It gave the odd sense of a marionette with a single string being pulled.

"What woman?" he said.

"Another one to blame on Tygard?" Monks said contemptuously.

"What woman?"

Monks blinked. He had not sensed much that was genuine from Kenneth Bouldin, but this had that ring.

"Gloria Sharpe," he said. "Walker Ostrand's assistant."

The rest of Bouldin turned. "When did this happen?"

"I found her a couple of hours ago," Monks said. "In her shop, South of Market. Somebody came to get her body and set the place on fire."

Bouldin's gaze swung the other way, fast this time, fixing Hearne.

Hearne shook his grizzled head emphatically. "It wasn't us." He was looking angrier by the minute.

"Is this some kind of a ploy, Monks?" Bouldin said. "A move to distract us?"

"You can smell the smoke on me, for Christ's sake."

Bouldin wheeled and strode toward the metal door. Monks watched, surprised, and then astounded, when it opened to show Ronald Tygard flopping around, struggling against his bonds and snarling through the gag.

The shots had been blanks.

Bouldin crouched and roughly pulled the duct tape gag loose.

"You son of a bitch!" Tygard shouted. His eyes were wild with rage and fear. "I didn't try to kill Lex! I didn't set up the hit on *him*." His head jerked to indicate Monks.

"If you lie to me on this one, I really will have you shot," Bouldin warned. "What do you know about a woman named Gloria Sharpe?"

"I never fucking heard of her! Let me go!"

Bouldin slammed the door, cutting Tygard's despairing yell to silence.

Bouldin took a hard plastic rectangle from his coat pocket. It was just bigger than a credit card, with an LCD readout.

"We use an internal email system for high-security communications," Bouldin said. "You access with one of these, connected to the company mainframe. It assigns you a new code every time. It's almost impossible to hack somebody else's personal channel.

"But Tygard claims that I authorized the assault on you, using my code. He swears it was my voice. But I didn't give that order, Monks. I didn't know it had happened until after the fact. So I assumed that Tygard was lying."

If not, it implied someone who could hack an elaborate firewall. Copy a voice. Manipulate the company's clandestine operations. All the while, staying hidden behind the scenes. There were probably dozens of employees at a place like Aesir with that level of technical skill. But the 'someone' had to have one more element: a reason to commit murder. Judging from the targets, that reason was self-defense—eliminating those who were out to expose him, or her, or them.

"I'm assuming you're all lying," Monks said. "But *somebody* tried to murder Lex. Probably murdered Walker Ostrand. Very definitely, Gloria Sharpe. If it wasn't Tygard and it wasn't you, you've got a killer loose in the house. It's time to open this up, Bouldin. Your worries go way beyond me now."

He watched Bouldin's reaction tensely, trying to read if this was still a bluff intended to make Monks drop his guard. If so, Bouldin was playing it well. He looked confused now, even frightened.

"What do you suggest?" Bouldin said.

Monks was not going to give up the information about Kwon: Kwon could be eliminated, and the prostitutes intimidated into silence. That had to go to someone who *could* be trusted.

"Look for whoever was in on the research with Walker Ostrand," Monks said. "Find out who hired him, who funded him, who had contact with him. The records have probably been wiped out, but your specialists should be able to recover them."

Bouldin hesitated, but then started punching keys on his handheld computer.

"Now you can tell me," Monks said to Hearne. "How did you locate us tonight?"

"Lex described the van you were using. We had units patrolling the hospital area. One of them spotted you."

Monks exhaled. It was like in the ER: You could do a thousand things right, but all it took was one piece of bad luck.

A small *beep* sounded. A video monitor above the door to the hall-way showed someone approaching: Audrey Cabot.

Hearne looked at Bouldin. "You want to keep this private?"

"Audrey can keep a secret," Bouldin said. "Let her in."

Hearne stepped to the door and opened it. Audrey's floor-length gown was rose-colored silk, adorned with a diamond necklace that would have graced a queen. Her skin was like alabaster and her gaze like frost. Monks could not help picturing the recent object of her affections, now hog-tied and thrashing in his cell only a few yards away.

"What are *you* doing here?" she said to Monks.

"Ms. Cabot," he said. "I admire your style."

Her eyes narrowed, that same stiletto look he had seen through the binoculars, but then she ignored him, turning to Bouldin.

"Lex is ready to mingle with the crowd," she said. "He's shaky. Let's stay close with him and keep it short."

Bouldin said, "Do you know the name Walker Ostrand?"

She frowned. "Not offhand. What about him?"

"He was a subcontractor. I want to know who hired him. Where he *came* from."

"Ken, I am not an employment service. I have no idea. If it's not absolutely urgent right now, I'm baby-sitting a billion dollars up there."

Bouldin nodded curtly. "I'll be right up." Audrey stalked out of the room.

Perhaps ninety seconds later, with Bouldin working at his keyboard again, the intercom clicked on. A man's voice said:

"Mr. Bouldin, Lex Rittenour's been shot. We need a doctor up here quick." The strain came through the voice, even with the static, as with paramedics in the field.

Bouldin closed his eyes and lowered his face into his hands, a gesture so defeated that Monks almost felt sorry for him.

Monks said, "Get me to Lex."

On his way to the door, he paused to look Mickey Hearne in the face.

"That's a good cop, sitting in that car," Monks said. "Let him go."

Hearne nodded stiffly.

Monks trotted after Kenneth Bouldin to the stairs at the end of the hall.

TWENTY-FOUR

The room where Lex Rittenour lay on the floor was upstairs in the north wing of the house, in the guest quarters for executives, separated from the public areas. A plainclothes security guard with an Uzi on a sling stood in front of the door. Audrey Cabot was in the hallway, pressed back against a wall, her composure finally gone. She looked ashen and her voice trembled.

"My god, I only left him for a minute," she said.

Another security guard was kneeling beside Lex, with a wadded bloody bedsheet pressed to the left side of Lex's back. There was no stain on the carpet underneath—no large exit wound—but the danger of internal bleeding was high.

Bouldin said urgently, "Lex. Who was it?"

Lex shook his head, a barely perceptible motion. "Don't know. Got hit and fell." Monks registered a floor lamp that had been knocked over and two ugly gouges in the wall, undoubtedly from missed gunshots.

Monks knelt opposite the guard and said, "I'll take over." His hands and senses worked automatically, checking the vital signs. Lex's pulse was rapid and thready from shock, his breathing shallow.

"Get a helicopter coming," Monks told Bouldin. "The closest trauma center is at Bayview."

Bouldin frowned. "That's not going to look good. We'll take him in a limo."

"The hell with looking good," Monks said heatedly. "He needs full medical attention, fast."

Bouldin's mouth tightened, but he nodded and stepped out into the hall.

"We gotta stop meeting like this," Lex mumbled. The words were labored, but he was not sucking for air.

"Save your breath," Monks said. His forefinger found the entry wound, a hole a little smaller than a dime, in the upper left quadrant of Lex's back. The shoulder blade had probably stopped it from hitting the heart.

"How'm I doing?"

"Okay."

"Really?"

"Really," Monks lied.

"I need a shot," Lex breathed. "The guards have it. Doling it out just like you, the pricks."

Monks hesitated, but then nodded to the waiting guard. He handed Monks a syringe and vial of Demerol—the precious healing balm that Lex had come in out of the cold for. Monks gave him the shot in the forearm, IV, and felt the tensed flesh start to relax under his hands.

"Sorry about that, tonight. Lost my nerve." Lex's eyes were closed, his face dreamily peaceful.

"Stay quiet, goddammit," Monks said.

"I was going to get some more money and dope and take off again," Lex said. His eyes opened and rolled up with that same flattened, fish-like gaze Monks had seen in the ER the first night. "I was having a hell of a good time, being out there."

Abruptly, his lips parted in a sad little belch of laughter. A bubble of blood bulged out between them, collapsing in a tiny spray.

"*Bouldin*," Monks said. "The *chopper*."

The guard in the hall leaned back in the doorway. "It's on its way."

"Get the paramedics up here on the run. Tell them to bring a MAST suit."

"A what?"

"A *MAST* suit, M-A-S-T. They'll know."

Bayview Hospital was only a few miles away. But Monks was sure now that there was severe bleeding into the chest. It was nothing he could hear or see. It came through another sense he could not name, perhaps a feel through his palms. He kept them pressed firmly on Lex's back, the best he could do to slow the internal wound. But he could feel Lex's consciousness slipping too, as if it were flowing away with the blood.

"When you're over this, we're going to take another road trip," Monks said, quietly, leaning close to Lex's ear. "Nobody on our ass this time. Just drugs, women, and booze." He could not tell if Lex heard him. "We'll go up to Montana, I've got a crazy brother there. He knows every good bar in the state."

Monks started to feel the helicopter, a barely perceptible disturbance on the far perimeter of awareness. His body knew what it was before his mind did, bringing the sour taste of bile far back in his throat, a Pavlovian response to what it portended: bloody men on stretchers being rushed out of medevac flights, landing on a navy hospital ship in the South China Sea.

Through the room's windows he could see the rapidly approaching glow in the sky, quickly coalescing into a narrrowing funnel of light as the chopper dropped down through the mist onto the grounds outside, met by signaling security guards. Two paramedics jumped out, carrying gear and a stretcher, running with the guards toward the house.

"Come on, Lex," Monks said. "You're a *fighter*."

He helped the paramedics get Lex, unconscious now, into the bright orange MAST suit and inflate it. Its help to the chest wound might be slight or even nil, but it was all that could be done until surgeons could get in. They strapped Lex to the stretcher and carried him downstairs. Monks followed.

A man in a suit stepped in front of him. "I'm sorry, sir, but Mr. Bouldin wants you to stay here."

Monks recognized Andrew, the heavy who had been with Tygard in the emergency room that first night. With sudden rage, Monks grabbed him by the lapels and shoved him against the wall.

"That's Lex Rittenour and I'm his doctor," Monks said into his face. "Don't you fucking *dare* try to stop me." Monks strode after the paramedics. No one followed.

He exited through a ground-floor doorway at the building's rear. Outside, the night was cool and wet, the fog turning to drizzle. Above him, on the rear balcony, a crowd of party-goers had gathered to watch the helicopter and the man being rushed toward it. He could see the consternation on the faces, the mouths moving as information or rumors flew around. He caught a glimpse of Bouldin circulating, talking, palms raised in a calming manner.

There were going to be some blistering headlines in the next hours.

"Could I get you to take another look at this?" a voice said.

Monks wheeled, startled.

Pete Hazeldon stepped out of the building's shadow, holding up his injured hand. Frizzy-haired and boyish, he had the air of wearing sneakers, even in black tie.

"I know it's a pain, people coming up to you at a party and asking for advice," he said, "but I'm afraid it's getting infected."

Monks stared at him, incredulous. His hands started rising to shove Hazeldon out of the way, while the words, *Are you crazy? Lex is dying!* formed in his brain and were on their way to his tongue.

But he stopped them. Hazeldon's other hand was in his jacket pocket, gripping something. It was just visible: the butt of a high-caliber automatic, its barrel pointed at Monks.

The injured hand was swollen badly, the flesh puffy and red around the bandage. Monks remembered the wound, with its ragged punctures from being crushed between the powerful jaws of machinery—not likely to get infected, as it obviously had.

But something played at an edge of his consciousness, a quick eidetic byte:

Himself, sitting in the van a few hours ago, watching ghostlike as Hazeldon scurried across the Bank of America plaza with the furtive air of a man on a guilty mission.

Just about the time when Gloria Sharpe was murdered.

The hand, crushed between powerful, infective jaws.

The jaws of an attack dog.

Monks told himself it was impossible. He had seen many dog bites—he would have recognized the sharp punctures of teeth. Hazeldon's wounds had been larger, ragged, gaping.

But arranged in the narrow V-shape of a Doberman's jaws.

Monks swallowed tightly. Something in him insisted that Hazeldon had deliberately torn the punctures open further; that in spite of his shock and agony, he had rent his own tormented flesh to disguise the wound's real origin, so that no one would think to connect him with Gloria after she disappeared.

"Come on with me," Hazeldon said. "We'll find a quiet place." His eyes were very bright and focused with absolute intensity.

It came to Monks with gut-level certainty that Hazeldon's pistol was the weapon that had killed Gloria Sharpe.

He glanced quickly toward the helicopter. It was more than a hundred yards away, the rotor drowning out sound around it. The paramedics and security guards were occupied with loading Lex in. There was no one closer.

"Okay," Monks said.

They moved toward the dock, staying in the shadows. Hazeldon took the pistol out of his pocket, pointing it at Monks's spine. The barrel ended in a silencer that looked homemade. Monks stepped with careful precision, on edge for cues from his captor, bristling with dread.

At the end of the dock, the dragon prow of the Viking longboat was lit and the boat's main body dark, giving the impression that its inventors had intended a thousand years ago: of a fearsome monster rising from the sea. Back on shore, the sound of the helicopter's rotor increased. The chopper lifted off, carrying Lex to Bayview Hospital. Everyone else had left the area. The boat looked deserted too.

Hazeldon gestured with the pistol barrel toward the mooring ropes. "Untie them." Monks unwound the two heavy ropes from their cleats and tossed them up onto the boat. "Now you," Hazeldon said. Monks climbed the ladder up the boat's side, with Hazeldon following.

When Monks stepped over the gunwale, the wet wind stung his face, bringing an image of the Viking warriors who had shivered and starved under the brutal North Sea storms. But the *Mjollnir*'s resemblance to those old-time crafts ended there. The deck was teakwood furnished with cushioned seats. The cabin was shielded by curved glass and housed a control panel that glowed with digital readouts. The galley below, down a short stairway, revealed a luxury bar with leather-upholstered chairs. The bottles of premium liquor lining the backbar flickered like flames in the dim light.

"You ever run a boat?" Hazeldon said.

"Smaller ones."

"I'll coach you."

They walked to the cabin, rocked in a greasy seesaw by the chops of water lapping against the hull. Hazeldon motioned Monks to stand at the console.

"That switch there will heat the plugs," he said, pointing with the gun. "Give it thirty seconds, then hit the starter."

Monks did. The big Cummins diesel turned over and caught instantly, settling into a powerful, throaty purr.

"Now put it into forward and give it just a little throttle," Hazeldon said.

"Where are we going?"

"Sausalito. Go ahead, take it out."

The boat lurched as Monks put it in gear. He took the wheel, eased the throttle lever back, and pulled slowly away from the dock. When they were clear, he swung the prow to head directly into the chop.

Sausalito was a little over a mile west, its lights dimly visible through the fog. Farther south, glimmers of the San Francisco skyline appeared and vanished in the swirls like a distant fairyland.

"Keep it slow," Hazeldon said. "Four, five knots."

Monks adjusted the throttle, risking a covert glance back toward shore. A floodlight had come on over the dock.

Hazeldon half sat on a cabinet, his bandaged hand held away from him, the pistol in his other hand balanced across his thigh. It jittered nervously.

"You must have taken chemistry, huh?" Hazeldon said.

"A long time ago."

"You remember Maxwell's Demon?"

"Not really," Monks said warily. "No."

"You've got this box full of hot and cold molecules," Hazeldon explained. "The law of entropy says they're going to mix randomly. Equal numbers of hot ones and cold ones everywhere. But there's this little demon in the middle who separates them, keeps the hot in one half, the cold in the other. He defeats the law of entropy. Imposes order on chaos.

"Except he doesn't really exist. Well, that's who I was. The invisible demon, putting in eighteen-hour days, making it all work. But nobody knew I was there."

Monks started to get a glimmer of what might lie behind the madness that had erupted in Pete Hazeldon. He was a man who considered himself brilliant, but he labored in the shadow of a true genius—Lex Rittenour—with all the resentment, jealousy, and rage that could engender. Worse, Lex was a genius who made it look easy, who made a mockery of the earnest worker bees. Monks recalled Hazeldon's words in the Aesir offices that first night:

He's like an idiot savant. We have to go back and fill them in, to make it all work.

"You're very important, from everything I heard," Monks said. "Head of R and D. One of the chief Aesir."

Hazeldon made a disgusted sound, spitting air. "Are you kidding?

They threw me a bone because they needed me. Look at Ken and Audrey, they're like European nobles. Lex is shooting dope and living glossy, with the girls nibbling his heels. Me? I'm Howdy Doody, the nerdy kid in the background. But they didn't dream I had them wired. I had *everybody* wired."

They were in the open waters of Richardson Bay now, the boat bucking across the white-tipped chop. Monks was watching for a chance to run for it and dive, or to slap the weapon out of Hazeldon's hand. But he was trapped in the cabin, with Hazeldon vigilant and too far away. Monks searched for a distraction, trying to push aside the fear that clouded his brain.

"What were you aiming for?" Monks said. "With your research?"

Hazeldon stared at him, looking puzzled. "Do you have any idea what's going on these days?" he said, in the tone of speaking to the simpleminded. "Rich people are standing in line for a chance to buy genetically perfect grandkids. Whoever gets on top of *that* is going to rule. Forget Lex Rittenour."

Hazeldon stood suddenly, the gun barrel rising. "Take off your clothes," he said.

"*What?*"

"Payback. Did you like sticking that needle in my ass?"

"I was giving you penicillin, for Christ's sake. You asked for it, remember?"

"Toss them over here."

Monks kicked off his shoes, then stripped off his sweatshirt and jeans. He threw them at Hazeldon's feet.

Hazeldon gathered them up, then stepped back out of the cabin. Monks heard the click of an electronic lock, trapping him inside. Hazeldon laid down the pistol and shrugged out of his own clothes, grimacing as he pulled jacket and shirt sleeve past his bandaged hand. Monks saw that there was something tied or taped to his thin white waist: a small black rectangle with a tiny red light. Hazeldon's hand went to it, one finger searching, then pressing. The light started to blink.

He stepped into Monks's jeans, buckling them awkwardly with one hand, and pulled on the sweatshirt. He opened the door again and kicked his own pile of discarded clothes inside, pistol held ready.

It was sinking into Monks what the device on Hazeldon's waist was: a detonator. Hazeldon had not been wiring the boat for a communications system. He had been wiring it with explosives.

"Put on my clothes," Hazeldon said.

"This isn't going to fool anybody," Monks said. "You know that."

The gun muzzle flashed along with a quick little sound, a sort of *putt* that had a leaden weight, like a dead bird being dropped. A chunk blew out of the cabin roof just above Monks's head. He flinched, hands flying to cover his face. Beads of glass sprayed him like shrapnel.

"Put them on," Hazeldon said.

Monks lowered himself to his right knee, a motion as familiar as breathing to his body from thousands of boyhood genuflections, and gathered the clothes. He struggled into the pants. They were tight and short. He knelt again and picked up the wadded shirt. Hazeldon looked at his watch.

Monks flung the shirt at his face and lunged, shoving off the console and diving low with his arms outstretched, going for the gun. Hazeldon flailed blindly at the shirt and fired two shots. Monks heard them crash into the console behind him. His left hand caught Hazeldon's gun forearm while his right clawed for a grip, getting hold of a fistful of sweatshirt. Hazeldon twisted like a cat, with desperate, unbelievable strength. Monks could feel the forearm muscles flexing like cables, forcing the pistol barrel toward Monks's body. It fired again and again. Their legs fought a battle of their own—shoving, kneeing, struggling to trip.

Monks let go of the sweatshirt suddenly and drove his right fist into Hazeldon's belly. He felt the torso double inward, heard the sudden harsh *whuuunh* of expelled breath. But the pistol fired another round, this time so close to his face he could feel the slap of air.

Monks punched again, planting his right foot and coming up hard off it, giving it all the shoulder he had. Hazeldon caved in further, wrapping himself around the fist. His face fell on Monks's shoulder in insane intimacy.

Then his teeth tore into Monks's flesh.

Monks roared, a ferocious bark of pain. His groping right hand found Hazeldon's other forearm and worked its way down to the bandage, moving spiderlike, clinging to the sleeve.

When it got there, Monks crushed Hazeldon's wounded hand in his own with every bit of strength he could summon.

Hazeldon threw his head back violently and howled, a long, eerie wail that might have come from the murdered dogs.

"Drop the gun!" Monks yelled. He felt the forearm twisting, trying to point the pistol at him. It fired several shots, a wild spray that crashed around the cabin, shattering plastic and glass.

Monks crushed the hand again, twisting it viciously. Hazeldon shrieked, a despairing sound that tore at Monk's ears.

"*Drop the gun!*"

This time, Monks felt the forearm relax, and heard the thump as the weapon hit the deck. He stepped back and spun Hazeldon around, keeping his grip on the bandaged hand, then bringing it up tight behind Hazeldon's back in a hammerlock.

"We've got to get off!" Hazeldon croaked. His voice came out in sobbing gasps. "It's going to blow in less than three minutes!"

Monks shoved him ahead, out of the cabin and toward the long-boat's stern. A light had appeared on the water to the east, in the direction of Angel Island. It was about a mile away and only showed in glimpses through the fog, but it seemed to be gaining on them fast—like a Coast Guard cutter.

"I'm not lying!" Hazeldon bawled the words into the wind.

Monks was dimly aware that his ordinary consciousness was no longer in control of his mind. Some part of it—a part that was usually buried deep, that was primitive and ferociously bent on survival—had been operating his body.

Now he had the distinct sense of another facet coming into play: asking something or someone what to do.

And if no answer came, this voice requested mercy.

Monks stared at the approaching light, estimating the seconds that remained out of three minutes.

The answer came.

He shoved Hazeldon to the starboard gunwale and shouldered him over, to fall flailing into the sea. Monks dove after him, burying his face in his arms. He slammed into the hard surface tension of the bay and plunged down into instant shocking cold. The saltwater bit fiercely where Hazeldon's teeth had ripped his neck.

Monks's groping hand found Hazeldon's sweatshirt—*Monks's* sweatshirt. For dizzy seconds Monks twisted, all direction lost, until a decades-old memory from scuba training led him to follow upward the bubbles from his thrashing. He struggled for the surface, his air almost gone, dragging the burden of the other man—starting to understand that he was not going to make it.

Then the burden was gone: slipped away like a fish out of a net, leaving Monks holding only the empty sweatshirt. He let it go.

His head broke the surface just before blackout and he managed to suck in one breath before a wave caught him and filled his mouth. He clawed and kicked and hacked the burning saltwater from throat and nose until finally he was afloat and breathing, and thought returned.

He looked for Hazeldon, pumping his legs in an eggbeater kick, striving to rise out of the water. There was nothing but the foaming whitecapped chop. Two hundred yards away, the *Mjollnir* was starting to roll, with no hand at the wheel. The approaching vessel was within a quarter mile now, the low, lean shape of a cutter becoming visible through the fog. Its spotlights were focused on the Viking boat.

Monks raised a hand in a futile wave.

A ball of flame appeared where the *Mjollnir* had been an instant before—a yellow flash the size of a house, erupting like a giant Roman candle into a spray of burning debris. A thunderous *boom* rolled across the water. The flaming chunks started to land, a couple of them falling close to Monks. He went underwater again and stayed as long as he could.

When he cautiously came up, what was left of the *Mjollnir* was outlined in flames. The central section, with the cabin, was mostly gone, with great gaping holes blown in the hull. The boat was filling quickly with water and the stern was sinking.

Within another minute, the dragon prow began to tip backward, seeming to rear up out of the sea as the stern dragged it down. Then it slipped quickly under water, its only visible remains the scattered flaming chunks of debris.

The cutter moved in, its lights playing over the wreckage. But it was still a quarter mile away. Monks understood that he would not be able to stay afloat for many more minutes. The chances of the cutter seeing him, a tiny white face amidst the fog and chop, were almost nil.

He started his slow journey toward Sausalito, about a half mile away. He tried to angle north, fearing the currents that could pull him from the calm of Richardson Bay into San Francisco Bay itself, where he would have no hope of making it. He moved in a mix of breaststroke and dog paddle, pausing to rest when a wave furthered him a few yards. Slimy tendrils of kelp tugged him back, and once he imagined the brush of a sea creature, curious or hungry.

Quickly, he was all out of energy and heat, his body sucked clean. Moving his arms was an increasingly impossible task. Something started to happen that he had felt once before. It was like an iron band tightening, not around his flesh, but around whatever lived inside. It was pitiless; not painful, just impossible to endure.

He had almost fallen into a dream that he was never, afterward, able to recall, when he felt sand squish between his toes.

Monks reluctantly came awake. He could tell from the lights that he was just south of Sausalito, facing a deserted stretch of coast. He plodded forward, rising from the sea like a creature emerging from the primeval soup. When he reached dry ground, he fell to his knees and then his face. The sand clung to his bloodless outer flesh, bringing warmth and peace.

Then he was aware of someone beside him. There was a distinct sense to the presence. It seemed to be urging him to look *out there*.

Monks lifted his face out of the sand. In the bay, the last burning chunks of the great longboat drifted in the mist like the remains of a Viking funeral.

But there was no one standing near him after all.

TWENTY-FIVE

It was just past dawn the next morning when Monks drove up his own driveway, and his own house came into view. He had never been so glad to see any place in his life.

He switched off the ignition of Martine Rostanov's Volvo, got out, and opened the passenger door for her. They walked slowly up the porch steps, his arm around her waist, both of them beyond exhaustion. They had been up all night talking to police.

Inside, she dropped her purse on a chair, looking around at the comfortable but tasteless bachelor digs he lived in. The house was dark and cold. There were no cats to be seen.

"The vodka's in the cabinet left of the sink," Monks said. "Ice and a lemon twist for me. I'll make a fire."

He crouched in front of the iron stove and built a rising pyre of crumpled newspaper and kindling topped by larger splits of oak. It started crackling at the touch of the match, flames shooting upward in the strong draft through the slightly open door and wide-open damper.

Martine came to him, holding two brimming, ice-filled glasses with crescents of lemon on the rims. She and Monks touched the glasses together and drank, but it was not the celebration they had talked about. Her face was pale, her eyes dark and hollow. She had been silent during most of the drive here.

Lex Rittenour had died in the helicopter on the way to Bayview Hospital. Surgery would not have saved him even if he had made it there. He had simply lost too much blood.

"Why don't you take a bath and get some sleep," Monks said to her. She nodded, holding the vodka glass in both hands like a child.

"What are you going to do?" she said.

"I'm going to have one more drink," he said. "Maybe two or three. Then I'm going to sleep too." There were going to be many more meetings with law enforcement authorities, attorneys, media people. But Monks had insisted on taking a break. They had dispersed—Stephanie to her mother's to be pampered, Larrabee to John's Grill on Ellis Street to drink under the portrait of his hero, Dashiell Hammett.

Martine had insisted on coming with Monks.

He showed her where things were and got her clean towels and a robe. Then, hesitantly, he pushed open the door to a medium-sized bedroom, with posters of rock stars on the walls and stuffed animals on the bed.

"This is Steffie's room," he said. "I want you to be comfortable."

Martine touched his cheek in the way she had done before. It could have signaled anything: *Thanks, you're sweet. I was wrong to come here. Good-bye.* She stepped into the bathroom and closed the door firmly.

This time, walking down the hall, he had company: all three cats had appeared, winding through his feet, glaring at him for bringing someone else into their home, but not so angry that they failed to herd him toward the kitchen. The food in their bowls was relatively fresh—a stack of mail and newspapers on the table showed that Emil Zukich had been coming by, as he had promised—but Monks got out clean bowls and doled out generous portions of Kultured Kat Kidney Feast, a guaranteed favorite.

Monks brushed his teeth and washed at the kitchen sink, hissing as water found its way beneath the bandage on his neck. He took a couple of filet mignons from the freezer and put them on the counter to thaw. Then he poured another vodka and walked out onto the deck. Clouds hung low over the surrounding hills and stretched to a solid gray front toward the Pacific, promising drizzle soon and later, a rain that might last days. But it was getting toward the end of that season.

He had put together enough information by now for a basic grasp of the forces that had interacted behind the scenes: Pete Hazeldon's rage at living in Lex Rittenour's shadow; Walker Ostrand's sadistic penchant for playing with human subjects; Gloria Sharpe's hard-heartedness and greed. The details would be coming under an intensive investigation. The Korean pimp, Kwon, had been arrested, and the process of questioning his stable of women for their sad stories would begin soon.

Hazeldon was presumed dead, although his body had not yet been found. In all probability it was lost in the deep murky waters of the bay, where, with currents and kelp and scavengers, it probably never would be. But Monks could not shake a touch of dread. Robby Vandenard had supposedly been dead for fifteen years, during which he had murdered an unknown number of people.

The shock waves of all this were going to reverberate fiercely and worldwide. The IPO had been called off. Kenneth Bouldin was already maneuvering with high-powered smoothness, declaring grief for Lex, deploring Hazeldon's research, denying any responsibility for himself or Aesir Corporation—deciding which of the underlings, like Tygard, would be thrown to the wolves.

And Monks was already sure that Bouldin had been right: REGIS was far from dead. On the contrary, for all the public outrage that the research would arouse, it would affirm, to the elect, that health, beauty, even immortality—things that had been the sole province of heaven—were coming available here on earth. If the cost was heavy to the damned, that was the way it was ordained.

Then there was Lex.

Monks went down to the car and got his grip. The blood sample was where he had left it, rolled up in a towel. He took the glass tube out of its plastic bag and held it in his hand, his mind moving again to some realm of faith or superstition

As near as he could tell, Lex had died at just about the time that

Monks had washed up on the beach—the moment when he had imagined that presence beside him.

When he climbed back up onto the deck, Martine was there waiting. He saw with surprise that she was not wearing the terrycloth robe of Stephanie's he had found for her, but one of his own, an old buff-colored chamois. It came to her ankles and her hands were lost in the sleeves. She was sipping his drink.

She looked fresh now, her hair damp, her faded makeup washed away. The hot water had given her skin a faint rosy flush. But her eyes were filled with hurt from all that had happened.

He had not intended to show her the tube of blood, but he could not hide it now.

"Steffie nicked it from the hospital," he said.

"She told me."

"I'm sorry for you, losing him. It must be hard."

"I cared for him enormously," she said. "But these last years—we both got very far from who we'd been. I just got lost, but Lex was used up. In pain: not physically, but in his being. He tried everything to stop it, but he kept getting backed farther into a corner."

She took the tube and held it between her palms, as if trying to warm it.

"What are you going to do with it?" she asked.

"I have a safe. I could make it into a reliquary."

"A place where they keep holy bones, that sort of thing?"

"Yeah."

"You were with him last. Was he scared?"

"I think he was ready to cut loose and voyage," Monks said.

He offered her the rest of the vodka in the glass. She shook her head. He drained it.

"We need to rest," he said. "When we wake up I'll grill steaks."

"That sounds wonderful."

He walked to the door and opened it. She watched him without moving, her eyes dark and anxious.

"I'd like you to hold me," she said. "But I'm afraid."

"Of what?"

"That you won't want me after you see me."

Monks walked back to her.

"Let me see you," he said.

Slowly, still holding his gaze with her own, she tugged her belt undone.

Monks parted the robe with his hands, resting them lightly around her waist. He took his time looking her up and down. The brace was off, her thinner leg as naked as the rest of her. It was delicate, fawnlike, just bent at the knee, toes touching the deck and heel slightly raised.

Monks started kissing her: lips, neck, small rose-nippled breasts. Her eyes were closed now. He knelt, working his way down, finding the soft flesh inside her thighs, then clasping her and pressing his face against her until she knelt too, and shook the robe back off her shoulders and pulled him down.

Acknowledgments

The author is deeply indebted to many people who helped in the making of this book. Special thanks to:

Kim, Lois, Chuck, and Jeff Anderson; Frank and LaRue Bender; Carl Clatterbuck; Dan Conaway; Mike Koepf; Georgia, Barbara, and the two Dans McMahon; David and Dick Merriman; Bob Rajala; Kuskay Sakeye; Nikola Scott; Xanthe Tabor; Jennifer Rudolph Walsh.

And Eric Warfield Johnson, builder, educator, and longtime comrade, who carried many aspiring writers on his broad Viking shoulders.